Genetic Power Play

GenePlay Series
J. Alan Childs

Flamethrower Productions

Copyright © 2025 by J. Alan Childs

All rights reserved.

Book cover designed by Touhid Wahid

No portion of this book may be reproduced in any form without written permission from the publisher or author, except as permitted by U.S. copyright law.

Flamethrower Productions
Savage, MN USA

flamethrowerprod@gmail.com

Print ISBN: 9798882172052

Dedication

There are many people who have help me on this journey to write this book.

First and foremost, to my wife, Candy, my partner of 40 wonderful years of marriage. You have been my rock, my muse, and my greatest supporter. Your unwavering belief in me has fueled every word, every sentence, every page. I am forever grateful for the life we've built together and the adventures still to come.

To my five amazing children, Courtney, Cory, Jace, Bailey, and Brody. You are my pride and my joy. Watching you grow, dream, and thrive has been one of the greatest privileges of my life. Thank you for always challenging me, grounding me, and inspiring me with your own unique talents and perspectives.

To my grandchildren, who bring light and laughter into every corner of my world. You remind me every day why stories matter, why imagination matters, and why the world is always brighter with curiosity and wonder.

This book owes its spark to Brody and the summer of 2008, when a comic about a lacrosse-playing superhero lit a creative fire that still burns today. That little comic became the seed of the Flamethrower lacrosse books, and now it has led us here. Brody, your creativity all those years ago reminds me that every idea, no matter how small, has the power to grow into something extraordinary.

GENETIC POWER PLAY

And to Zeus, my ever-faithful writing companion, your quiet presence, loyal watch, and occasional demands for attention ensured I was never truly alone in this journey. Whether pacing the room, snoozing at my feet, or nudging me for a well-timed break, you were always there.

The Note

"Victory is not just about winning. It's about rising above fear, failure, and the shadows of doubt that try to define us." – Coach Boucha

There were exactly three hundred and fifty-four days between losing to Team USA and stepping onto the ice in Toronto. Liam Desjardins had counted every one of them. Now nineteen thousand seats waited to be filled with fans who demanded redemption in this opening game against Finland. The World Junior Championships had returned to Canadian soil, and with it, the weight of an entire nation's expectations. For Team USA, last year's game had been a victory. For Liam, it had become an obsession.

A mounted TV in the corridor caught his attention. TSN's pre-game show running through their ritual analysis. His reflection in the dark screen caught his eye for a moment, the same mixed-race features that had made him stand out in team photos since childhood, now bearing the weight of leadership. Last year's gold medal game played in silent loops behind the analysts, each replay of Team USA's celebration like a fresh wound.

"...youngest captain in Team Canada history," one commentator was saying, "and still only seventeen. The pressure on Desjardins..."

"But that's what makes this tournament special," another cut in. "These kids, under twenty, playing for their countries, fighting for gold, and NHL scouts watching their every move. Two weeks that can change..."

Liam turned away. He didn't need reminders of what was at stake, or how many NHL teams had representatives in the building tonight. From Boxing Day until the gold medal game, the eyes of the hockey world would be watching.

Liam leaned against the cold concrete wall, listening to the distant echoes of last year's Team USA cheers. Today, though, the air buzzed with something different, a quiet hum of belief. He closed his eyes, feeling the moment settle over him like armor. This was his chance to seize what had eluded him, to transform the bitter taste of defeat into glory. Opening his eyes, Liam pushed off from the wall and resumed his walk. He passed by the equipment room where Paul gave him a nod. A silent conversation passed between them. No words were needed. Teammates like them understood without speaking.

Liam's pregame routine was meticulous, a blend of mental and physical precision. He began with stretches that challenged every muscle, his six-foot-two frame moving with the fluid grace of someone who'd spent countless hours perfecting each motion. Next, he practiced stickhandling drills with a weighted ball, his wrists snapping back and forth, seamlessly weaving a spell of agility.

"Light it up," he whispered to himself as he worked through the movements.

The jitters were there, sharpening his focus. He welcomed them, they were old friends by now. Channeling that energy, Liam visualized each play unfolding, each pass sharp, each shot finding the back of the net.

"Ready to play the hero today, Liam?" Julian Broten's voice cut through his concentration. The Vancouver native's lean six-foot frame leaned against the corridor wall, his perfectly styled dark hair never looking out of place even after practice. His smirk carried its usual mix of confidence and disdain as he watched Liam prepare for the game.

"Someone's gotta be the hero," Liam said with a wry smile, tightening his grip on his stick.

Julian clapped him on the shoulder before moving on, that characteristic swagger in his stride that came from believing he was the best player in the room. The hallway filled with more players emerging from the locker room, their voices echoing off the concrete walls. At the end of the corridor, a group had gathered around playing hacky sack, feet flicking it up, keeping it airborne, their laughter mixing with the nervous energy that crackled in the air. It was a small distraction, a way to shake off the weight of what was to come, but Liam couldn't join in. His mind was elsewhere.

Liam took one last deep breath before heading back toward the locker room. His pulse quickened, his focus sharpening as he walked. He paused at the door, hand on the knob, allowing himself just one more moment to gather his nerves within him. The hacky sack banter faded behind him, replaced by the sharp focus of the game ahead. It was time.

The locker room door swung open, and Liam took a step forward. A movement caught his eye, a figure lurking in the shadows where the fluorescent lights flickered. Something about the man's stance triggered a memory Liam couldn't quite place. The lab coat partially concealed under a dark jacket seemed familiar, like an echo from countless medical evaluations. An ID badge peeked from his pocket, and Liam caught a glimpse of an unusual logo: what looked like a stylized DNA helix wrapped around the silhouette of an animal. The badge disappeared as the man hastily stuffed it deeper into his pocket.

"Liam." The quiet call of his first name made him stop. There was something in that voice, something that pulled at his memory. The stranger's hands fidgeted in his pockets, sweat dotting his forehead.

"You shouldn't be here." Liam's voice was calm but carried an edge that matched the question in his eyes. He studied the man's face, trying to place where he'd seen him before. Those evaluations at VSM's facility? The endless tests Ben insisted were routine?

The man's eyes darted to Liam's right shoulder, the exact spot where they'd placed the sensors during last spring's testing. He seemed to struggle with himself before speaking. "Everything you think you know..."

A folded piece of paper appeared in his trembling hand. "My name is Ryan," he said softly, extending the note.

Liam's brow furrowed as he accepted it, fingers brushing against the man's palm. There was no time for this. No time for distractions. But that specific glance at his shoulder, the familiar way Ryan carried himself... "Wait," he called sharply, taking a step forward, but the man was already gone, vanishing around the corner with surprising speed. Liam looked down at the paper, his heart rate climbing for reasons that had nothing to do with hockey.

The note was plain, just words typed in black ink. Liam's stick clattered to the floor as he read it once, then again, each word threatening to unravel seventeen years of certainty. His hands tightened around the paper before he smoothed it out, hoping he'd gotten it wrong. But no, the words remained unchanged, burrowing into his mind like an insidious whisper.

He snatched up his stick and searched again for Ryan, but he was gone. As Liam entered the locker room, his carefully built pre-game focus began to crack. His teammates were caught up in their own routines, oblivious to the reality Ryan had just dropped in his lap. He felt Julian watching him, unsure if the look was curious or mocking.

"Everything alright there?" Julian's voice broke Liam's concentration with an edge.

Liam forced a tight-lipped smiles. "Just focusing on what needs to be done," he replied with measured nonchalance.

Liam shifted his focus from Julian to Coach Dave Boucha, who had just entered. The presence of Team Canada's coach instantly drew everyone's attention, his broad-shouldered six-foot-one frame filling the doorway with the same commanding presence he'd carried through his playing days.

His weathered face, dark with the natural tan of his Ojibwe heritage, bore the sharp intensity that could silence a room. As Coach cracked his knuckles, a habit that always preceded his most important speeches, the overhead lights caught the old hockey scar on his cheek, a souvenir from a high stick years ago.

His steel-gray eyes swept across the room as he began outlining game tactics, his deep, gravelly voice carrying the weight of experience. While Coach Boucha rallied the team's spirit for victory, chewing his ever-present gum with determination, Liam couldn't shake a feeling that gnawed at him, something was off about today's game.

As the team made their way from the charged environment of the locker room to the ice, the tension among them was evident. Liam, lost in his thoughts, barely registered the shift from the dim hallways to the bright arena lights. The crowd's roar built around them, a stark contrast to the silence of his teammates. The cold air bit at his skin, a reminder of the reality that awaited them. It was in this walk, this passage from strategy to execution, that Liam's doubts whispered the loudest. Yet, as they stepped onto the ice, the familiar chill underfoot, the sound of blades cutting into the surface, everything but the game ahead began to fade. The moment of truth was near, the faceoff that would set everything in motion.

The din of the arena dwindled to a faint buzz as Liam took his position at the faceoff dot, the tension thick enough to slice through. Opposite him stood a Finnish center, his eyes locked on Liam with a cold, mocking stare. Their skates carved shallow grooves into the ice, both players shifting subtly, trying to out-position the other before the puck dropped. Liam straightened, refusing to break eye contact, his breath steady but his pulse quickening. The Finnish player smirked, as if daring Liam to make the first mistake.

Out of the corner of his eye, Liam caught the official skating toward them. The official's movements were deliberate, almost slow-motion in the heat of the moment, and both players tracked him closely. The puck dangled in the official's hand, ready to drop. Liam tightened his grip on his stick, his body coiled and ready to spring. The two centers leaned in slightly, their sticks hovering just above the ice, anticipating the moment they would strike.

The puck fell, spinning in a blur between them. Liam lunged, but the Finnish center was quicker, his stick meeting the puck first as Liam's stick caught nothing but cold air. The sharp clack of stick against ice echoed, followed by a collective intake of breath from the crowd. It was a rare miss, the kind that sent a ripple of uncertainty through the arena, a sound that lingered in the chilled air.

Moments later, the play shifted, and Liam was back in motion, dashing along the wing with the puck now at his feet. The ice opened up before him, the perfect opportunity to redeem his blunder. This was it, his hallmark shot, the one he'd perfected a thousand times in practice. His teammates' voices faded as he lined up the shot, but then, in a split second, Ryan's note crept into his thoughts, an insidious distraction.

His wrist flicked the puck toward the goal, but something was off. The 'ping' of the puck striking the post reverberated through the arena, mocking him, amplifying the dismay that gnawed at his focus. He could almost feel the weight of the crowd's collective sigh as his shot missed the mark.

Despite his teammates rallying and securing a goal, Liam felt like an imposter in his own skates. Liam received a pass in the offensive zone, a chance to tie the game. But as he maneuvered for a shot, a Finnish defenseman closed in. The urgent shouting of his teammates sounded distant, and in a critical split-second, he hesitated. The puck was stolen, the counterattack swift and brutal. The red light flared behind Canada's net, and Liam's failure was laid bare under the arena lights.

The final buzzer cut through the air, confirming what they already knew. Team Canada's players, once so full of hope and determination, now drifted from the ice with heads bowed and spirits frayed. The scoreboard loomed above them. A glaring reminder of their shortcomings. Finland 3, Canada 1. Liam felt the weight of each point like a physical blow, his skates carved tracks of regret into the ice as he left the rink.

The loss stung more because Liam knew he hadn't been himself out there. The note had done its work well, unraveling him thread by thread until he was a shadow of the player he was known to be. Passes slipped by him, shots went wide, and his usual fluid confidence had been replaced by hesitation. He felt the eyes of thousands upon him, heavy with expectation turned to dismay.

In the locker room, the air was thick with silence. Players undressed in a ritual of disappointment, their movements slow and heavy. No one spoke, what was there to say?

Julian leaned back against his locker, arms crossed, a smug smile tugging at the corner of his mouth. His eyes locked onto Liam, then deliberately dropped to the crumpled note still visible in Liam's bag. With exaggerated casualness, he stood and adjusted his jersey. "Guess some of us crack under pressure, eh?"

Without looking up, Liam focused on his skates, fingers working the laces with mechanical precision. Each pull of the lace was an anchor, keeping him from rising to Julian's bait. But Ryan's words from the note kept echoing, mixing with each missed opportunity that played through his mind like a highlight reel of mistakes.

A pat on his shoulder broke through Liam's inner turmoil, Coach Boucha stood beside him, an island of calm in a sea of tension.

"Walk with me," Coach said simply.

Liam stood without a word and followed him out of the locker room and down the hall.

"Look," Coach Boucha began as they walked side by side, "it's just one game. I've seen you play, you're better than what we saw out there today."

Liam let out a breath, pausing, "I know, Coach. I don't know what happened out there."

Boucha stopped walking and faced Liam squarely. His eyes were sharp but not unkind, eyes that had seen many players rise and fall and rise again.

"We all have off days," Coach said firmly. "What matters is how you bounce back. You're not just some rookie anymore, you're a leader on this team."

Liam focused on Coach Boucha, drawing strength from his steady presence and the grounding weight of his words amidst the storm Ryan's note had unleashed.

The press conference room was a tempest of anticipation, buzzing with probing questions that felt inescapable. Cameras pointed accusingly while microphones thrust forward aggressively, as if ready to battle. Liam sat down at the table alongside his teammates, feeling every eye upon him, their silent questions louder than any reporter could shout. Coach Boucha took his place at the podium and began addressing the media, his voice steady as he spoke of teamwork and resilience.

Liam listened but didn't hear. The words washed over him like water over stone. His mind kept circling back to Ryan's note, its meaning sinking in deeper with every replay.

When it came time for Liam to speak, he looked straight into the sea of cameras before him and spoke with conviction that belied his inner turmoil.

"We didn't get the result we wanted today," he said firmly, "but this isn't over, not by a long shot." His voice carried through the room with an authority born from necessity, the necessity to believe in himself once more.

Harper Sinclair entered the room with the practiced ease of someone who had spent years navigating the rhythms of the sports world. Her lean five-foot-seven frame moved with the confidence of a former athlete, commanding respect despite being one of the few women in the press pool.

She slipped her reading glasses into her blazer pocket, a habit before any interview, and pulled her dark blonde hair into a tighter ponytail, a practical solution to the controlled chaos of game-day coverage.

Her keen hazel eyes swept over the room, not just searching for a story but finding familiar faces. When her eyes landed on Liam. Harper had been tracking his career since he was just a rising hopeful, long before the pressure truly set in.

But today, something was different. Harper could see it even from across the room. There was a flicker of uncertainty in Liam's stance, a small crack in the confidence. Her instincts kicked in, sharpened by years of studying both the game and those who played it. She knew his game, how a flick of his wrist or burst of speed could ignite the ice. But now, in this moment, it wasn't his skill that caught her attention. It was the hesitation, a hesitation she'd never seen in him before.

As the floor opened for questions, Harper stood, notepad in hand. A brief nod passed between her and the other reporters, a silent recognition of her seasoned presence. She caught Liam's eye across the room, and for a moment, there was a flicker of something unspoken between them, a shared history that allowed her to understand more than what his words could ever reveal.

"Liam," she began, her tone measured but carrying the warmth of someone who knew him well, "you've been incredible this season. We've all seen how you've taken your game to the next level. But today..." she paused, tilting her head slightly, giving him space to fill in the gap. "Something felt off. What's your read on it? How do you rebound from a day like this?"

Liam looked toward her, and for a split second, Harper noticed a flicker of vulnerability breaking through his usual calm exterior. He straightened in his chair, his broad shoulders tensing beneath his Team Canada jersey as he leaned forward into the microphone. She had written about him so many times before, sung his praises in her columns, but now, she sensed there was more beneath the surface.

"Every team faces adversity," he said, his words deliberate, carefully chosen. "Today was one of those days. But one game won't define us or where we're headed. We'll regroup and come back stronger." Then, showing the polish expected of Team Canada's captain, he offered the same message in French, not perfectly, but with the determined effort of someone who understood what it meant to lead the Canadian national team. His eyes flicked briefly away, toward Julian, but Harper caught the tension in his shoulders. Something else was weighing on him.

She hesitated, sensing the pressure he was under, but pressed forward gently. "And you, personally?" she asked, her voice soft but firm, knowing he'd expect nothing less from her. "You've set a standard, Liam. Your fans look to you to lead this team. Can they count on you to be the one who brings them to gold?"

Liam looked at her for a moment longer than usual, as if carefully weighing how much he could reveal. "I'll do whatever it takes for this team," he said quietly but with conviction. "We're focused on one goal. To win gold for Canada."

Satisfied for the moment, Harper gave a slight nod and sat back down, letting the other reporters take their turns. Pete Marston from Arete Sports Agency leaned over from the next seat.

"NHL scouts are practically climbing over each other to get a better look at him," Pete whispered. "Most of these kids are already drafted, playing with their NHL rights secured. But the undrafted ones like Desjardins?" He shook his head. "They're the ones everyone's really watching. Especially with the draft only six months away."

Harper nodded slightly, knowing Pete was right. At eighteen and nineteen, most players had already heard their names called at the NHL draft. But it was the handful of draft-eligible players like Liam who drew the heaviest scrutiny. Every shift, every decision, every response in pressers like this, it all fed into their draft stock.

The press conference wrapped up with familiar promises of regrouping and strategy, words as predictable as they were urgent. As reporters dispersed and players filed out, Harper lingered, watching Liam's departure. She'd built her career on noticing what others missed, and tonight, something was definitely off with Team Canada's star player.

Stepping into the brisk Toronto evening, Harper knew one thing for sure: whatever had shaken Liam today went far beyond a single lost game.

Family Ties

"We don't choose the challenges we face, but we choose how we face them, together." – Tammy

Silverware clinked, the low hum of conversation wrapping around Liam as he sank into the plush seat at the hotel restaurant. His parents, Jim and Tammy Desjardins, sat across from him. His father's solid build and expressive brown eyes surveyed him with that steady Manitoba prairie watchfulness. Beside him, his mother's elegant frame and darker complexion offered a striking contrast to Jim's weathered farmer's skin, her composed posture revealing the quiet strength she'd carried north from her Saint Paul roots.

His mother had taught him to carry his brown skin with quiet confidence, though he still caught the occasional glance from other diners. After years in Manitoba's predominantly white hockey culture, these looks were nothing new, especially not with his parents beside him, their presence a reminder of who he was and where he came from.

"Rough game out there today," Jim said, breaking the bread with a decisive tear, his tone firm but not accusatory. It was the same voice he used when leading his team at work.

Liam gave a small shrug, his hand moving absently across his plate, pushing vegetables around with his fork. "Yeah," he murmured, "I wasn't on my game."

Tammy reached across the table, her fingers brushing his wrist, a small gesture, but one filled with the quiet strength she'd always passed on to him. "One game doesn't define who you are, Liam. You've got so much ahead of you," she said softly, but with that edge of steel in her voice that always reminded him of the resilience she embodied.

Liam tried to smile, but it felt like a mask, heavy and unfamiliar. He could feel the note burning a hole in his pocket, its weight pressing against him, crushing him. The words inside it had burrowed deep into his mind, distracting him in ways he hadn't anticipated.

"I know," he whispered, but the lie in his voice rang louder to him than anything his parents could have said.

Jim leaned forward, folding his hands on the table, his gaze steady. "You're gonna bounce back from this. You always do."

The certainty in his father's voice was a tether, something solid in the growing confusion inside his head. It was Jim who had instilled that relentless drive in him. But tonight, even those words felt distant, like he was hearing them from the other side of a thick wall of ice.

"And we'll be right here, cheering for you," Tammy added, her eyes crinkling at the corners with pride.

Liam forced a deep breath and let it out slowly, feeling the air catch in his throat. He looked between them, these two people who had been his foundation for as long as he could remember. They saw him as their champion, their rising star destined to light up the rink, yet he felt like an imposter, weighed down by something they couldn't see, something he couldn't even explain.

"I won't let you down," Liam said, though the words tasted bitter as soon as they left his mouth.

"You never could," Tammy said quietly, with the kind of certainty that should have been comforting. But tonight, it only added to the pressure closing in around him.

They continued eating, conversation drifting to lighter topics, Jim's stories from work, Tammy's latest book club discussions. Normally, the sound of their voices would have eased his tension, but tonight it all felt like background noise, as if he were watching them from a distance. Liam nodded at the right moments, smiled when appropriate, but his mind wasn't there. The pressure in his chest kept building, the weight of expectations, his own, his parents', the fans', the team's, bearing down on him with relentless force.

The note pressed against his leg, a weight he couldn't shake. He couldn't escape it, couldn't shove it into the back of his mind like he did with missed plays or lost games. It was there, pressing harder with every passing minute.

Jim caught Liam's distant gaze and tilted his head slightly. "Something else on your mind?"

Liam straightened a little, masking his unease. "Just... thinking about the next game," he replied, the lie slipping out more easily than he expected. He took a sip of water, as if that could wash away the knot tightening in his gut.

Jim studied him for a moment longer before a flicker of understanding crossed his face, his expression softening. "I get it. Focus is everything."

Liam dipped his head slightly, grateful his father hadn't pressed further. But even as the dinner conversation shifted, as the waiter cleared their plates and laughter filled the space, Liam felt like he was suffocating under the weight of something unspoken. His parents, his two biggest supporters, had no idea how close he was to falling apart.

Liam looked up to see Benjamin LaFleur, his six-foot frame sharply dressed in a tailored business suit, his affable smile as polished as the leather shoes he wore. His light brown hair was cut short and professional, image was everything to him. Ben never had to demand attention, people just gave it to him.

"Ben!" Jim boomed, his face lighting up as he stood to shake hands with the man who had become a fixture in their lives. "Good of you to drop by."

Ben returned the greeting with equal enthusiasm, his handshake firm, his posture relaxed. His fingers absently brushed the fidget spinner in his pocket, a habit few noticed. "Jim, Tammy, always a pleasure." His brown eyes shifted to Liam, gleaming with a mix of warmth and something sharper, professional pride, expectation, a keen assessment. "Liam, tough break out there today, but don't let it get to you. You've got what it takes to bounce back stronger."

Tammy smiled, the fondness in her gesture unmistakable. "Care to join us, Ben? Coffee or dessert, perhaps?"

Ben shook his head with a polite, easy refusal, adjusting his tie, a subtle tell of nervousness he couldn't quite suppress. "I appreciate the offer, but I'll have to pass this time."

He turned his attention to Liam, his tone casual, though his eyes sharpened slightly. "I wanted to drop in for a quick chat," Ben began, letting his words linger just long enough to shift the mood. His prominent watch caught the restaurant's dim light as he checked the time, a habit that always preceded his more serious conversations. "Heard some concerns about focus out there today. People are wondering what's going on with you." His affable smile remained, but a subtle edge crept into his voice. "You know how quickly chatter spreads."

Liam felt a knot tighten in his stomach. The message was unmistakable: his lack of focus had drawn attention. "Yeah, I get it," he replied, striving to sound composed despite the weight of Ben's words pressing down on him. "I'll be ready for the next game."

Ben's smile remained, but there was a lingering intensity in his eyes. He absently adjusted his watch, a power move as much as a nervous tic. "Good to hear," he said, giving Liam's shoulder a light pat. "Just remember, everyone's watching. You know what you can do, stay locked in." The easy tone could not mask the seriousness beneath.

With a final wave and nod, Ben made his departure. As the Desjardins family exchanged quiet looks of reassurance, the unspoken tension lingered. Benjamin LaFleur wasn't just an agent, he was the one guiding Liam's career toward bigger contracts, brighter lights, and higher stakes. But with that guidance came an increasingly heavy web of commitments and expectations, a weight that grew each time they crossed paths.

Liam watched Ben go, unsure if his support was a blessing or a leash. It wasn't just his parents' faith he carried, it was the belief of people like Ben, people who had invested in his success, who had made his rise their mission. And that belief came with its own set of pressures.

As they rose from the table and made their way into the hotel's grand lobby, the cold Toronto air nipped at Liam's heels. The weight of defeat clung to his broad shoulders, making each step heavier, as if the missed opportunities on the ice had aged him. Eyes followed him as he walked, whispers from fans buzzing in the air like a swarm, filling the silence with murmurs of speculation.

Liam's gaze remained fixed ahead, his mind swirling with the thoughts of the game, and the silent battles waged far beyond it, until a familiar figure emerged from the shadows of the lobby's golden light.

Ryan stood near a towering potted plant, stiff and uneasy. Their eyes locked, and for a brief moment, something unspoken passed between them, a silent acknowledgment of the tension simmering just below the surface.

Liam didn't hesitate. He strode over to Ryan, his heart pounding harder with every step. "You," he said, his voice low and sharp. "What is this supposed to mean?" He thrust the crumpled note into Ryan's hands, the weight of its contents pressing against his chest like a leaden anchor.

Ryan glanced down at the note, his eyes flickering over the words before meeting Liam's gaze. "I had to tell you," he murmured, barely loud enough to be heard over the hum of the hotel.

"Tell me what?" Liam's voice cracked, raw and cutting. "That Jim and Tammy aren't my parents? What kind of sick joke is this?" His words cut through the noise, though his disbelief wavered on the edge of anger.

Ryan shifted uncomfortably, his hands twitching as though they wanted to return the note but couldn't. "It's no joke, Liam," he said quietly. "They aren't your biological parents. I'm sorry you had to find out this way."

The words settled like ice in Liam's gut, a cold doubt he couldn't shake. Heat rose in his face, his pulse hammering in his ears. His hands clenched into fists, nails biting into his palms. "What the hell are you talking about? My mom, my dad they are my parents."

Ryan glanced around, his own nervousness growing as the lobby's busy flow of people moved past them, oblivious to the bombshell that had just dropped. "They are your parents," Ryan said softly, "in every way that counts. But not biologically."

He stared at Ryan, searching for some sign that this was a cruel prank, but all he saw was the weight of uncomfortable truth etched into Ryan's face. The doubt gnawed at him, sharp and unrelenting, yet it was there, slowly seeping into his bones.

"You're lying," Liam snapped, though the words felt hollow as soon as they left his mouth. He didn't want to believe it, but the pieces of the puzzle, Ryan's seriousness, the note, the timing, began to click into place in his mind.

Ryan shook his head, his voice barely above a whisper. "I wish I were. But you deserve to know."

Liam shook his head, trying to fend off the rising panic. "Why now?" His voice was hoarse, the edges fraying with frustration. "Why tell me this in the middle of Worlds?"

Ryan hesitated, his breath catching. "Because it matters now more than ever," he said finally, the weight of the statement hanging between them like an unresolved question.

Not far away, hidden among the flurry of hotel guests, Harper Sinclair leaned against a wall, arms crossed as she quietly observed the exchange. She hadn't intended to be here, but her instincts had led her right to this moment, and now everything in her told her to stay silent and watch.

Liam wanted to lash out, to rage against Ryan, against the truth that threatened to dismantle everything he thought he knew about his family. This was no time to fall apart, there were games to play and a championship to win.

He stepped back from Ryan, the crumpled note still clenched in his hand like a piece of himself he wasn't ready to confront. "You're wrong about this, Ryan," Liam said, shaking his head.

Harper caught the name. Ryan. She tucked it away, this was the thread she'd been waiting for. As Liam turned on his heel and stormed off, leaving Ryan standing alone in the opulent hotel lobby, Harper lingered, her gaze narrowing as the puzzle began to take shape.

Harper remained motionless for a moment longer, blending into the flow of hotel guests as she watched Ryan retreat into the shadows of the lobby. She didn't need to rush. *Who was this person that had Liam so agitated?*

Her gaze narrowed as she moved closer, slipping through the crowd with practiced ease. Ryan, his attention fixed on his phone, didn't notice her approach, a fact she used to her advantage.

"Ryan?" Harper's voice was smooth, calm, as if she were picking up an old conversation. She didn't offer her hand just yet, she wanted him to feel cornered, not comfortable.

Ryan looked up, his movements deliberate and controlled. "Ms. Sinclair," he said, surprising her by knowing her name.

"Harper Sinclair, True North Hockey," she confirmed, studying his composed demeanor. "You and Liam seemed to have an interesting exchange just now. Care to fill me in?"

"Ryan Patel," he replied. "And I'm afraid that conversation was private. VSM takes confidentiality very seriously."

"VSM?" Harper's journalistic instincts sparked to life. Victoria Sports Management didn't usually send representatives to corner players before games.

"As I said, private." Ryan slipped his phone into his pocket, his manner professional but distant. "Now, if you'll excuse me—"

"You've piqued my interest, Mr. Patel," Harper said, watching him shift from foot to foot, his lab coat wrinkled under his jacket. "And I don't lose interest easily."

"That's what makes you good at your job." Ryan stepped past her, then paused. "But sometimes, Ms. Sinclair, curiosity can be... complicated."

Harper watched as Ryan walked away, disappearing into the night. Curiosity was buzzing in her mind, and she was determined to dig deeper and find out what was really going on.

Her phone buzzed in her pocket, pulling her back to reality. The screen flashed with her Editor-in-Chief's name, Frank Taylor didn't appreciate delays.

"Sinclair," she answered, keeping the excitement out of her voice as best she could.

"Harper, where are we on Desjardins? I need a fresh angle on Game 1, and fast," Frank's voice came through with clipped efficiency, no-nonsense but with a hint of urgency.

Harper's gaze swept over the lobby as she spoke, catching sight of Liam just as he moved toward the elevators. "He had a rough game, but there's more to it than just an off night," she said, her tone calm but deliberate.

"Good. Give me something real. I don't need a hunch, I need a hook," Frank replied, his tone direct but not harsh. "Facts, not guesses."

"Count on me," Harper replied, her words carrying the assurance of a reporter with a solid lead. "I'll deliver something deeper than box scores."

The line clicked off before she could say more, but Frank's message was clear, no speculation, just results. Harper pocketed her phone, her mind already racing through the possibilities.

As she glanced back up, her eyes met Liam's across the lobby. For a moment, their eyes locked, and she caught a flicker of something in his expression, guarded, tense, like he was carrying the weight of more than just a bad game. Then, without a word, he turned and disappeared toward the elevators, leaving Harper with one certainty: this story was far from over.

Harper exhaled slowly, resisting the urge to chase after him. Trust wasn't built overnight, and she knew that pressing too hard could push Liam away.

Phenom in the Making

"The ice doesn't care about your potential. It only reveals the work you've put in and the fire you bring." – Coach Boucha

SIX YEARS BEFORE WORLD JUNIORS

An unblemished sky stretched above the frozen pond, the sun's rays glinting off the ice. The crisp air rang with the sharp clack of pucks on sticks, skates carving deep lines, and the fleeting clouds of breath from young competitors. A young Liam, barely twelve, moved with purpose across the frozen pond, his favorite battleground.

He was a comet on ice, his jersey billowing like a flag in the chill breeze as he navigated through his peers with a puck on an invisible string. His skates etched patterns into the surface, a silent testimony to his natural prowess. The scrimmage was a blur of motion, yet on the edges of the ice, dreams quietly built themselves, step by step.

Jim and Tammy Desjardins stood behind the boards that surrounded the rink, their faces reflecting a blend of hope, pride, and the colors of sacrifice. Jim kept his hands deep in his coat pockets, shoulders curled inward to fend off the chill. A subtle smile graced his lips, a father's quiet recognition of burgeoning talent.

Tammy, her dark skin wrapped in a thick scarf that did little to conceal her animated features, clapped her gloved hands together as Liam executed a spin-o-rama that left two defenders colliding like mismatched puzzle pieces. Her voice was a warm beacon in the frigid air. "That's it, Liam! Light it up!"

The other parents and children cast admiring glances at Liam, some tinged with envy, recognizing that they were witnessing something extraordinary. Even at twelve years old, Liam carried an aura of inevitability around him, greatness seemed not just possible but predestined.

"Heard they're doing those new genetic tests on all the prospects," one parent said, watching Liam's explosive acceleration. "Trying to predict who'll make it to the show." Jim pretended not to hear, but his jaw tightened slightly. The idea that raw talent and hard work might not be enough anymore troubled him deeply.

At the far end of the rink, a figure in a dark coat made notes on a tablet, occasionally lifting a phone to record Liam's movements. Tammy noticed but said nothing, pulling her scarf tighter.

Jim leaned in, his voice just above a whisper. "He's got it, Tam. That thing you can't teach."

Tammy nodded, her eyes never leaving their son. "He does. But we've got to keep him grounded, Jim. Remember where we come from."

"I know," Jim replied softly, a quiet determination settling in his expression as he thought about the long hours at Maple Prairie AgriTech and Tammy's weekend shifts at the bookstore. All for the skates, sticks, and endless travel, a future they were building, one stride at a time.

The scrimmage pressed on, unaware of the dreams being built by the parents watching from the sidelines. Liam cut in, lifted the puck clean off his opponent's blade, and was gone, a streak of red and black slicing through the ice. He faked left, his opponent bit, and then snapped right before firing a wrist shot that sang past the goalie's glove into the top corner of the net.

Cheers erupted from onlookers, even players from both teams couldn't help but tap their sticks in appreciation. But none cheered louder than Jim and Tammy.

Liam circled back to center ice with a grin that could have melted all the snow in Manitoba. He raised his stick in salute to his parents, acknowledging their sacrifices without saying a word.

* * *

FOUR YEARS BEFORE WORLD JUNIORS

The frozen ponds of his childhood felt like a distant memory now, replaced by the cold, calculated precision of real rinks. At fourteen, Liam's world had expanded beyond his hometown, yet every time his skates touched the ice, the same fire burned within him.

Young hockey prospects skated across an icy surface, their breaths misting in the air as they followed the drill instructions with focused precision. Liam was among them, his strides long and powerful, his mind singularly tuned to the puck at his stick's end. As a young teenager, he already stood out, not just for his height but for that spark of potential that seemed to electrify his every move.

Coach Boucha's voice boomed over the rink, echoing off the high ceilings and reverberating in Liam's chest. "Keep your head up, watch your passes!" The coach was a fortress of a man, his presence alone demanding excellence from every young player on the ice.

Liam executed a crisp pass to his teammate, pride swelling within him when Coach Boucha nodded in approval. He knew he had much to learn, but moments like this made him believe in what he could become. Each time he touched the puck, it felt like holding a bolt of lightning, wild and unpredictable, yet under his control.

Off to the side of the rink, leaning against the cool barrier, stood Harper Sinclair. Her eyes were trained on Liam with an intensity that matched his own focus on the game. She followed each move he made, noting his strengths and potential areas for growth. Harper, a journalist for True North Hockey, possessed a talent for discovering emerging athletes and highlighting them in her articles.

As Coach Boucha called for a water break, most players slumped toward the bench, their breaths coming in heavy gasps, legs wobbling from the intense session. But not Liam. While his teammates collapsed onto the bench, gulping water and wiping sweat-soaked faces, he continued gliding across the ice, working on his edges, practicing his signature toe drag sequence again and again.

Julian Broten slumped on the bench, taking long pulls from his water bottle, his Vancouver Thunderbirds practice jersey dark with sweat. His eyes tracked Liam's continued practice with barely concealed annoyance.

"Show-off," Julian muttered, loud enough for nearby players to hear. But Harper noticed how he straightened up, forcing himself back onto the ice despite his obvious fatigue. Even Julian's natural talent couldn't match Liam's seemingly endless stamina.

As practice wound down and players started to leave the ice, Harper pushed off from her spot against the boards and approached Liam as he skated toward the exit. She adjusted her dark blonde hair, now escaping from its messy bun after hours of rink side observation, and pulled her battered notebook from her jacket pocket.

"Hey there," she said, her voice friendly but carrying an edge of purpose. "Liam Desjardins, right?"

He came to a stop before her, a little breathless from exertion. "Yeah, that's me." A flush of surprise warmed his cheeks as he realized who she was. "You're Harper Sinclair."

"In person." She smiled, though it was more polite than warm. "I've had my eye on you. You're quite skilled."

Liam couldn't help but feel flattered, someone from True North taking notice of him felt like another step toward his dreams. "Thanks," he said with a shy grin. "I'm just trying to get better, you know?"

"I know," Harper affirmed. She shifted slightly, angling her body toward him casually. "You played with Ethan Bernard last season, if I'm not mistaken?"

Liam's heart hitched at Ethan's name, his friend and teammate, the one who made him play his best. "Yeah, Ethan and I... we have good chemistry on the ice."

"I saw some of your games together. You two play like you're reading each other's minds."

"That's hockey for you," Liam chuckled softly, nodding earnestly. "Ethan's great."

Harper glanced away for just a moment as if weighing her next words carefully before returning her attention to him. "I'm looking forward to seeing you both tear it up for the Brandon Wheat Kings this winter."

"We'll light it up," Liam promised, his confidence blossoming.

"I don't doubt it for a second," Harper said, conviction in her voice. She offered her hand, and as he shook it, Liam noticed the jagged scar running across the back of her hand, evidence of the surgery that had pieced her bones back together after a brutal slash in youth hockey. That same determination that had kept her playing after the injury had carried her through college hockey and onto Team Canada's women's gold medal team. Their handshake was firm, and Liam felt a connection, a feeling of being truly seen for all he was striving to become.

As Harper made her way back to the press area, a small group of journalists stood nearby, their voices a low hum, exchanging the day's observations. She joined the conversation smoothly, picking up on their chatter.

"Have you noticed the way these kids are coming up?" Greg Marshall, a seasoned beat writer from Hockey Insight, tapped his iPad thoughtfully. "Some of them are making moves like the toe drag that would make McDavid proud, or pulling off Crosby's signature backhand roofer."

Murmurs of agreement rippled through the group. Harper folded her arms, leaning casually against the rink's barrier.

"It's more than just skill," she mused. "They push harder. Recover faster. Almost like they're built for it."

"How?" Anita from SportsNet asked, her brow knitting in curiosity.

Harper hesitated, leaving the thought open-ended. "I don't know, maybe it's just advanced training. But they're pushing past limits we didn't even realize existed."

"Training's gotten better, no doubt," Greg added. "Specialization, diet, high-level coaching, it's no surprise they're making waves."

"Maybe that's all it is," Harper murmured, but the question lingered in her mind: *What was really behind this new generation of athletes?*

As Harper turned to grab her Tim Horton's coffee, a familiar figure approached the rink's barrier from the opposite side, drawing her attention away from Liam's form. It was Benjamin LaFleur, no longer the carefree college hockey player she remembered, but now a sharp-suited agent with an air of confidence that bordered on arrogance.

"Still hunting stories, Sinclair?" Ben smirked. "Some things never change."

Harper arched a brow. "Surprised you're here without a phone glued to your hand."

He chuckled, glancing down at the ice. "Can't miss watching Liam. Kid's got a comet's tail, one hell of an upward trajectory."

"Mmm," Harper hummed, noncommittal. "Seems you've carved a decent path for yourself since our days at the University of Toronto."

For a fleeting moment, she saw the old Benjamin, the one who had matched her drive on and off the ice. Their eyes met, and a mutual recognition of the past flickered between them, an acknowledgment of what once was, though neither lingered on it.

"Times change, Harper," Ben said with a knowing smile. "It's all about making the right moves, both on and off the ice."

As Ben's figure retreated, Harper found herself puzzling over the changes in her former college boyfriend. The polished agent he'd become, that calculated confidence, the way he'd deflected her questions about his athletes.

She pulled out her notebook, jotting down a few observations. Old habits died hard, especially for a journalist with a curious mind.

Genesis

"Furever didn't just give me back Max, they gave me back the warmth, the joy, and the memories that made every day brighter."
- Furever client

*T*WENTY TWO YEARS BEFORE WORLD JUNIORS

Fireworks exploded over Furever Genetics' Seoul headquarters, their brilliance reflected in the glass and steel of the building, a decade of miraculous rebirths written across the night sky. The air was thick with the heady aroma of success and expensive cologne.

Dr. Kim Jung-So, his wiry five-foot-four frame garbed in a tailored suit that spoke of both affluence and intellect, navigated the crowd. Despite his slight stature, he carried an intensity that commanded attention. Years in the laboratory had left his complexion sallow, the artificial lights of his research facility having replaced the sun. Behind sleek, understated glasses, his dark eyes moved calculatingly through the gathering, already assessing, always observing.

Screens around the room showcased the crowning achievements of Furever: a majestic racehorse prancing with an owner's pride, a loyal golden retriever bounding into the arms of a tearful child, camels racing across the sands, their identical forms blurring into one. At the center of the room, an ornate phoenix ice sculpture glowed under soft lights. Nearby, a screen looped footage of near-extinct pandas and tigers frolicking, living proof of Furever's work.

"Dr. Kim! The Arabian Oryx project was truly inspirational," a sheikh complimented, shaking his hand with vigor.

"Though not everyone shares your enthusiasm," Dr. Kim replied diplomatically, noting the small cluster of protestors visible through the floor-to-ceiling windows. Their signs about 'Playing God' cast shadows in the fireworks' glow. A recent controversy over Furever's successful cloning of the extinct Pyrenean Ibex had sparked heated debates about the ethics of resurrecting species that nature had selected for extinction. But tonight wasn't about debates. It was about celebration.

As the evening wore on, anticipation rippled through the assembly as Dr. Kim ascended the podium for his speech. A hush fell over the room, all eyes turned toward him.

"Ladies and gentlemen," he began, his voice rich and assured, "we stand at the precipice of what many believed impossible in animal cloning. From beloved family pets to prized racehorses, each creature you've seen tonight represents a triumph of our proprietary process," he continued, gesturing to the screens where DNA helices spiraled in an elegant dance. "Our breakthrough in preserving the cell's energy centers, the mitochondria, has achieved success rates that were once thought impossible. When others said perfect animal cloning couldn't be done, we found a way."

The screens shifted to show side-by-side comparisons of original and cloned specimens, identical golden retrievers playing fetch, champion polo ponies in mid-stride, their features perfectly matched. "Where others failed, we succeeded. Whether it's preserving endangered species or reuniting families with their cherished pets, each new life we create isn't just a copy, it's a continuation of life itself."

He paused, letting his gaze sweep over his audience before continuing.

"But as we marvel at these scientific wonders, let us not forget that at the heart of every innovation is emotion, the joy when a child reunites with their beloved pet, or the awe when we see an extinct species take its first breath anew."

A tender smile softened Dr. Kim's features as he gestured toward his son to come on stage, Dae-Song.

"As I look at my son, I realize more than ever how fragile those bonds can be..." The words hung in the air for a moment, heavy with unspoken grief.

"Life does not offer second chances, not for my wife, not for the mother who gave her life so that he could have his. That love, so pure and final, lives on in him. And in that love, I find the strength to push forward."

The applause swelled, filling the room with warmth and appreciation. Dr. Kim bowed slightly, his professional demeanor returning as he stepped from the podium. Moving through the crowd of well-wishers, he found Ryan Patel waiting with a quiet, "Another success for the books, Dr. Kim."

Dr. Kim responded with a small smile, gesturing toward Ryan as they briefly paused near the sheikh. "Ryan Patel has been integral in overseeing some of our largest projects, including the tiger rewilding initiative. His contributions cannot be overstated."

Ryan nodded respectfully. "It's been an honor to work on something so meaningful."

Dr. Kim gave a curt nod, already moving toward the next conversation. Ryan stepped away seamlessly, his quiet departure unnoticed by most, but the few who caught his eye exchanged knowing glances, aware that his influence ran deeper than appearances suggested.

The celebration at Furever Genetics' headquarters was winding down, but Dr. Kim Jung-So still felt the warmth of success, or perhaps it was just the champagne. As the crowd thinned, he found himself relying on each handshake and congratulatory pat to maintain his balance, the room gently spinning around him like a slow-motion carousel.

"You've had quite a bit to drink. Let me get you a car," Melanie said gently, her voice carrying more than just concern, it carried the weight of years spent watching him try to hold his world together after it shattered once before.

Melanie had worked alongside him through the dark days after his wife's death, had seen the grief he tried so hard to hide. Her concern tonight wasn't just about his drinking, it was about the weight he still carried.

He laughed off her suggestion with an airy wave of his hand. "Nonsense, Melanie. I'm perfectly capable of driving myself home."

"I insist, Dr. Kim," Melanie pressed, her eyes reflecting years of unspoken concern. "Let me call you a car service."

"I appreciate your concern," he muttered, drawing himself up with wounded dignity, "but I am perfectly capable of handling myself." The words were meant to be firm but came out slurred.

Melanie opened her mouth to protest again but thought better of it. She could only watch helplessly as Dr. Kim waved her off and made his unsteady way toward the parking lot, where his sleek car waited beneath the silver glow of moonlight.

A momentary flash of doubt cut through the haze, had Melanie been right? But his pride drowned it out, as it always did. A deeper sadness, long buried, briefly stirred within him, thoughts of her, his wife, who hadn't been given a second chance. Her absence, always there in the shadows, sharpened the momentary fear that he wasn't protecting Dae-Song well enough. He shook it off, he had promised, he would protect him from everything life had taken away from them before.

The engine purred to life, a familiar and comforting sound, and he pulled out onto the road with only the ghostly echo of his son's laughter for company.

The city lights blurred into streaks as he drove, colors merging into an abstract painting only he could see. It was as if reality had taken on a dreamlike quality, each turn and stop sign coming up on him too quickly or too late.

A sharp cry from Dae-Song's booster seat in the back jolted him back to attention.

"Daddy? Where are we going?" The little voice was sleepy and confused.

"Home," Dr. Kim replied with an attempt at reassurance that fell flat even to his own ears.

But home would remain out of reach tonight.

His hands felt disconnected, heavy, as he gripped the wheel tighter, trying to focus on the road, but each streetlight blurred past like the flicker of dying stars. A wave of dizziness washed over him, and a dark voice in the back of his mind whispered what he already knew, he was losing control.

No screech of tires, no warning, just a shift, almost gentle, before the world spun into chaos. The car twisted, weightless for a moment, a ballet of steel and glass before the darkness swallowed him whole.

When Dr. Kim's senses returned to him, he was lying sideways, strapped by his seatbelt in what remained of his car. Shattered glass littered the darkness around him.

Sirens wailed in the distance, red and blue lights flashed across the asphalt. Panic surged through him as he remembered Dae-Song. His hand reached blindly for the backseat, finding only empty space and cold leather.

"Dae-Song!" His voice cracked as he called out for his son.

First responders swarmed his car. Voices shouted instructions, metal groaned under pressure.

"Sir, stay still! We're going to cut you out," someone commanded over the buzz of a saw.

But Dr. Kim's eyes were fixed on the small form being lifted from the wreckage and placed into a waiting ambulance.

"No! My son!" The words tore from his throat as realization hit him.

The ambulance drove away with urgent speed, sirens blaring. Dr. Kim could only watch, helpless as his son disappeared into the night. Every mistake he'd made led to this moment, this consequence of driving drunk.

The jaws of life screeched against metal as rescuers worked to free him. For all his brilliance, for all his power, he was utterly powerless.

Unspooled

"The truth has a way of surfacing, no matter how deeply it's buried beneath layers of ice and lies." – Harper

Silence filled the hotel room, absolute and heavy, with only the echoes of skates carving ice and the distant roar of a crowd long gone. Liam sat on the edge of his bed, a lone figure against the backdrop of a neatly made comforter and drab hotel art that tried too hard to seem like home.

In his hands, he held a photograph, its edges worn from being thumbed over time. His calloused fingers, hardened from countless hours of stick handling, traced the creased edges with unexpected gentleness.

The image was a snapshot of joy, frozen in glossy permanence, a younger Liam, gap-toothed and beaming with the kind of innocence that comes before life starts asking hard questions. Beside him, Jim's proud grin stretched ear to ear, while Tammy's embrace engulfed him as if she could shield him from any off-ice hit life might throw.

"Look at us," Liam whispered to himself, tracing the contours of their faces. "Just look at us."

The warmth in that photograph seemed at odds with the chill that now seeped into his bones, a chill that had nothing to do with Canadian winters or poorly heated rooms. It was an internal coldness, one that spread from the pit of his stomach to the tips of his fingers as he clutched the photo.

His mind raced back to Ryan's words, every syllable etching itself into his memory. *Not your biological ones.* The phrase was a puck slammed into his gut, leaving him winded and disoriented.

A short, bitter laugh escaped him. How could he not see himself in them? The set of Jim's jaw when he was determined, that was Liam's stubborn tilt when staring down an opponent. And Tammy's calm under pressure? He lived for that in shootouts.

"Blade," he muttered to himself, reaching for his nickname like a stick-tap for good luck. "Light it up."

But what did lighting it up even mean when you felt like someone had just dimmed all the lights around you? His thoughts spun faster than he ever could on skates, a dizzying whirlwind that offered no clear path forward.

He needed air, needed to feel something other than this oppressive stillness.

With swift movements born from restless energy rather than purpose, Liam stood and crossed to the window. He pressed his forehead against the cool glass, staring out at Toronto's skyline as if it held answers among its clustered lights and towering structures.

Below him, life moved uninterrupted, cars honking in their late-night urgency and pedestrians wrapped up in their own little worlds. None of them knew about the turmoil in room 1428 or cared about the implications of a single piece of paper.

"Maybe it doesn't change anything," he spoke to his reflection in the window, a ghostly version of himself superimposed on the cityscape. "You're still you."

Yet doubt crept in like shadows at dusk, subtle and insidious. *Could genetics unravel everything he thought he knew about himself? Did they have that power?*

He turned away from the window abruptly, as if by looking away he could also dismiss these intrusive thoughts.

"Stay focused," he chided himself, repeating Coach Boucha's words from earlier conversations meant to steel him against less personal challenges.

His phone buzzed against the nightstand, the screen illuminating with a message from Jim: *You're still my boy out there tomorrow. Show 'em what prairie hockey looks like.*

Before he could look away, another text rolled in, this one from Tammy: *Sweetheart, please call when you can. We love you.*

Liam's throat tightened. Their messages, so normal, so them, only twisted the knife deeper. Three missed calls from earlier blinked accusingly on his screen: two from Jim, one from Tammy. He could almost hear his dad's worried voice, his mom's gentle prodding. Seventeen years of love and everything he thought he knew about himself, all wrapped up in those simple texts.

With a frustrated grunt, he tossed the phone onto his pillow. The soft thud as it landed felt like a door closing between him and the only parents he'd ever known.

* * *

Morning sunlight pierced the Toronto skyline as Liam made his way through the hotel lobby. He moved with his usual focus, though today it served more to fortify him against thoughts of his lineage than prepare him for the game ahead.

Liam forced a smile on his face when his teammate, Jensen, walked past with their usual fist bump and "Wheel, snipe, celly, eh?" He managed a weak "Beauty," but his reaction betrayed his stress. He wasn't okay. How could he be, when everything he thought he knew about himself was suddenly up for debate?

"Desjardins!" The sharp call cut through the morning quiet.

Liam turned, his eyes landing on Pete Marston. The fit six-foot agent moved with practiced confidence, his dark hair graying stylishly at the temples, custom suit and luxury watch marking him as one of hockey's power players. Pete's smile was as slick as fresh ice. "Liam, got a minute?"

Liam gave Pete a guarded glance. "Sure," he said, the word crisp and final like the crack of a puck against the boards.

Pete steered Liam toward a pair of plush armchairs, strategically placed away from prying eyes. His keen, observant gaze never wavered as he crossed his legs with an air of casual authority. "You're quite the talk of the town, kid," Pete began. "You know you're sitting on a goldmine of potential, right?"

"I'm aware," Liam replied, voice even but cool.

Pete leaned in, his eyes gleaming with persuasive intent. "VSM's good, sure. But what I can offer you—"

"I'm good with VSM," Liam interjected without hesitation. "Ben's been solid for us."

Pete chuckled softly. "Loyalty. Admirable. But sometimes loyalty can cost you opportunities."

Liam's voice hardened with competitive resolve. "And sometimes it can build something worth more than opportunities."

Undeterred, Pete unfolded a glossy card from his jacket and slid it across to Liam. The front boasted an athlete mid-stride, muscles taut with promise and power. "We're not just about contracts and endorsements," Pete said smoothly. "We're about building legends."

Liam glanced at the card but didn't touch it. His thoughts darted to Ben, the man who had stood by him through thick and thin, whose guidance had become as much a part of his career as his own right hand on the stick.

"Look at you," Pete pressed on, mistaking Liam's silence for consideration. "The future of sports isn't just about training anymore, Liam. It's about optimization. Enhancement. Evolution. We work with partners who are... shall we say, ahead of the curve."

Despite everything, the cryptic note, the tumultuous game, it was that same sense of integrity that anchored Liam now. His voice was firm as he spoke: "I appreciate what you're saying, Pete. But Ben's got my back."

Pete leaned back in his chair, smile unfaltering as if this was just another play in a long game. "You sure about that? You think VSM hasn't kept secrets from you?"

The insinuation hung between them like fog over morning ice. Liam felt a familiar surge of defensiveness for his team, both on and off the ice.

"Everyone's got secrets," Liam said pointedly. "Doesn't change where my loyalty lies."

Pete sighed theatrically and stood up. "Well then," he said smoothly, tucking the card away. "The offer stands if you ever change your mind."

As Pete sauntered away, Liam remained seated for a moment longer. He thought about what Pete had said about legends and enhancement, words that might have tempted someone else. But Liam knew better, knew who he was, or at least who he wanted to be.

"Light it up," he whispered to himself as he headed toward practice. Today, those words meant more than just hockey.

* * *

Harper Sinclair hunched over her laptop in the busy press room, searching through social media accounts, stories, and public documents. The world around her faded as she focused on her target: Ryan Patel.

"Come on, where are you hiding?" she murmured, scrolling through another dead-end LinkedIn profile. Her usual knack for sniffing out details seemed to falter against Ryan's elusive online presence. Dozens of Ryan Patels populated the professional network, but none matched the nervous man she'd encountered at the hotel.

She cross-referenced employment histories against VSM's company records, but nothing connected. It was as if someone had methodically erased his digital footprint.

A contact on her phone caught her attention. Mary Davidson, an old teammate from her playing days who'd traded her stick for Silicon Valley success. She typed hastily.

Hey Mary, need a favor. Looking for info on a Ryan Patel. Can you help?

The three dots blinked in response before a message popped up.

Harper! Long time. Pretty vague ask. Got anything else? Current employer? Education?

Claims some connection to VSM, but I can't find a trace. Mid forties, South Asian. That's all I've got.

VSM? The sports management company? Interesting. Let me dig around, but no promises. What's this about?

Harper hesitated, fingers hovering over the keys. *Just following a lead. Might be nothing.*

Your 'nothing' usually turns into something big. Give me a day.

She leaned back in her chair, crossing her arms with a sigh. The World Juniors press box was filling up, two hours until puck drop. Team Canada, still stinging from their opening loss to Finland, needed this win against Sweden.

* * *

The hockey arena thundered with anticipation. Harper stood among the sea of red and white jerseys, but her attention wasn't on the scoreboard showing 2-1 Canada over Sweden midway through the second period. Her eyes tracked Ryan, who lurked near the media entrance, his movements betraying his nervous energy.

A collective groan rippled through the crowd. Julian Broten had just taken a holding penalty, his piercing blue eyes flashing with defiance as he argued the call. The penalty put Canada down a man against Sweden's lethal power play unit.

Sweden's top unit took the ice, their crisp passes probing Canada's penalty kill formation. Julian sat in the penalty box, seething.

A Swedish defenseman wound up for a one-timer from the point. Liam read it perfectly, dropping to block the shot. The puck ricocheted off his shin pads and fluttered toward center ice.

"Go, go, GO!" The crowd erupted as Liam exploded from his defensive stance, accelerating past the Swedish defensemen. His skates cut deep into the ice, each stride eating up distance as he broke free.

Harper's stood up, leaning forward, she'd seen this acceleration countless times. There was something almost superhuman about his speed.

The Swedish defender, desperate to stop the breakaway, lunged from behind. His stick clipped Liam's skates just as he crossed the hash marks, sending him airborne, a helpless projectile hurtling full speed into the goalie. The impact sent both players crashing into the goal post, which tore free from its moorings with a sickening metallic screech.

The arena fell silent. The Team Canada medical staff rushed out, their equipment bags bouncing against their sides. Players from both teams circled at a respectful distance, most taking a knee.

Liam lay motionless, crumpled against the displaced net.

Harper's knees buckled slightly, her grip tightening on the press box desk. Her concern for Liam was undeniable. She glanced back and spotted

Ryan, who was now on the move, eyes locked on his phone, his movements deliberate and controlled.

Harper rushed out the press box and pushed her way through the stunned crowd, keeping Ryan in sight as he navigated the corridors. The concrete hallways echoed with the muffled sound of medical calls from above.

"Ryan!" Her voice bounced off the walls.

He turned, his composure breaking just enough to seem genuine. "Not here," he said quietly, glancing past her shoulder with calculated concern.

"Victoria Sports Management?" Harper stepped closer, blocking his path to the exit. "Because I can't find a single record of you ever working there. Or anywhere else."

Ryan's expression shifted subtly. "Some records are meant to stay hidden." His voice was low but steady. "You don't understand what's at stake. Liam's not just a hockey player—"

"Then make me understand." Harper's voice was steel, her reporter's instincts screaming that she was close to something big. "Because right now, a kid is lying on the ice, and you're acting like it's more than just a hockey injury."

The crowd erupted in applause as Liam slowly got to his feet and skated toward the bench, headed for the locker room. Harper knew she needed to get there too. As Ryan moved to leave, Harper grabbed his arm. *Not this time*, she thought, steering him down the hallway.

Buried Promises

"We bury not just the ones we love, but the future we imagined with them." — Mourner

The fluorescent lights of Seoul Memorial's ICU corridor cast a harsh, sterile glow, exposing Dr. Kim Jung-So's unsteady state. His vision blurred, the remnants of alcohol in his system turning the hallway into a shifting maze.

His legs felt like lead, each step heavier than the last as though the hallway itself was conspiring to slow him down. The air grew thick, every breath a labor, as if the hospital itself were closing in on him.

A nurse, her face a blur of pastel uniform and concern, caught his arm as he stumbled past the reception. "Sir, you can't go in there without..."

But her words fell away as Dr. Kim shook off her grip, propelled by an urgency that transcended protocol. He had to find him. His son, Dae-Song. The little boy who'd been laughing in the backseat just hours before, now somewhere behind these cold walls, fighting for his life.

The corridors whispered with hushed voices and soft footsteps, none of it mattered. His world had narrowed to a single point of focus: Dae-Song. A sign read 'Intensive Care Unit,' and he burst through the doors without hesitation.

There he was, his boy, enshrouded in tubes and wires, a small chest rising and falling with mechanical precision. Monitors beeped a jarring rhythm that measured the thread of life still holding Dae-Song to this world.

Dr. Kim's knees buckled as he approached the bedside, his hands trembling as they reached for his son's pale fingers, dwarfed by bandages and IV lines.

"Dae-Song... my boy... I'm here," Dr. Kim's voice cracked, the words catching in his throat like shards of glass.

Dae-Song lay still, cocooned in white sheets, a stark contrast to the vibrant child who had once chased butterflies in their garden under the sun's gentle embrace.

For a moment, just one fleeting moment, Dr. Kim convinced himself that if he could just will it hard enough, if he could just speak his son's name loud enough, the machines would reverse their course, the beeping would stabilize, and his son would open his eyes.

"Please... please..." It was all he could muster, a father's desperate incantation against the unyielding march of fate.

Dr. Kim's trained eye caught every detail he didn't want to see: the dropping oxygen levels, the irregular heartbeat pattern, the subtle signs of organ failure.

But it was the warmth leaving his son's small fingers that shattered him. The moment he had feared, the moment he had refused to believe, had arrived.

Dae-Song was gone.

Dr. Kim collapsed into sobs that wracked his body with such force it seemed as though his soul was trying to escape the cage of his ribs, to chase after Dae-Song into whatever lay beyond this realm of beeping machines and whispered condolences.

Nurses rushed forward, their faces blurring as they tried to console him, but Dr. Kim couldn't hear them over the roar of grief that filled his ears, a torrential downpour that drowned out everything else. His tears fell onto Dae-Song's hand, saltwater tributes mingling with memories of laughter and bedtime stories whispered in the dark. A floodgate had opened within him, spilling forth all the love he had failed to protect, his son from harm, himself from regret.

* * *

Three days after Dae-Song's death, the world seemed to shrink to the confines of the funeral, its walls draped in white. Dr. Kim Jung-So stood motionless in his white hemp hanbok, the numbness in his heart rivaling the stillness of his son's portrait at the memorial altar. Dae-Song's face, captured in a moment of youthful exuberance, smiled back at him, a cruel reminder of what was lost.

Four years ago, that same smile had been his salvation after Min-Seo's death. While others saw only tragedy in losing his wife during childbirth, Dr. Kim had found purpose in his son's eyes. Every milestone, first step, first word, first question about the world, had been both joy and heartache, knowing Min-Seo wasn't there to share them.

Mourners clad in white moved past him like specters, bowing deeply before Dae-Song's portrait and the offerings laid before it. Their murmured condolences fell on deaf ears as Dr. Kim clutched a white chrysanthemum in his trembling hand.

His gaze never left the portrait as he clutched a white chrysanthemum tightly in his hand. Just last week, he'd been reviewing preschools, imagining Dae-Song in a tiny uniform, ready to begin his education. The applications still sat unsigned on his desk at home, next to the children's science kit he'd bought, a father's eager attempt to share his passion for discovery with his son.

Now those dreams, like the flower in his trembling fingers, would never bloom.

The procession to the grave felt endless, each step slower than the last.

His son had been everywhere. A voice echoing through the lab after daycare, *Why, Papa?* A tiny hand reaching for his on their walks through the park. Soft laughter tangled in bedtime stories, the kind of nights where work could wait, because nothing mattered more than being there.

Now, he was nowhere.

All because he'd broken his most sacred promise to Min-Seo, to always protect their child. One moment of weakness. One drink too many. One fatal drive home.

The graveside was adorned with more chrysanthemums, their whiteness stark against the dark soil that had been freshly turned. He watched as others placed their flowers on the grave with reverent care before stepping back into the crowd.

But Dr. Kim remained rooted to the spot, unable to let go of his flower or move away from his son's final resting place. He stood there as an embodiment of sorrow, a father whose future had been buried along with his child.

The chrysanthemum trembled in his hand as a memory flashed: Dae-Song running through his lab, laughing at the bubbling solutions, asking endless questions about what Papa did at work. Such curiosity, such potential, now forever stilled.

As people began to disperse, leaving quiet footprints in their wake, Dr. Kim finally moved forward with a heavy heart and trembling hands. He laid his chrysanthemum upon the grave and dropped to his knees as if the weight of his loss had finally become too much for him to bear standing.

"I'm sorry," he whispered hoarsely into the wind, "I'm so sorry." His words were meant for Dae-Song, for himself, for a universe that had allowed such injustice.

The cold earth beneath him seemed to call out for him to join his son, to lay down and never rise again, but he knew he could not succumb to that temptation. His tears fell freely now, soaking into the soil.

Around him, attendants waited at a respectful distance, knowing that it was not their place to interrupt this private moment between father and son.

The sky above threatened rain as if even the heavens mourned Dae-Song's passing. Dr. Kim remained at the graveside long after everyone else had left, unwilling to leave and unwilling to let go. The connection between him and his son transcended life and death, it was etched into every fiber of his being.

He knew he had promises yet unfulfilled, promises made through tears over Dae-Song's still form in the hospital, promises that gave purpose to each breath he now took without his son by his side.

Eventually, Dr. Kim rose stiffly from beside the grave, each movement an act of defiance against despair. He took one last look at Dae-Song's final resting place before turning away, a piece of his soul forever interred with his child beneath the weeping sky.

As he walked from the grave, his grief began to crystallize into something else entirely. Something that burned with purpose.

"Papa can fix anything," he had always told his son.

And he would.

Shattered Blade

"Secrets have a way of settling in the air, as unmistakable as the chill of an unspoken truth, both lingering and impossible to ignore." – Harper

The locker room's chill clung to Liam's skin, burrowing into his muscles. The sharp bite of antiseptic stung his nostrils as the medical team worked around him. Ice packs and gauze became their weapons of choice, hands moving with practiced efficiency. The trip had left him battered, a physical toll that mirrored the chaos inside.

Through the walls came the muffled roar of the crowd, punctuated by bursts of music after another Team Canada goal. Liam winced. The announcer's voice boomed through the corridors: *"Hat trick for Julian Broten!"* The words hit harder than the ice. *"Team Canada leads Sweden 4-1!"* Liam's grip tightened around the edge of the treatment table, his knuckles pressing white. Stuck here while Broten took center stage? That wasn't part of the plan.

Liam could picture it perfectly, Julian circling the ice with that practiced smile, mouthguard hanging half out while he chirped at the Swedish players, making sure every camera caught his best angle. Always the showman, turning every goal celebration into a photo op. The thought of Julian soaking up the spotlight made his grip on the table tighten further.

"You're gonna be alright, kid," Ben murmured, hovering close enough for Liam to feel his agent's warm breath against his ear. His eyes scanned Liam's face, searching for reassurance that wasn't there.

Liam winced as a doctor prodded gently at his shoulder, her fingers expert and precise. "Does this hurt?" she asked.

"Just a bit," Liam grunted, his voice betraying more discomfort than he intended.

Ben, VSM's golden boy agent, stood at Liam's side like a general surveying his top soldier. With the NHL draft mere months away, every bruise was scrutinized, every grimace dissected.

Ben's phone buzzed again, another text from Montreal demanding updates. Minnesota's scouts were in the building, watching their potential first overall pick, and VSM couldn't afford any setbacks. Not now. Not with everything they'd invested in Liam.

"Keep him iced and get an MRI," Ben instructed without taking his eyes off Liam.

This was World Juniors, every team was watching, and every mistake could cost millions.

Liam watched the flurry of activity around him through half-closed eyes. Doctors nodded at Ben's commands while trainers scurried back and forth with medical supplies. He'd become an island in a sea of concern, a commodity everyone wanted to protect.

The trainers applied another layer of ice to his shoulder with practiced care. To VSM, every movement, every treatment was about protecting their investment.

"How's that leg feel?" another doctor asked as she inspected his knee.

"Tight," Liam admitted, allowing himself this small truth among so many uncertainties.

"We'll wrap it up tight. Rest it tonight," she said with a smile that was meant to be comforting but couldn't quite mask her professional concern.

Rest wasn't what Liam wanted, he wanted answers about who he was beyond what the ice could tell him.

Ben pulled up a stool and sat down beside him, exuding an air of confidence that felt at odds with the sterile environment of the locker room. "Look at me," he said softly.

Liam turned toward him, locking eyes with his agent. In Ben's gaze was something fierce and unyielding, a promise that no matter what lay ahead, they were in it together.

"We've worked too hard to let anything derail us now," Ben said with conviction. "You're going to light it up in the pros just like you do every time you hit that ice."

Liam could feel the weight of expectation settle on him like a mantle, heavy but not unfamiliar. It was part of being Liam Desjardins: always striving for more, always reaching for greatness.

"We got this," Liam said finally, feeling the truth of those words deep in his gut.

Ben clapped him on the back, his hand skimming just short of the worst bruises, an unconscious reflex after years of managing fragile million-dollar bodies. "Yes, we do."

As Ben stood up to speak with one of the doctors again, Liam set his jaw, channeling the same mental reset he used between periods. The pain was still there, both physical and emotional, but so was something else: determination.

"Tell Coach I'm good to go," Liam called out to anyone who would listen. The sound of another Team Canada goal celebration echoed through the halls.

Ben leaned over, voice firm. "You're up 5-1 on the Swedes, and Broten's handling the scoring just fine. You're not going anywhere." The words stung worse than the ice on Liam's shoulder. While Julian was out there building his draft stock, Liam was stuck here, watching his own slip away minute by minute.

The chatter and clank of equipment subsided as the staff trickled out of the locker room, leaving Liam alone with his thoughts and the echo of a dull ache where the bruise on his shoulder throbbed beneath the skin.

Liam's gaze drifted to the doorway, drawn by a flicker of movement in the hallway just outside the locker room.

There, standing under the harsh fluorescent lights, was Harper, her brow furrowed as she spoke with Ryan. The murmur of their conversation didn't carry through the door, but their body language spoke volumes, Harper's hands gesturing animatedly, Ryan's head nodding with a certain reluctance.

Liam straightened up as Harper glanced inside. Their eyes met, a silent exchange heavy with unspoken words. In that brief connection, he saw concern etch lines around her hazel eyes, and it unsettled him. He didn't need to hear their conversation to know what stirred that worry in her gaze. Ryan must have told her about the note, about Jim and Tammy not being his biological parents.

He could almost hear her journalistic mind whirring behind those eyes, calculating, digging for the truth beneath layers of guarded secrets. It gnawed at him, this notion that Harper knew something so personal, something he had barely begun to process himself.

Liam's body was still, but his mind shifted uneasily, the tension settling deep in his muscles, a sensation he often felt when navigating unfamiliar outdoor ice, not the kind he could skate across with practiced ease, but the treacherous, unseen cracks beneath the surface of life's uncertainty. It was a place he didn't visit often, Liam thrived on control, predictability, the clear path from puck drop to goal horn.

Ryan's presence here bothered Liam more than he wanted to admit. VSM was meticulous about who got access to their athletes, Ben had drilled that into him since he was fourteen. *So how did this guy get past security to give him a note?*

But life had thrown him a curveball, or more fittingly, a puck that wobbled unpredictably on its edge before veering off in an unexpected direction.

"Hey." Harper's voice was quiet but firm as she stepped inside. "Got a minute?"

Liam took in a deep breath and let it out slowly. "Sure," he replied with a nod. His voice was even, years of post-game interviews had taught him how to mask turmoil with calmness.

Harper's investigative instincts faced off against her compassion, she'd seen enough athletes destroyed by scandals to know timing was everything. But this was different. This wasn't about performance enhancing drugs or contract disputes. This was about identity itself.

"I won't pry," Harper started, leaning against the opposite row of lockers with casual grace. "I know you've got enough on your plate."

Her voice carried a note of sincerity that chipped away at Liam's defenses. She wasn't here just as a journalist, there was empathy in her posture, the way she held herself back just enough to give him space.

Liam let out a chuckle without humor. "Seems like everyone knows I've got a full plate these days."

She gave him a wry smile. "Comes with the territory when you're 'Blazing Bolt', doesn't it?"

"Light it up," Liam corrected reflexively before pausing. His catchphrase felt hollow now, like an old jersey worn and faded from too many washes.

Harper nodded understandingly. "You do that on the ice," she acknowledged before her gaze softened further. "But you're more than just your game stats and a draft prospect."

He didn't know how to respond to that, how could he when he wasn't sure who 'more than' was anymore? Was he still Liam Desjardins if part of what made up that name wasn't true?

"You're handling it better than most would," she continued quietly.

"I don't feel like I'm handling anything right now," Liam admitted, his voice barely above a whisper.

For a moment, they just stood there, two individuals caught in an orbit of shared knowledge and unasked questions. The silence stretched between them like the calm before overtime.

Liam studied Harper's face, looking for any sign that might reveal the extent of what she knew, or perhaps, what she believed. The overhead lights cast a stark contrast on her features, accentuating her resolve.

"Ryan says he works at VSM," Harper said, her tone careful. "Ever see him before?"

Liam shook his head. "No, never seen him 'round there. VSM's a big place though." The answer felt hollow, an attempt to rationalize the presence of a stranger who had somehow burrowed into the fabric of his life.

The VSM logo on his hockey bag stared back at him, a brand he'd worn proudly since childhood. Now, it felt less like an emblem and more like a piece of a puzzle he couldn't solve.

"Did he say anything about... about my parents?" Liam's voice was barely audible over the humming silence of the locker room. His heart thrummed in his chest, each beat echoing against the metal lockers.

Harper paused, considering her words carefully before responding. "He suggested that Jim and Tammy are not your biological parents."

The finality in Harper's voice made Liam's stomach churn. The words 'biological parents' echoed in his head like a slap shot ricocheting off the boards. Each time he tried to dismiss them, they came back harder, faster.

He searched Harper's face again, this time for a lifeline, some sliver of doubt that could make the reality less stark. "Did he say I was adopted?"

"I'm skeptical of what Ryan is claiming," Harper said carefully. Not *I don't believe him* or *He's lying,* but *skeptical.* That distinction mattered.

"Skeptical?" Liam repeated, latching onto the word like a life raft amidst stormy seas.

Harper nodded firmly. "I need to follow up on this." Her eyes locked onto his with an intensity that seemed to hold him in place. "Don't think we can trust him right now."

The warning rang in Liam's ears, a distant alarm amidst the fog of confusion.

"Something about the way he is acting and presenting himself," Harper continued. "I think he's up to something."

Up to something? The words unsettled him, curling in his gut like a slow-building storm. That same instinct that warned him of an incoming check now whispered of something worse. This wasn't just about hockey anymore. It was about who he was. And someone, somewhere, was working hard to keep him from finding out.

Furever

"Grief whispers impossible promises, and desperation listens. But at what cost do we take back what was never meant to return?" – Dr Kim

Dr. Kim Jung-So wandered the dimly lit corridors of Furever Genetics, the silence of the evening pressing in around him. The burn scars on his hands, testaments to countless lab accidents, caught the faint light as he traced them absently, a habit born of recent sleepless nights.

Deep lines etched his face, grief and stress aging him prematurely in the weeks since the accident. The weight of his recent tragedy bore down on each step, visible in his tired but relentless expression, a haunted look that never truly left his dark eyes. Yet as he passed the towering portraits lining the walls, a flicker of pride managed to break through his grief, momentarily lighting up features that had grown sharper, more gaunt with each passing day.

The first portrait was a majestic polo horse named Sultan, its mane flowing like silk, eyes alight with competitive fire. Sultan was one of Furever's earliest successes, a clone engineered for agility and strength that had since become a legend on the fields of Argentina. The owner, a wealthy magnate with a passion for the sport, had once embraced Dr. Kim with tears in his eyes, grateful for the return of a champion he thought lost forever.

Next came a series of photographs featuring camels with coats as smooth as velvet, their long lashes casting shadows over wise eyes. These creatures were more than just clones, they were embodiments of heritage for their Middle Eastern patrons. They bore riders through desert storms and across dunes with the same endurance as their beloved progenitors. The owners held their heads high, knowing that their culture's treasured beasts would continue to stride for generations to come.

As Dr. Kim's gaze drifted to another frame, he beheld a thoroughbred racehorse captured mid-gallop, muscles taut and nostrils flared. It was an animal that embodied speed and grace, a product of Furever's meticulous work. Its owner, an oil tycoon with an affinity for the racetrack, boasted endlessly about the horse's lineage and the genetic marvel it represented.

Through the window, he watched his driver, Mr. Park, waiting patiently in the black Mercedes, another reminder of the mercy he'd never wanted. The judge's words still echoed in his mind: "The loss of your son is punishment enough." The jury had wept during his confession, moved by a father's raw grief. They hadn't understood that their compassion was the cruelest sentence they could have imposed.

Dr. Kim pulled out the newspaper clipping he kept in his wallet, creased from countless readings. "Grieving Father Spared Prison," the headline declared. The article praised the court's wisdom in showing leniency, citing his immediate confession and profound remorse. But they hadn't seen how their mercy had trapped him in an endless cycle of guilt. Every morning, as Mr. Park drove him past the accident site, he forced himself to look, a perpetual penance that the courts had denied him.

He tucked the article away, his attention returning to the success stories lining the walls. Each clone represented a second chance, a restoration of something precious that had been lost. But while he could resurrect prized horses and beloved pets for others, his own loss remained irreversible. Or so the world believed.

The corridor turned to showcase livestock, cloned cattle, hogs, and sheep vital for agriculturalists who prized specific traits in their herds. They stood proud and strong in green fields, indistinguishable from their forebears except to those who knew them intimately. Farmers shook Dr. Kim's hand with calloused fingers, gratitude resonating in their voices for the preservation and improvement of their stock.

Pets came next, beloved dogs and cats whose owners could not bear parting with them. They sat perched on laps or curled beside children in photographs that radiated warmth and comfort. Each picture told a story of reunion and joy, moments that Dr. Kim cherished as tokens of success amidst ethical quandaries that often plagued his field.

The final portrait was different from the rest, an exotic animal that Furever had cloned not for profit but for conservation purposes. A Sumatran tiger stared back at him from behind glass, its stripes were dark rivers flowing across a vibrant coat, a genetic echo of a creature whose roar was fading from the wilds. This particular project had drawn international attention and acclaim, it was a beacon of hope in an otherwise often controversial enterprise.

Dr. Kim stood before these images as night deepened outside his company's walls. The pride swelled within him, pride for what he had accomplished for his clients, pride in his team's ability to push boundaries no one else dared approach.

Yet beneath it all lay an undercurrent of disquiet, each success brought with it reminders of what he could not replicate or replace, his own flesh and blood, his son Dae-Song. No amount of scientific prowess could fill that void.

As he passed the lab where he'd once let Dae-Song "help" with an experiment, carefully guiding his small hands through the motions, Dr. Kim felt the weight of emptiness press against his chest. His son had been so curious, so eager to learn about Papa's work.

As he turned to leave, his phone buzzed. A message: *A client insists on thanking you personally. Can you meet them in the lobby?*

He sighed, intending to refuse. But something pulled at him, a need to distract himself, if only for a few moments.

The elevator chimed softly as Dr. Kim stepped into the lobby. A family stood waiting, a man, woman, and a child no older than eight. In the mother's arms, a tiny puppy wriggled, identical to the pet they had lost. It squirmed free, licking the boy's face as he erupted into giggles.

"Dr. Kim!" The father stepped forward eagerly, extending his hand. "We can't thank you enough. You've given us our family back."

Dr. Kim shook the man's hand absentmindedly, his gaze fixed on the child. The boy's eyes sparkled with the kind of joy only children know, holding the puppy as if reuniting with a long-lost friend. "He's perfect," the boy said, his voice light with awe. "He's just like Max used to be!"

Dr. Kim felt his chest tighten. The boy hugged the puppy tightly, his laughter echoing in the lobby.

"It's more than we could have hoped for," the father continued. "We're so grateful for this second chance."

The words landed heavily on Dr. Kim. A second chance. His heart ached, memories of Dae-Song's laughter piercing through his grief. He watched as the child caressed the puppy's soft fur, the family's joy enveloping them.

"Thank you, Dr. Kim," the mother said softly, her eyes brimming with tears. "You've made us whole again."

Dr. Kim forced a smile, but inside, he was crumbling. As the family left, the boy's laughter lingered in the air. He watched them disappear through the lobby doors, the child holding the puppy close, oblivious to the cruel finality that Dr. Kim knew all too well.

Dr. Kim stood frozen in place, the scene replaying in his mind, the child's innocent happiness, the reunion that had been impossible just months ago. He had made it happen. He had given them what they thought was lost forever.

But what about him? What about his son?

His hands trembled as he turned and walked back down the familiar halls, the portraits of his successes watching him like silent judges. The boy's laughter echoed in his ears, blending with the sound of Dae-Song's voice, laughter that he would never hear again. Not unless...

He couldn't stop the thought from forming, creeping into his mind like a thief in the night. Could he bring back Dae-Song?

The weight of that possibility hung heavy in the air, suffocating him. He stopped in front of a portrait of a cloned dog, its eyes bright and full of life. He had done it before, for others. Why not for himself? Why not for Dae-Song?

The internal struggle between his ethical code and his overwhelming grief threatened to tear him apart. Human cloning was forbidden, banned across the world. The consequences would be catastrophic if anyone found out. But the emptiness inside him, the ache that gnawed at him every day, whispered something darker. If he could do it for animals, why not for his son? Was there truly such a vast difference between them?

Years of scientific ethics conferences flashed through his mind, countless lectures about the sanctity of human genetic boundaries. He'd given some of those lectures himself. But what did ethical boundaries mean to a father who'd killed his own son?

As he reached his office, the moonlight spilling through the window bathed the room in silver. He picked up the framed photograph of Dae-Song, his fingers tracing the edges of his son's face, feeling the sharp sting of longing flood his senses. The boy's smile was bright, captured in a moment frozen in time, yet that was all Dr. Kim had now, moments, memories, fragments of a life torn away too soon.

The portrait of Dae-Song seemed to watch him, those bright eyes holding both accusation and possibility. He'd failed as a father once. The thought of failing again, of not even trying when he had the means... That would be a different kind of death.

His computer screen glowed with Dae-Song's preserved genetic profile, a complete map of his son's DNA, taken during that final hospital visit. The data waited like a dormant possibility, a scientific key to unlock death itself.

In his darkened office, Dr. Kim stared at Dae-Song's genetic profile on his screen. Unlike Frankenstein's creature, built from disparate parts, this would be pure, perfect reproduction. He wasn't creating a monster, he was bringing back his son. The distinction felt important, even if only to him.

The temptation grew stronger with each passing second. What if he could hold his son again? What if he could undo what fate had cruelly taken from him?

But deep down, he knew this was a line no one should cross. It wasn't just about science, it was about the sanctity of life itself. Yet, as he stared into the eyes of his son, the darkness within him whispered sweet promises.

Dr. Kim closed his eyes, his hands shaking. The ethical walls he had built around himself were crumbling, brick by brick. The joy in the family's reunion, the laughter of that little boy, it was a reminder of what he could never have again. Not unless...

No. He couldn't.

But then again, why not?

The questions swirled, unanswered, but powerful. What if he could succeed? What if he could clone Dae-Song and no one ever knew?

He set down the photograph and turned to the window, gazing out at the sprawling city of Seoul. The skyline twinkled like stars, oblivious to the turmoil roiling within him.

He was a pioneer in genetics. He had already achieved the impossible. So why stop now?

Centuries of ethical boundaries, international laws, professional oaths, all designed to prevent exactly what he was about to attempt. But they hadn't designed those rules for a father who had the power to bring back his son.

He would bring back Dae-Song, and in doing so, he would either become humanity's greatest pioneer or its most dangerous criminal. Perhaps both.

As he stood in the silent office, staring out into the abyss of night, Dr. Kim knew that the decision had already been made, even if he refused to acknowledge it aloud.

He would bring back his son.

Dark Designs

"Loss is the ultimate innovator, driving us to places reason would never dare tread." – Dr. Kim

Dr. Kim sat in his dimly lit office, the tablet's glow flickering across his face. A new document awaited, encrypted with security protocols meant for Furever's most classified work. But this wasn't about pet cloning anymore.

His fingers moved across the screen, listing what he'd need:

- Advanced genetic sequencers
- Micromanipulators for nuclear transfer
- PCR and testing equipment
- Specialized cryopreservation systems
- Class 100 clean room facilities
- Human cell culture media
- CO_2 incubators for embryo development
- Staff compensation
- Facility acquisition

The numbers were staggering, even for him. Furever's success had made him wealthy, but this project demanded more than wealth, it required discretion.

He glanced at the live feed on a secondary monitor. Technicians moved through Furever's halls, badges visible, their every step recorded. Every employee, visitor, and delivery was logged in meticulous detail. His current facility was a fortress of documentation, exactly what he couldn't use for this project.

The cameras that had once made him feel secure now seemed like accusatory eyes. He needed somewhere off the grid, yet sophisticated enough to support the delicate process of human cloning. Somewhere beyond the reach of Korea's biotech regulators.

Seoul's sprawling industrial districts offered possibilities, abandoned facilities that could be converted under the guise of research and development. The Incheon area, with its maze of biotech startups and pharmaceutical companies, would provide perfect cover. A shell company, properly structured, could operate without drawing attention from Korea's oversight committees.

Incheon's busy port would provide cover for equipment deliveries, while its dense network of biotech firms would make one more research facility unremarkable.

Dr. Kim opened another file, this one containing contact information for Furever's most elite clients. The successful cloning of Lou Booker's dog Zeus had demonstrated Furever's capabilities to wealthy individuals worldwide. People who understood discretion, who had the means to fund projects that existed in ethical gray areas. People who might understand the price of bringing back the irreplaceable.

His gaze drifted to the family photo on his desk. Dae-Song's smile beamed back at him, forever frozen in that moment. Soon, he told himself, that smile wouldn't just be preserved in a photograph. But he'd need more than equipment. He'd need extraordinary funding.

The sooner he acted, the better. Each day without Dae-Song was another day lost forever.

Every employee at Furever had signed ironclad NDAs, but human cloning was beyond any normal confidentiality agreement. He'd need people willing to risk everything, people who understood that discovery meant not just unemployment, but imprisonment.

Dr. Kim leaned back in his chair, the silence of his laboratory amplifying the magnitude of what he was planning. Each step would take him further from the respected scientist he'd been, closer to becoming something else entirely. But when he looked at Dae-Song's photo, the choice seemed inevitable. Science had always advanced through bold action, through crossing lines others feared to approach.

Dr. Kim pulled up the contact information for Lou Booker. The Canadian sports magnate had first approached Furever about Zeus, his cloned Saint Bernard, but their relationship had deepened after successfully cloning Triple Crown winner Northern Dynasty. Though the racing community officially banned cloned horses, Lou had helped keep the project quiet while connecting Dr. Kim to other sports figures who valued both innovation and discretion. More importantly, he had access to private funding, people who understood that breaking new ground sometimes meant breaking old rules.

The cursor blinked as Dr. Kim composed his message to Lou. Each word was carefully chosen: *Recent breakthroughs suggest exciting possibilities for expansion. Your insight into specialized markets would be valuable. I will be in Montreal this week, let's meet at VSM.*

The implied opportunity would appeal to Lou's ambition. The man had already pushed ethical boundaries with animal cloning, perhaps he'd be willing to go further. Much further.

The respected scientist in him knew this path led to darkness. But the grieving father in him didn't care. He would build his hidden lab, find his trusted team, and bring back his son.

Whatever the cost.

* * *

Dr. Kim studied Lou Booker's office as he waited, taking in the calculated display of power and success. Stanley Cup photos lined one wall, signed jerseys another, while the third showcased a collection of framed magazine covers featuring VSM's greatest success stories. The fourth wall was nothing but windows, offering a commanding view of Montreal's skyline.

Zeus's photos held a place of prominence near Lou's desk, the massive Saint Bernard's soulful eyes captured in various moments of triumph. Show ribbons and Best-in-Show awards flanked the photos, testament to the clone's perfect replication of the original Zeus's championship bloodline.

A soft padding of heavy paws drew Dr. Kim's attention to the door. Zeus entered first, his massive frame moving with surprising grace, followed by Lou's booming presence. Lou Booker's heavyset six-foot-eight frame filled the doorway, his expensive suit and gold watch glinting under the office lights. His dark hair and well-groomed beard gave him the polished look of ambition, though a slight flush colored his face, the mark of too many late nights closing deals.

"He never misses a chance to greet visitors," Lou said proudly, his thick French-Canadian accent mixing English and French as Zeus approached Dr. Kim, tail wagging. "Especially the man who gave him a second chance at life."

"Hello, old friend," Dr. Kim said softly, letting Zeus sniff his hand before giving the giant dog a gentle pat. The Saint Bernard settled near Lou's desk, watching them with intelligent eyes.

Lou's handshake was firm, practiced, the grip of a man who'd built an empire on first impressions. His dark brown eyes pierced through Dr. Kim with their usual calculating intensity. "When you asked for this meeting, I thought of that day I first came to you about Zeus. The emptiness in my life after losing him..."

"Loss changes us," Dr. Kim said quietly, his hand unconsciously moving to his jacket pocket where he kept Dae-Song's photo. "It makes us see possibilities we never considered before."

Lou studied him for a moment. "You speak from experience."

Dr. Kim withdrew the worn photograph, offering it to Lou. "My son, Dae-Song. Four years old when I lost him recently." His voice remained steady, but his fingers trembled slightly as Lou took the photo.

"I remember the funeral," Lou said, his usual boisterous tone softened. Zeus, sensing the shift in mood, moved closer to his master.

"When you came to me about Zeus, I listened to your pain." Dr. Kim's gaze drifted to the Saint Bernard. "I did not fully understand your sorrow then. But, science gave you back your family. What we did with Zeus... it was just the beginning."

Lou's expression sharpened. "What exactly are you suggesting?"

Dr. Kim's eyes never left Lou's face. "I need to get my son back."

The silence stretched between them, broken only by Zeus's gentle panting. Lou's expression shifted from confusion to dawning comprehension, then to disbelief.

"You plan to clone your son?" Lou said, the words falling heavy in the quiet office.

Dr. Kim nodded once, his composure never wavering.

Lou pushed back from his desk, standing abruptly. Zeus lifted his head, alert to his master's sudden movement. "That's—that's impossible. Not to mention illegal. Every country in the world has banned human cloning."

"Laws change," Dr. Kim said softly. "Science advances—"

"No." Lou cut him off, his voice sharp. "This isn't like Zeus. This is human cloning. It's immoral, it's unethical, it's..." He shook his head. "I can't be part of this."

"You understand loss," Dr. Kim pressed. "You understand what it means to get back what was taken—"

"A dog is not a child!" Lou's voice boomed through the office. Zeus whined softly at the tension. "I'm sorry about your son, truly. But this... this is madness. I won't risk everything I've built on something so dangerous."

"You've built an empire, Lou," Dr. Kim said, his voice low and steady, as though reading the turmoil in Lou's mind. "Empires aren't built without compromise."

A muscle twitched in Lou's cheek. It was true. Compromise had been part of the game from the beginning. But this, this was too far. This wasn't just bending the rules, it was breaking them completely.

"Think beyond my personal loss for a moment," Dr. Kim continued, gesturing to the wall of NHL jerseys. "Imagine what this technology could mean for VSM. For hockey."

Lou's eyes narrowed. "What exactly are you suggesting?"

"The same precision we achieved with Zeus. Perfect replication. Perfect health. Perfect traits." Dr. Kim paused, letting the implications sink in. "While your competitors chase conventional talent, you could be creating it."

"Cloning hockey players?" Lou's voice was barely a whisper, but his eyes darted to the Stanley Cup photos.

"I'm talking about controlling the future of sports itself." Dr. Kim's voice remained calm, but his eyes gleamed. "Zeus proved the technology works. Now imagine applying that precision to athletic development. Your agency wouldn't just represent the best players, you'd own their very creation."

Zeus lifted his large head, sensing his master's tension. Lou absently scratched the dog's ears, his mind clearly racing with possibilities.

"It's still illegal," Lou said, but his tone had shifted from outright rejection to careful consideration. "And more than that, it's immoral."

"Is it?" Dr. Kim challenged softly. "More immoral than watching talented athletes destroy their bodies with steroids? More immoral than the genetic lottery that determines who gets to play professional sports?"

"The risks would be astronomical," Lou said, but Dr. Kim noted he was now weighing consequences rather than dismissing the idea outright.

"As are the potential rewards." Dr. Kim stood. "You built VSM by seeing opportunities others missed. This isn't just about my son anymore, Lou. It's about the future. Your future. VSM's future."

Lou moved to the windows, Zeus following loyally. The Montreal skyline stretched before them, a concrete testament to ambition realized. He looked down at Zeus now standing by his side.

"I can't help you," Lou said finally, his voice quiet but firm. "But..." he hesitated, looking at his beloved dog. "I understand why you'd try."

Dr. Kim studied Lou's reflection in the window, the empire builder and his faithful companion, both products of pushing boundaries. Of crossing lines. He nodded once and turned to leave, knowing that understanding was all he needed. For now.

The soft click of the door closing echoed in the quiet office, leaving Lou alone with Zeus and the dangerous whisper of what-ifs.

VSM

"The truth has a way of slipping through cracks, no matter how carefully someone tries to seal them." – Harper

Harper's phone buzzed. Mary Davidson's number.

"Please tell me you found something," Harper said, dropping onto her hotel room couch. The World Juniors game schedules lay scattered across the coffee table, marked up with her investigation notes.

"Maybe." Mary's voice crackled with static. "But it's weird. Most of VSM's financials are what you'd expect, standard contracts, marketing deals, the usual sports management stuff."

Harper sat up straighter. "But?"

"I found two crypto transactions from over twenty years ago. Both seven figures, both supposedly belong to a company called GeneCore Solutions in Seoul." Mary paused. "They tried to hide it through multiple wallets and exchanges, but they made a rookie mistake, used the same shell company's name in the blockchain metadata."

"How did you even trace that?" Harper asked, already reaching for her laptop.

"Remember that crypto forensics software I helped develop at FinTech? Most people think early crypto was untraceable, but that's not true. The transactions were old, but crypto leaves fingerprints if you know where to look. They converted the money through five different cryptocurrencies, bounced it through dozens of wallets. Someone really wanted to hide these payments."

"And GeneCore Solutions?"

"That's the thing, no website, no business registration, no physical address. The company's a ghost, but the money? That's very real. And Harper..." Mary hesitated. "Be careful. People who go through this much trouble to hide money usually prefer staying hidden."

Harper ended the call, staring at the new email in her inbox. Two carefully hidden payments to a ghost company in Seoul. The trail might be digital, but it was there, and it led straight to VSM.

"Got you," she whispered, opening the files. The trail might be faint, but she hadn't won Olympic gold by giving up when things got tough.

She scribbled down notes, connecting dots. Korea. Ryan's lab. VSM's mysterious payments. Her phone buzzed again, a text from her editor at True North Hockey.

Need your Desjardins piece by midnight. Focus on the hockey, not conspiracy theories.

Harper snorted. If he only knew. She typed back: *On it. Story's bigger than you think.*

She dove into the archives, searching for any trace of Seoul businesses from twenty years ago. Nothing on GeneCore Solutions, but something else caught her eye, a series of news articles about breakthrough genetic research in Korea.

"Come on, give me something," she muttered, scrolling through archived pages. A photo made her pause, a younger Lou Booker shaking hands with an Asian scientist at some kind of tech conference. The caption was in Korean.

Her phone rang again.

Harper watched Ben's name flash on the screen, remembering their time at University of Toronto. Back then, she'd trusted him completely. Now? He was VSM's man, and she had learned the hard way that friendship meant nothing when careers were on the line.

She let it go to voicemail. Better to have concrete proof before confronting anyone at VSM. The photo of Lou Booker with the Korean scientist was interesting, but it wasn't enough. Not yet.

"One breadcrumb at a time," she muttered, turning back to her research. The truth was out there, in shell companies and twenty-year-old payments and Korean scientists.

And Harper Sinclair was going to find it.

* * *

Later that day, Harper left the press box office and headed down as Team Canada was practicing. The chill of the rink bit into Harper's skin as she pressed against the boards, watching as Team Canada ran through their drills.

In the far corner, away from the action, Liam glided slowly across the ice, testing his injured leg. Even from here, she could see the ice pack strapped to his shoulder.

Liam glanced up and caught her eye. Veering off from his solo skating, he made his way to where Harper stood, his movements more cautious than usual.

"Sinclair," he greeted, his breath fogging in the crisp air.

"Desjardins," Harper nodded back. "How's the leg?"

"Been better." He adjusted the ice pack on his shoulder. "Doc says I will be ready for the medal round."

Harper studied him. The physical injuries were obvious, but something else weighed on him. "And the rest?"

Liam's eyes searched hers, looking for something, an answer, a clue, anything. "Any more on Ryan?"

"I'm working on it," she admitted carefully. She didn't have enough yet to share her suspicions, but she couldn't ignore the worry in his voice. "Nothing concrete, but I'm following some leads."

"My parents..." he started, then glanced at his teammates running drills. Julian scored and celebrated with an exaggerated fist pump. Liam's shoulder twitched. "They've been great, supportive. But something feels off. Like they're worried about more than just my injuries."

"Give me time," Harper said softly. "I need to be sure before I say more."

Liam nodded slowly, understanding. On the ice, Coach Boucha's whistle pierced the air, calling the team to gather.

"I should get back," Liam said, but hesitated. "You'll let me know? If you find anything?"

"You'll be my first call," Harper promised. "Just focus on healing. Let me handle the digging."

He pushed off, skating back to his teammates, each movement measured and careful.

* * *

Later that evening, after practice, Liam sat between his parents at a cozy restaurant in downtown Toronto. The familiar rhythm of family dinners settled around them, with Jim and Tammy bantering lightly about their day. Yet to Liam, the easygoing conversation felt distant. His mind lingered on Ryan's note, each cryptic word sinking deeper.

"So, Dad," Liam began cautiously, steering into safer waters first. "That guy who mistook you for the conference keynote speaker, did you ever tell him you were just there for the AV setup?"

Jim's face brightened as he launched into the story, his energy lighting up the table. Tammy chuckled beside him, playfully adding her own teasing remarks. Their laughter filled the small booth, a sound that had always comforted Liam, but tonight, it seemed muffled, as if he were listening from another room.

Liam's smile was there, but thin, as his thoughts continued to drift. He had grown up with these stories, the anecdotes and playful jabs that had shaped his understanding of family, but now, under the weight of Ryan's note, they felt more like carefully curated memories rather than spontaneous truths. A subtle doubt took root, and Liam couldn't ignore it.

After a moment of quiet, Liam shifted gears, edging closer to the questions he truly wanted to ask. "Mom," he began, his voice softer, careful not to draw too much attention. "How did you and Dad meet? I mean, what's the real story?"

"It was at an agriculture conference in Winnipeg," Tammy said. "I was helping with the library archives display, and your dad was handling the event logistics."

Jim reached across the table to squeeze Tammy's hand. "She was trying to find the right spot for her display on Manitoba wheat farming history," he chuckled, "and I completely mixed up the conference rooms."

"And I should've known then what I was getting into," Tammy teased back, smiling at her husband.

Liam chuckled along, the sound barely escaping his lips. The story was unchanged, just like every time they had told it before, but tonight, the repetition only amplified his doubts. It felt rehearsed. But was that his mind playing tricks on him, or was there something more he had never seen before?

Liam pressed on, his tone more reflective now. "What about when I was born? Any stories from then?" His heart quickened, but he kept his voice steady, careful not to betray his growing unease.

Tammy's expression softened further as she reminisced. "Oh, Liam... It was a blizzard that night. We barely made it to the hospital on time."

Jim nodded in agreement, his pride unmistakable as he recounted the details. "You were so eager to come into the world," he said, shaking his head with a smile.

Liam listened, nodding along, but his thoughts were elsewhere, weighing every word against the shadow Ryan had cast. These stories, so woven into his identity, suddenly seemed fragile. Were they real, or had they been crafted to hide something? The doubt gnawed at him, yet he couldn't bring himself to confront it directly, not yet.

"And after that?" Liam asked, his voice almost casual as he leaned back in his chair. "When I was little?"

Tammy smiled again, clearly pleased by the trip down memory lane. "You were always so focused," she said with affection. "Even with your toys, you'd line them up by size or color, and heaven forbid anyone messed up your system."

Liam smiled at that, but his heart wasn't in it. He could feel the questions rising within him, pressing against his chest, but he wasn't ready to ask. Not yet.

"You were always such a tough kid," Jim added, pride evident in his voice. "Remember that time you took that header off your bike? the doctor said it should've laid you up for weeks, but you were back on skates in a week."

"Your father nearly had a heart attack," Tammy said, her smile fading slightly. "But you always did heal quickly."

The memory triggered another, one Liam had almost forgotten. He'd been twelve, in the emergency room after a bad hit during playoffs. The doctor had been reviewing his chart, asking about blood types for a possible transfusion.

"Must've been scary," Liam said carefully, watching their faces. "That time in emergency room during playoffs. The doc was confused on my blood type. I'm AB positive and you're both O negative."

Jim's hand tightened slightly around his water glass. "Ancient history now, son. You did bounce back like you always do. And will again."

Tammy smoothly changed the subject, steering the conversation toward Liam's upcoming game, but Liam caught the quick glance between his parents, the same one they'd shared in the hospital when the doctor had mentioned blood types.

Liam hesitated, feeling the familiar change of subject. For a brief moment, he considered pushing forward, letting the question slip from his lips. But he wasn't ready, not without more information, not without certainty. As the conversation drifted back to lighter topics, he let the familiar rhythm of family carry him through the evening, even as the undercurrent of doubt pulled at him, deeper and deeper.

Buried Truths

"The ethical line isn't a sudden chasm but a slope, each step down rationalized until the unthinkable feels inevitable." — Ryan

Harper watched the hotel entrance from behind a frost-covered hotel partition. Ryan's presence here was no coincidence, his calculated movements and frequent glances over his shoulder confirmed her suspicions. She maintained her distance, letting the evening crowd mask her pursuit.

She glanced down at her phone, reviewing the photos Mary had sent. Something about Ryan nagged at her memory, his methodical movements, his careful observation of everything around him.

Ryan tensed when he saw Liam emerge from the hotel with Jim and Tammy. They looked relaxed, caught up in conversation and laughter. But as they walked toward a nearby restaurant, Ryan's attention locked onto them.

Harper's mind raced through possibilities. Corporate espionage? Family secrets? Or something deeper, connected to the mysterious payments she'd uncovered?

She remained vigilant as Ryan kept his distance from the Desjardins, positioning himself at a café across the street. He ordered coffee but hardly touched it, his attention fixed on the restaurant's frosted windows. Harper noticed how his hand occasionally strayed to his laptop bag, where a corner of what looked like a scientific journal peeked out.

The winter evening deepened around them, street lights casting pools of yellow light on the snow. Through the restaurant window, Harper could see the Desjardins family sharing a meal, unaware of the scrutiny they were under. The normalcy of their family dinner contrasted sharply with Ryan's focused surveillance.

A woman at the next table struggled to calm her anxious service dog, startled by a car alarm outside. Ryan's demeanor shifted instantly. Without a word, he knelt beside them, his movements gentle and practiced. The dog settled under his quiet attention, showing years of experience working with animals.

When the Desjardins finally emerged from the restaurant, their voices carrying across the quiet street, Harper seized her moment. She approached Ryan's table with purpose, noting how he tensed at her footsteps.

"Ryan Patel," she said quietly, sliding into the seat across from him. "What's your interest in Liam?"

His hand jerked, coffee sloshing against the rim of his cup. His composure cracked for just a moment before he forced his features neutral.

"I don't know what you mean," he said, but his voice had lost its earlier confidence.

Harper leaned forward. "Cut the act. You've been watching them all evening, just like I've been watching you. And you're not listed as an employee at VSM. So, who are you really?"

Ryan swallowed hard. She saw the internal struggle play across his face, fear warring with something else. Pride? Passion?

"I used to work for a company called Furever," he admitted finally. His eyes lit up despite his obvious anxiety. "We did incredible things there, preserving endangered species, reuniting families with lost pets. The genetic possibilities were... extraordinary."

"A pet cloning company?" Harper pressed. "What's that got to do with Liam?"

Ryan's gaze dropped to his coffee. "We helped people hold onto what they loved most. You can't imagine what it means to see a child's face when we bring back their beloved pet, or to help save a species from extinction." His voice cracked slightly. "Sometimes the hardest losses drive the greatest innovations."

Harper noticed his hand move unconsciously to his chest, where a thin chain disappeared beneath his collar. "What kind of loss, Ryan?"

His fingers found what must have been a pendant under his shirt. "My sister, Mira." The words came out barely above a whisper. "Thalassemia. A genetic blood disorder. I was in my second year of college when..." He stopped, composing himself. "That's what led me to genetics. To understanding how tiny changes in our DNA can mean the difference between life and death."

"And Furever gave you that chance?"

"They gave me purpose. A way to make a difference." Ryan straightened suddenly, as if remembering himself. "But I made a mistake. Crossed a line I shouldn't have."

"What kind of mistake gets a geneticist fired from a pet cloning company?"

Ryan's eyes darted away, and Harper saw real fear there now. The secret he carried seemed to hollow him out from the inside.

Ryan's fingers tightened around his coffee cup, the steam long since dissipated. Beyond the café window, snow fell beneath Toronto's amber streetlights, while forgotten Christmas lights in the window cast multicolored shadows across their table.

"I wasn't fired," he said finally. "I left. There's a difference."

Harper leaned back, studying him. The café had emptied as evening deepened, leaving them nearly alone among scattered empty tables. "Tell me about Dr. Kim Jung-So."

Ryan's head snapped up. "How do you—"

"I'm good at my job," Harper interrupted. "And you're not as subtle as you think."

A long pause followed, filled only by the soft jazz playing through the café's speakers and the distant scrape of snowplows. Ryan touched the chain around his neck again, and Harper noticed it held a small silver pendant shaped like a double helix.

"I met Dr. Kim at a genetics conference twenty-five years ago," Ryan began. "I was fresh out of graduate school, presenting my research on genetic disorders. Specifically, Thalassemia." His voice caught slightly.

"Thalassemia attacks the blood at a genetic level," Ryan continued, his scientific training showing through his emotion. "It's hereditary, a DNA mutation that destroys red blood cells. We watched my sister's body betray her, one transfusion at a time."

"She was my whole world. After watching her suffer through endless transfusions, experimental treatments... I dedicated my life to understanding genetic diseases. I thought if I could just unlock the right combination, find the right solution..." He trailed off, lost in memory.

"How does Dr. Kim fit in?"

"He attended my presentation, just another face in the crowd back then. But afterward..." Ryan's fingers drummed against the coffee cup. "He found me in the empty conference hall, and we talked for hours. He'd just lost his wife during childbirth. Min-Seo. He told me about raising his son alone, about his work with genetic preservation."

Harper shifted in her seat, her recorder hidden beneath her scarf on the table. Years of experience had taught her the value of letting sources talk without the intimidation of obvious documentation. "Furever was already well-established then?"

"They were the leader in pet cloning. They'd done everything from race horses to endangered species. But Dr. Kim saw something in me that day. Maybe it was our shared loss, or my passion for the science. He offered me a position on the spot."

Ryan's gaze drifted to the window, watching the snow fall. "You should have seen the lab in those early days. We were doing incredible things, Harper. Helping families preserve their beloved pets' genetic material, cloning endangered species. I remember this couple from Dubai, their champion racing camel had died, and we managed to create a perfect clone. The look on their faces..." He shook his head. "We were giving people back something precious they'd lost."

"But something changed?"

Ryan's expression darkened. "Everything changed when Dae-Song died. Dr. Kim's son." He lowered his voice. "Car accident. Dr. Kim was driving. The guilt... it consumed him."

Harper felt a chill that had nothing to do with the winter night. "What did he do?"

"At first, nothing obvious. More late nights in the lab. Obsessing over success rates with primates, pushing the boundaries of what we'd achieved with other mammals. Each success brought us closer to his real goal."

"Then the questions started, theoretical discussions about human applications." Ryan's hands trembled slightly, moving from his coffee cup to the double helix pendant, then back again. His chair scraped against the floor as he shifted position, unable to stay still. "We'd already perfected the techniques with many different mammals. The leap to human genetics wasn't as large as you might think."

"You helped him clone his son?" Harper kept her voice neutral, professional, as she steadied herself.

Ryan stood abruptly, pacing the small space beside their table. "I should have seen it coming. Should have stopped it. We weren't just pushing boundaries anymore, we were obliterating them." He turned back to Harper, his face haunted. "Do you know what it's like to watch someone's ethical lines blur? To see rationalization after rationalization, each small step leading to something unthinkable?"

"When did you leave?"

Ryan's voice dropped to barely a whisper. "Success with Dae-Song wasn't enough. There were others, powerful people who saw the potential. Who wanted to push further." He glanced nervously at the door. "When I realized we weren't stopping with Dae-Song..."

Ryan's hands clenched at his sides, his eyes darting toward the cafe's front windows. "We shouldn't... this isn't the place." He scanned the nearly empty cafe, paranoia evident in every movement. "There's a booth in the back, away from windows. Away from phones and cameras."

Harper studied him carefully. The scientist's earlier confidence had cracked, revealing something raw beneath, fear, maybe, or guilt. Possibly both. She gathered her recorder and notebook, careful to keep her movements casual.

"Lead the way," she said quietly.

As they moved deeper into the cafe's shadows, Harper pulled up the photo Mary had sent earlier on her phone, Dr. Kim shaking hands with someone just out of frame, the VSM logo barely visible in the background. Her finger hovered over the image, pieces starting to align in her mind.

What exactly had happened in that lab? And more importantly, what did it have to do with an seventeen-year-old hockey prodigy?

The booth Ryan chose sat in a darkened corner, far from the cafe's windows where snow continued to fall, covering Toronto in its silent blanket. Here, in the shadows, perhaps she'd finally learn just how deep these secrets went.

The Next Generation

"Control the talent, and you control the game. Create the talent, and you own the future." — Lou

Lou Booker stood in Furever Genetics' equine facility, his breath visible in the climate-controlled air. The stable's polished steel and glass interior was a far cry from the traditional wooden barns of his youth in Bromont. Digital displays monitored every vital sign, every genetic marker of the specimens housed within.

His phone buzzed, another message about Desert Crown Golf poaching one of VSM's rising stars. He silenced it without looking. The Saudis had rewritten golf's rules with their checkbooks, just as Qatar's sportswashing was changing the world of sport. VSM was falling behind.

"Impressive facility," Lou said as Dr. Kim approached. His voice echoed off the steel walls, competing with the soft whir of environmental controls.

"We've expanded significantly since your last visit." Dr. Kim gestured toward the first stall. "I believe you'll find our latest achievements... enlightening."

A magnificent stallion occupied the space, its muscled frame rippling beneath a gleaming coat. Lou had seen hundreds of thoroughbreds in his career, but this one was different. The muscle definition, the proportion, the very way it carried itself, all familiar, yet enhanced.

"Arabian Cipher," Dr. Kim said. "Three-time Dubai World Cup champion. Sheikh Mohammed commissioned six clones after his first victory." He tapped the digital display beside the stall. "Each one genetically optimized for performance."

"Optimized?" Lou moved closer to the display, studying the scrolling data.

"Enhanced oxygen utilization. Increased fast-twitch muscle fiber density. Optimized recovery rates, improvements that would take generations of traditional breeding."

They moved deeper into the facility. Each stall housed another testament to Furever's capabilities, champions bred from champions, enhanced and replicated with scientific precision.

"My clients understand potential," Dr. Kim continued, stopping at another stall. "This racing camel's bloodline has dominated every major Gulf race for three seasons." He lowered his voice. "Each success requires significant investment. Lab costs, specialized equipment, absolute privacy. The facilities alone..." He gestured at the pristine surroundings. "In this world, Lou, innovation outweighs inconvenience."

Lou watched the camel's powerful movements, commenting. "They're rewriting the rules for everything. Soccer teams, NHL, NBA, Formula One teams."

A sleek monitoring drone hummed overhead, checking vital signs and collecting data. Lou's mind raced with possibilities. While Middle Eastern billions reshuffled today's sports landscape, the real power lay in controlling tomorrow's athletes.

"They buy the present," Dr. Kim interrupted, a hint of frustration in his voice. "But the future?" He hesitated, choosing his words carefully. "The future requires more than just money, Lou. It needs vision, discretion, and the right... partnerships."

Lou turned from the stalls, facing Dr. Kim directly. The scientist's eyes held none of the desperate grief from their previous meeting. This was a businessman now, offering a partnership in revolution.

"You're not just talking about horses anymore, are you?"

Dr. Kim's smile didn't waver. "Perhaps we should discuss this in my office. I have something to show you that makes these achievements..." he gestured at the stable of enhanced champions, "seem rather primitive."

Lou glanced once more at Arabian Cipher, at its perfect form and enhanced capabilities. His phone buzzed again in his pocket, another reminder of the changing industry, of power shifting to those who could afford to buy the future.

But what if you could build it instead?

"Lead the way," Lou said.

Behind them, the soft glow of genetic sequences scrolled endlessly across the monitors, spelling out tomorrow's victories in the language of DNA.

Dr. Kim's office felt like a fortress. As the door sealed behind them with a soft hiss, Lou noticed the subtle shimmer of privacy glass activating. No coincidence, nothing in this room happened by chance.

The office itself spoke of careful precision, sleek Korean modernism merged with scientific functionality. Multiple displays wrapped the walls, streaming real-time data from global sports markets and genetic research feeds. Behind Dr. Kim's desk, a single framed photograph caught Lou's attention: a young boy, maybe four years old, his smile hauntingly innocent among the surrounding scientific accolades and degrees.

Subtle security features punctuated the space, retinal scanners disguised as art pieces, encrypted keypads masquerading as climate controls. Everything about the room suggested power carefully contained, like a laboratory experiment under precise conditions.

"You understand what we're discussing?" Dr. Kim settled behind his desk, gesturing Lou to a chair. "The implications?"

"Human cloning." Lou remained standing, studying the genetic sequences flowing across wall displays. "Let's not dance around it."

"Yes." Dr. Kim activated his desk display. "But there are challenges beyond the science."

Dr. Kim's hand moved unconsciously toward the photograph before redirecting to his tablet. Even that slight gesture betrayed an emotional undercurrent beneath his clinical exterior. His carefully pressed lab coat and rigid posture couldn't completely mask the energy thrumming beneath, the excitement of a scientist on the verge of breakthrough.

"Like free will?" Lou turned, fixing Dr. Kim with a hard stare. "Even identical twins make different choices. What happens when your perfect athlete decides he'd rather play piano?"

Dr. Kim nodded, as if expecting this. "That's why implementation is crucial. Early intervention, careful guidance—"

"Control," Lou cut in. "You're talking about controlling every aspect of someone's life."

"We already do that with elite athletes. Training programs, diets, schedules."

"That's different. They choose that life." Lou's phone buzzed again. Another notification about someone else reshaping sports. He silenced it with more force than necessary. "You can't program passion into DNA."

Dr. Kim leaned forward. "Consider your current athletes. How many truly chose their path? Parents, coaches, circumstances, they all shape choices. We're simply being more... deliberate."

"And when people start asking questions?" Lou began pacing. "Birth records? Medical history? School records? One investigation and everything falls apart."

"Infrastructure is already in place." Dr. Kim pulled up documents on his display. "International facilities, discrete medical providers, carefully crafted backgrounds. Nothing appears suddenly, prodigies emerge gradually, naturally."

Lou stopped at the window, looking down at the lab below. "The legal exposure—"

"Is considerable," Dr. Kim finished. "But manageable through shell companies, offshore accounts, distributed operations. No direct connections."

"And the athletes themselves? Psychology, identity issues—"

"Comprehensive support systems," Dr. Kim interrupted. "Mental health monitoring, controlled social integration, career guidance. Everything managed through your existing sports programs."

Lou turned back. "Whistleblowers? DNA testing?"

"Genetic modifications appear natural. Untraceable enhancements. As for loyalty..." Dr. Kim's voice hardened slightly. "Their entire existence depends on discretion."

Dr. Kim rose, his movements deliberate as he approached one of the wall displays. The smart glass window behind him shifted subtly, revealing glimpses of the labs below where technicians moved through their precisely choreographed routines. The entire facility pulsed with controlled purpose, every element part of a greater design.

The implications hung heavy in the air. Lou resumed pacing, each step marking time between the old world and whatever came next.

"They bid against each other for what nature created," Dr. Kim continued, his voice carrying quiet conviction. "We're discussing something far more significant, designing excellence from the ground up."

"Nothing's perfect," Lou muttered. "Twins, triplets, identical DNA, they still turn out different."

Lou's empire had been built on finding and developing talent. But this... this was manufacturing it. His phone buzzed again.

"Time isn't on our side," Dr. Kim said quietly. "Others will eventually cross this line. The question is: will you be the one controlling that future?"

Lou stared at the CRISPR sequences dancing across the screens. Champions built from scratch. Perfect athletes under his control. His entire career had been about managing sports talent. This was about creating it.

Lou felt the weight of years in sports management pressing down on him. He'd built VSM from nothing, weathered scandals, fought off hostile takeovers, survived every shift in the industry. This was crossing a line that couldn't be uncrossed. And one mistake, one leak, one whistleblower, and it wouldn't just be jail, it would be the destruction of everything he'd built. His family's reputation. His legacy.

But then his phone buzzed again. The old guard was dying, suffocating under waves of foreign money. Adapt or die. Wasn't that always the rule?

"The facility requirements?" Lou's voice was barely audible.

"Substantial. Private location, sophisticated equipment, discrete staff."

"Cost?"

"Significant." Dr. Kim paused. "Beyond my current resources."

And there it was. The real partnership proposal. Lou's money, influence, and sports empire combined with Dr. Kim's scientific expertise.

"This crosses every line," Lou said finally.

"Lines exist until someone steps over them." Dr. Kim's voice was steady.

Lou looked down at his buzzing phone one last time. The sports world was changing. Stand still, and you die.

"Show me the details," he said.

Dr. Kim smiled slightly, reaching for a secure tablet. "Welcome to tomorrow, Lou."

The genetic sequences continued their endless dance across the screens, spelling out a future where champions weren't born or made.

They were engineered.

Another

"Every time I see Liam on the ice, I see Ethan too, his passion, his determination. It's like part of him is still out there." – Sue

Harper leaned forward, shoulders tensed, watching Ryan fidget in the shadowed booth. They'd moved to the back of the café, where high-backed booths created shadows within shadows. The illusion of privacy was punctuated by the distant clink of cups and fragments of conversation, each sound making Ryan flinch slightly.

Ryan's eyes darted between his coffee cup and the café's entrance, his shoulders tightening with each passing shadow. He'd insisted on this spot, back to the wall, clear view of both exits. Every time the door chimed, his shoulders tightened.

"You mentioned 'others' before," Harper said, keeping her voice low. "When you talked about Dr. Kim's work." She placed her recorder on the table, switched off. A show of trust. "Is that why you've been following Liam?"

Ryan's hand froze mid-tap. His gaze snapped to her phone, lying silent next to her notebook.

"The phones," he said. "They need to be off. Completely off."

Harper studied him for a moment, then powered down her phone. Ryan did the same, his movements precise, almost ritualistic. Only after both devices were dark did some of the tension ease from his shoulders.

"I've seen you," Harper continued. "At the arena. The hotel. You're not exactly subtle about watching him."

Ryan's laugh held no humor. "Subtle? No, I suppose not." He wrapped both hands around his coffee cup, as if seeking warmth. "But someone needs to watch. Someone needs to..." Ryan hunched lower in his seat as a server passed.

"Why Liam?"

The question hung between them. Ryan closed his eyes, throat working as he swallowed. When he opened them again, something had shifted in his expression, fear giving way to resignation.

"Because," he said, voice barely above a whisper, "Liam is one of them. One of the others I mentioned." He leaned forward, the words tumbling out now. "He's a clone, Ms. Sinclair. A clone, created in our lab."

Harper felt the words like a physical blow, but years of journalism kept her expression neutral. Her mind raced through every interaction with Liam, the interviews, the games, the casual conversations in arena hallways. A clone. The word hung in her mind, absurd and impossible.

"That's..." She paused, choosing her words carefully. "That's a significant accusation, Mr. Patel."

"You think I don't know that?" Ryan's voice cracked. He leaned closer, almost hunched over the table. "I was there. In the lab. Watching Dr. Kim perfect the process. First with Dae-Song, then..." He shuddered. "Then VSM."

Harper's face twitched with curiosity. "Victoria Sports Management? Lou Booker's company?"

Ryan nodded, his eyes constantly scanning the café. "They wanted NHL superstars. A perfect athlete, designed from the ground up." His laugh was bitter.

"Lou Booker approached Dr. Kim?" Harper pressed.

"Other way around." Ryan's voice dropped lower. "After Dae-Song died, Dr. Kim needed funding. Lou has vast family resources."

Harper thought of the files on her laptop. The money trails Mary had found, leading from VSM to shell companies in Seoul. The photograph of Lou Booker with Dr. Kim, hidden away in old news archives.

Harper's mind flashed to the hotel restaurant, watching Liam with his parents. "But that's impossible. I've seen him with Jim and Tammy. He looks exactly like them, he has Jim's jawline, Tammy's eyes. The way he moves, even his expressions..."

She stopped, watching Ryan's face. Something in his expression made her stomach tighten.

"That's what makes it brilliant," Ryan said, his voice taking on an edge of reluctant admiration. He took a deep breath before finally asking, "Do you know what CRISPR is?"

Harper's brow furrowed. "I've heard of it. Genetic editing, right? Something about changing eye color in animals. I remember reading about an octopus they engineered so its skin would be transparent, to study its organs without cutting it open."

Ryan nodded, relieved at her recognition. "Exactly. CRISPR is a tool that rewrites the blueprints of life. Imagine DNA as a string of beads, each bead a letter in life's code. CRISPR lets scientists remove, replace, or rewrite any part of that sequence."

"So, like editing a sentence in a story?" Harper ventured, her mind clicking through the analogy.

Ryan's shoulders relaxed slightly as he caught onto her understanding. "Exactly. You can remove words, add new ones, or change them to alter the entire meaning."

Harper leaned back, absorbing the information, but her mind was still locked on Liam. "And you're saying they used this on Liam? Edited his DNA?"

Ryan's nod was barely perceptible as he leaned closer. "Think of CRISPR like you having a set of tiny molecular scissors. We could cut out traits, replace them, even enhance them. At first, it was just about making racing animals better, stronger. But with Liam... they used it to make him look like he belonged in his family."

The weight of that confession settled over Harper like a heavy coat, uncomfortable but necessary as she prepared to weather the storm of implications it brought with it. The story she was uncovering would shake foundations far beyond sports, it delved into what it meant to be human and who had the right to dictate that definition. As Ryan spoke, Harper's thoughts zeroed in on his word choice, "we." He wasn't just a bystander to this project, he was complicit. The realization hit her hard, and she tried to keep her voice steady.

"And you think this... CRISPR editing hid Liam's true origins?"

Ryan's coffee cup rattled against its saucer as he set it down. His voice dropped to a near whisper, eyes fixed on the dark liquid. "His DNA was engineered to blend in, to mask who he really came from. And it wasn't just Liam."

Harper's eyes narrowed. "What do you mean, not just Liam?"

Ryan hesitated, then his shoulders sagged. "There were others. VSM used the same process for more than just Liam. Ethan Bernard, for example."

The name struck Harper with physical force. Ethan Bernard. She'd been rink side when it happened, watched him collapse mid-stride, saw the medical team's desperate efforts, felt the arena's collective breath catch as minutes stretched into eternity. Her notebook from that day still held the unfinished sentence where her pen had stopped moving.

"Ethan Bernard," she repeated, her voice tight. "You're telling me Ethan was part of this too?"

Ryan nodded again, slower this time. "He was... a clone. Just like Liam."

Harper's mind reeled, a dozen questions fighting to surface at once. "And you have proof of this?"

Ryan's breathing quickened as he leaned forward. "I don't have documents or anything concrete. But Ethan... he was just like Liam. Cloned, engineered to be a star athlete."

Harper leaned back, her skepticism flaring up again. This could be the story of her career, but she had to be sure. The accusations Ryan was leveling against VSM weren't just earth-shattering, they could destroy lives. "You realize how this sounds, don't you? You're accusing a top sports management company of playing god with human lives."

Harper's skepticism warred with the weight of his words. She had seen hoaxes before, been fed fabricated stories that unraveled under scrutiny. But something about Ryan's demeanor, the fear, the guilt, it felt real.

"I've said too much." The shadows in the booth's corners seemed to deepen, real fear crossing his face. "They're still watching. Always watching. And Liam..." He leaned forward, urgent now. "He doesn't know. None of them do. And VSM can't risk—"

The café door chimed again. Ryan practically jumped out of his seat, his face draining of color as he stared past Harper's shoulder.

"I have to go." He was already sliding out of the booth. "Be careful, Ms. Sinclair. Some truths..." His voice faltered as his gaze fixed on something, or someone, behind Harper. "Some truths are more dangerous than others."

Harper watched him hurry toward the back exit, her notebook filled with impossible revelations. Her phone lay dark on the table, and for the first time in her career, she wasn't sure she wanted to turn it back on.

Harper gathered her notebook and phone, still processing Ryan's abrupt departure. As she slid out of the booth, a white rectangle caught her eye, a business card, partially hidden under a napkin. Ryan must have left it behind in his hurry to escape.

New Horizon Fertility Clinic, Brandon, Manitoba was printed in neat blue letters on the front. But it was the handwritten note on the back that made her breath catch: *Bernard family - embryo donation program - NH1214*.

She turned the card over in her hands, her journalist's mind racing. The Bernards had never mentioned fertility treatments, but then again, why would they? She'd gotten to know them during Ethan's rising star years, not his early childhood.

The memory hit her with surprising force, Ethan Bernard's first profile piece. She'd been covering junior hockey in Brandon, tracking the emergence of what sports writers were calling a "once-in-a-generation talent." Tom and Sue Bernard had welcomed her into their home, proud parents sharing stories of their son's earliest skating lessons. Sue had served hot chocolate while Tom dug out old photo albums.

Now those warm memories collided with Ryan's desperate revelations. Clone. The word felt foreign, impossible. Yet here was evidence of something the Bernards had never mentioned, a fertility clinic's business card with a cryptic note about embryo donation.

Harper sank back into the booth, her earlier conversation with Ryan replaying in her mind. She'd been there that terrible day, watching Ethan collapse during the game.

She'd stayed with the story through all of it. The desperate ambulance ride, the hospital vigil, and finally, the devastating press conference where doctors admitted they had no explanation for why a seemingly healthy sixteen-year-old athlete's heart had simply stopped. She'd written Ethan's obituary, something no sports journalist ever wants to do.

Sue had found her that night, slumped over her laptop in the hospital waiting room, struggling to find words worthy of Ethan's memory. Without a word, Sue had sat beside her, pulled out a small photo album, and started sharing stories about Ethan's first steps on ice, his pre-game rituals, the way he'd always leave his gear bag by the front door no matter how many times they asked him not to. Through her own grief, Sue had helped Harper write not just about the hockey player, but about the son, the friend, the boy who'd light up any room he entered.

And in all the grief and confusion that followed, in all her conversations with Tom and Sue, there'd never been any mention of fertility treatments or embryo donations.

The café's ambient noise faded as she stared at the card. She knew the Bernards, their integrity, their honesty, their deep love for their son. Whatever this card meant, whatever part of their story remained untold, she knew they deserved more than an ambush of accusations based on a desperate man's claims and a mysterious business card.

Harper pulled out her phone, then stopped, her finger hovering over Sue's contact. The Bernards had always been more than just sources, they'd become friends during those dark days after Ethan's death. Now she was about to use that trust to probe into what might be their most private secret.

Her journalistic instincts battled with personal loyalty. If Ryan was telling the truth about cloning and genetic engineering, the Bernards might hold crucial answers about Ethan and Liam's uncanny abilities on the ice. But digging into those memories meant risking their friendship and potentially reopening wounds that had never fully healed.

The World Juniors tournament could provide a natural opening. The Bernards had stayed connected to hockey through Liam, she remembered how close the families had been, watching their boys light up the ice together for the Wheat Kings. The dynamic duo, everyone had called them.

Before she could second-guess herself, Harper dialed Sue's number. Each ring seemed to stretch longer than the last.

"Harper?" Sue's warm voice carried the slight raspiness she remembered. "What a lovely surprise."

"Hi Sue." Harper kept her tone gentle, personal. "I'm covering the World Juniors in Toronto, and with everything happening with Liam... I've been thinking about you and Tom."

There was a moment of silence on the line. "We've been watching every game," Sue said softly. "Poor Liam, he's carrying so much weight on his shoulders. Tom and I..." She paused, her voice catching slightly. "We're actually flying out tomorrow. Tom says Liam needs all the support he can get right now. And after everything..."

Harper heard the unspoken words: after losing Ethan.

"Every time I see Liam on the ice," Sue continued, her voice steadier now, "I remember them together. How they'd practice for hours, pushing each other to be better. Ethan would be so proud of him making it this far."

The weight of shared memories hung between them. Harper glanced at the business card on the table, then carefully asked, "Would you and Tom have time for coffee while you're here? It's been too long."

"Oh, sweetheart." The old term of endearment, coupled with genuine warmth, made Harper's throat tight. "We'd love that. It'll be good to see you, to talk about old times."

After ending the call, Harper's gaze was drawn back to the business card, its presence on the table like a weight pulling at her conscience. The warmth and openness of the Bernards only made this harder. In all the years she'd known them, through Ethan's rise in hockey, through the tragedy, through their grief, they'd never given her reason to doubt their integrity.

Her mind drifted to the scene at Brandon Memorial, the day after they lost Ethan. Sue had gripped her hand, whispering through tears about how the doctors couldn't explain it. How a perfectly healthy boy could just... stop. The medical reports had shown nothing, no underlying conditions, no warning signs. Just another tragic story of a young athlete lost too soon.

But what if there had been more to it? What if Ryan's wild claims about cloning weren't so wild after all? The business card felt heavy in her hands, its implications even heavier.

She reached for her laptop, then hesitated. Part of her wanted to start digging now, into the clinic's history, into embryo donation programs, into anything that might corroborate Ryan's story.

Maybe some mysteries were better left buried, but she'd never been very good at leaving things alone.

Inherited Lies

"Sometimes we keep secrets thinking we're protecting the people we love, but maybe we're just protecting ourselves from their hurt." — Tammy

Harper paced her hotel room, Ryan's words about cloning and genetic engineering burning in her mind. The Toronto skyline stretched beyond the window, its lights a reminder of the lives she was about to upend. Her phone felt like a grenade in her hand.

Taking a deep breath, she dialed Liam's number, she exhaled slowly, keeping the nerves at bay.

"Hello?" His voice came through, hesitant yet expectant.

"Hey Liam, it's Harper." She fought to keep her voice steady.

"Oh, hey Harper." His tone warmed slightly, waking up from an unexpected nap. "What's up?"

Harper's throat tightened. The truth about his origin, about Ethan, about everything VSM had built, threatened to burst out. "Liam, remember when we talked about Ryan's claims? About Jim and Tammy?" She paused, choosing her words carefully. "I didn't believe him at first, but... I've learned some things."

Liam's breath hitched audibly. "You found something?"

"I did. I tracked down some more about Ryan." Her knuckles whitened around the phone, the weight of what she knew threatening to spill out. "He's not exactly on VSM's roster but... he's got connections. And Liam, some of what he told you... there might be truth to it."

Liam's grip tightened on his phone. "What are you saying?"

Images of Dr. Kim's lab, of VSM's secrets, of Ethan's tragic end flashed through Harper's mind. "I think..." Harper pressed her lips together, choosing her words carefully. "I think there are conversations you need to have with your parents. About your past, about Brandon..."

"What kind of conversations?" His voice sharpened, ice creeping into the edges of his tone.

Her free hand clenched into a fist. Everything she'd uncovered about Furever Genetics, about Lou's empire, about the genetic engineering that had shaped Liam's existence, it all pressed against her conscience. "Liam, I know this isn't easy," Harper said, her voice gentle but firm. "But with everything that's happening, Ryan's claims, the draft coming up, you deserve answers."

She could feel him withdrawing into himself, his replies became shorter, more guarded. "What aren't they telling me?"

Harper tilted her head back against the chair, staring at the ceiling as if it might reveal how much to disclose without breaking him. "That's not for me to say. But I think there are things they've been protecting you from."

Liam fell quiet again. The silence stretched out between them like a taut string ready to snap.

"Look," Harper continued, fighting the urge to tell him everything right there, trying to navigate the delicate path between journalistic pursuit and human compassion, "I don't have all the pieces yet. But I'm on your side here, okay? Whatever you learn... it doesn't change who you are on that ice."

She could sense his skepticism, trust was not easily given in his world where every word could be a headline or a hidden blade. The irony of what she knew about his true origins made her chest ache.

"Uh," he finally murmured. The word was laden with uncertainty and appreciation mixed together like oil and water.

"And Liam?" Harper added before he could hang up, her voice cracking slightly. "Just remember they love you."

After the line went dead, Harper collapsed into her chair, the weight of what she'd set in motion crushing her chest. She turned her gaze back to the night outside her window, the darkness held no answers but promised that dawn was never too far away.

Liam stood frozen in the middle of his hotel room, the weight of Harper's words pressing down on him like a physical force. The Toronto skyline sprawled out beyond the window, indifferent to the tremor in his hands as he reached for his phone again.

With a sharp inhale, he finally selected Jim's number, Harper's warning still echoing in his mind. The ringing felt too loud, cutting through the silence of the room like a siren.

"Hey, champ! How're you holding up?" Jim's voice came through, warm and familiar, a balm to the unease swirling inside Liam.

Liam swallowed hard, his grip on the phone tightening. "Hey, Dad," he began, his voice quieter than usual, tentative. "Can we talk? You and Mom?"

There was a brief pause on the other end before Jim replied, his voice laced with concern. "Of course, son. Everything alright?"

Liam nodded, though Jim couldn't see it. "Yeah... I just... I just need to ask you something. Can I come to your room?"

"Room 714," Jim said without hesitation. "Come on over. Whatever it is, we'll figure it out together."

Liam's footsteps echoed through the hotel corridor, each step bringing him closer to a truth he couldn't ignore. The crumpled note in his pocket held four words that threatened to shatter everything: *Not your biological parents.*

The knock on his parents' door came too soon. His breaths felt like ice in his lungs as he hesitated, wondering if he was about to break something he couldn't put back together.

Jim opened the door, his face a picture of fatherly concern. Behind him, Tammy appeared, her soft voice reaching out to him like a warm embrace. "Come in, sweetheart."

Liam stepped into the room. The familiar presence of his parents should have been comforting, but tonight it felt like a façade about to crumble. Without a word, he pulled out the note and placed it on the table between them.

Jim and Tammy exchanged a look, one of those silent exchanges that Liam had witnessed so many times over the years. But this time, it carried something he had never seen before, something unreadable, something that made his stomach tighten.

"What's this about?" Jim asked, though his voice held a tremor.

Jim reached for the note, his hand trembling slightly. Tammy's sharp intake of breath suggested she already knew what it said. The paper seemed to carry the weight of years of unspoken truths.

Liam's heart pounded in his chest. "I got this note." His voice was steady, but it felt like it was coming from someone else. "It says... you're not my biological parents."

The silence stretched between them. Seconds became minutes. Liam watched his parents, the people he'd known his whole life, transform into strangers before his eyes. Jim sank heavily into the hotel chair, his shoulders curving inward. Tammy remained standing, her hand pressed against her throat, her eyes moving from the note to Jim to Liam and back again.

Liam felt the weight of their silence crushing him. "Say something," he whispered, his voice barely audible. "Please."

When Tammy finally spoke, her voice was quiet but firm. "We... we wanted you so much, Liam."

Jim nodded slowly, his eyes filled with a sadness that seemed to weigh on his very soul. "Liam, we did everything we could, because we wanted you more than anything."

Tammy took a step closer, reaching out to him, her hands trembling as she grasped his. "We went to clinics, explored every option. And when we couldn't... when it wasn't possible, we decided to use a donor embryo."

Tammy paused, then continued, "We were desperate, Liam. We just wanted a family. When nothing else worked... this was our only hope."

Her words washed over Liam like cold water, each one deepening the fissures spreading through his sense of self. He felt as though the ground beneath him had shifted, the foundation of his identity suddenly cracking wide open.

"I carried you," Tammy said, her voice thick with emotion. "I gave birth to you. You are our son in every way that matters."

Liam stared at her, searching her eyes for something, reassurance, maybe? A promise that this revelation didn't change everything. But it did. How could it not? He felt hollow, like a stranger in his own skin. The memories, the victories, the love, it had all been real, hadn't it?

But now, standing in front of the two people who had raised him, who had cheered for him from the sidelines and held him after every loss, it all felt fragile, like glass teetering on the edge of shattering.

"Why didn't you tell me?" Liam's voice was quiet, but there was a tremor beneath the surface, a crack threatening to widen if they didn't answer him honestly.

"We never wanted to lie," Jim said, his voice rough with emotion. "We just... we thought it wouldn't change anything. You were always our son. You still are."

Tammy's grip on his hands tightened. "We hoped you'd never have to know. We just wanted to love you. We didn't want you to feel different, less."

The words stung like a slap. All those times they'd praised his honesty, demanded his truth, while keeping this from him.

Liam nodded slowly, the weight of their words pressing down on him, but they couldn't erase the doubt gnawing at the edges of his mind. He'd always known who he was, or so he thought. But now? Now there were questions he didn't know how to answer.

"Did you know who donated?" His voice cracked, each word like a piece of ice breaking off and floating into an uncertain sea.

Tammy shook her head, tears brimming in her eyes. "No. We never knew. We didn't want to know. We didn't care where you came from, we only cared about you."

"The clinic was very strict about privacy," Jim added, his voice taking on an edge Liam had never heard before. "No medical history, no genetic profile, nothing we could trace. They said it was their policy, everything was confidential, sealed."

"But they must have had records," Liam pressed, searching their faces. "Some kind of documentation?"

Tammy's hands twisted together. "The clinic was clear, no information, no records, nothing to trace. But we didn't care. We were just so grateful to have you, we never questioned it."

Liam felt like he was standing on a sheet of ice, and the cracks were spreading faster than he could comprehend.

Jim stepped forward, placing a hand on his shoulder, the same gesture he had used countless times after games, after losses. "We're your family," Jim said firmly. "That hasn't changed. It never will."

Liam nodded reflexively, the words offering some small measure of comfort, but it wasn't enough to stop the fissures that were growing inside him. He couldn't shake the feeling that something essential had shifted, that a part of him was lost in the cracks of this new truth.

"I don't know what to think right now. I need some space to figure this out," Liam said, his voice distant. "I just need..."

Jim and Tammy both nodded, their understanding clear as they watched him turn toward the door. Their love followed him out, but for the first time in his life, it wasn't enough.

As Liam stepped into the corridor, the air felt too thin, like he couldn't breathe. His hands shook, and the hotel hallway felt longer than it had any right to be. His world was cracked wide open, and he wasn't sure how he'd ever put the pieces back together.

Outside in the cold night air, Liam walked aimlessly, his breath visible in the chilled air. The note still felt heavy in his pocket, but now it wasn't the note that weighed on him, it was the questions. Who were his biological parents? Why was Ryan involved? What else didn't he know?

The cold bit at him, sharp and unforgiving, as though the world was showing him the stark reality of what he'd just learned. For so long, Jim and Tammy had been his warmth, his certainty. He couldn't hate them, their love was real, he knew that much. But trust? That was as fractured as everything else.

Who was he now? Liam Desjardins, Jim and Tammy's son? Or someone else, someone reduced to a clinic number and sealed records?

The cracks had spread too far for him to see the whole picture. But tomorrow, on the ice, at least, he'd still be Liam. Hockey was real. His skill was real. Everything else... he'd figure out later.

The Genesis Code

"Desperation is the mother of loyalty. Offer salvation, and no one questions the strings you've attached to it." – Finn

TWENTY YEARS BEFORE WORLD JUNIORS

Dr. Kim Jung-So's fingers hovered above the sterile glass of the petri dish, trembling, not from the lab's controlled chill, but from the weight of the moment. Three blastocysts lay inside, each dividing with mechanical precision. The CRISPR modifications had taken hold perfectly, the enhanced sequences integrating exactly as designed.

Two of these lives carried the weight of a secret pact between science and ambition. The third, however, was something else entirely. A father's desperate love.

Dae-Song.

His son's name left his lips in a whisper, a prayer lost in the sterile air.

Dr. Kim adjusted the focus on the microscope, peering closer at the embryonic cells. Their division was a flawless dance, a perfect execution of genetic orchestration. He had achieved it, an audacious leap beyond nature's boundaries. For a moment, he allowed himself to marvel at what he had done. But in the marvel, there was fear. Each cell represented both a miracle and a transgression.

Footsteps echoed down the corridor, sharp and deliberate. **Lou Booker.**

The door hissed open, revealing his imposing silhouette, framed in the fluorescent glow. His gaze swept the lab, cold and calculating, before settling on Dr. Kim.

"Dr. Kim," Lou began, his voice thick with anticipation and something else, perhaps apprehension, perhaps awe.

Dr. Kim straightened up from the microscope and turned to face him. "Lou," he said solemnly, gesturing toward the scope. "Come see for yourself."

Lou's steps were deliberate, heavy with the weight of what they were about to witness. Dr. Kim motioned to the microscope.

"These are them?" Lou asked, his tone hushed, almost reverent.

"Yes," Dr. Kim confirmed. "The first step toward everything we envisioned."

Lou bent forward, pressing his eye to the microscope. His breath slowed. The room seemed to close in as he studied the dividing cells, his silence stretching into something reverent.

Finally, he straightened, his face unreadable, awe, maybe. Or fear.

"My God," Lou whispered, staring off into the distance as if the cells had already become the future stars they intended them to be, athletes molded from the raw material of greatness.

"This changes everything," Lou murmured, his mind already racing. "The draft. The league. The future of sports itself."

"If we succeed," Dr. Kim cautioned, checking the environmental controls again. "We're still days away from viable implantation, and months from knowing if the genetic modifications will express as designed."

Yet as he spoke, Dr. Kim felt the weight of everything he had sacrificed, his ethics bending under the weight of grief, his soul bargaining for one more chance to glimpse what he had lost. He had crossed the line long ago, but seeing it in Lou's eyes, he realized there might be no going back.

Lou began to pace, his movements jittery, his thoughts colliding with one another. He stopped and looked at the petri dish again, a glimmer of hesitation flashing in his eyes. "And the others?"

Dr. Kim's response was immediate, perhaps too quick. "Yes," he said firmly, though the doubt gnawed at him. "Everything is proceeding as planned."

Lou exhaled sharply, rolling his shoulders, as if shedding whatever uncertainty remained. "Good." He checked his watch, already shifting gears. "Let's talk next steps. When do we move to implantation?"

Dr. Kim turned back to the microscope, adjusting the focus unnecessarily. "Two weeks. We'll be ready."

The words settled between them, not as reassurance, but as inevitability. Lou took one last glance at the embryos before turning away, already thinking ahead.

"Mon Dieu," Lou whispered, sinking into a chair. Sweat beaded on his brow. "We're playing with something bigger than we understand."

"Progress always feels that way," Dr. Kim said, though even he wasn't sure if it was reassurance or deflection. The moral calculus? That was for someone else to debate.

He met Lou's gaze and saw it, the hunger, the need to win at any cost. It should have reassured him. Instead, it terrified him. "We're creating legends, Lou. The world will be astounded by what we can achieve."

Lou straightened, the word 'legends' igniting something in his eyes. His shoulders relaxed as he envisioned the future, the wealth, the dominance that VSM would enjoy. "You're right. The world has no idea what we can do."

Lou's shift in demeanor didn't entirely reassure Dr. Kim. His scientific mind knew the risks. He had learned to ignore the whispers of doubt that haunted him. But Lou? Lou was more driven by the end result than the process, and that frightened Dr. Kim. The moral ramifications of their work weighed heavily on him, but for Lou, it was about glory.

Footsteps in the corridor interrupted them, lighter, faster than Lou's had been. The door opened, and Finn Booker strode in, his lean five-foot-eleven frame wrapped in an expensive suit that seemed at stark contrast to the sterile lab environment. His dark blond hair was characteristically disheveled, as if he'd been running his hands through it too often, a nervous habit that betrayed the collected image he tried to project.

Dr. Kim noted how his pale green eyes darted around the room before fixing on the microscope with an unmistakable hunger. A thin sheen of sweat on his face aged him beyond his thirty-six years, exhaustion etched into his sharp jawline and thin features.

"How does it look?" Finn asked, his voice casual but his hands betraying him, tapping, twitching, never quite still. He pulled out a stick of gum and began chewing aggressively, another tell when he was trying to play it cool.

"Marvelous," Lou said, clapping his nephew on the back. "This is the beginning of something historic."

Dr. Kim watched the exchange, noting how Finn leaned into his uncle's approval. After the fraud conviction, after all the failed businesses, this was Finn's last chance, Lou had made that clear when he'd proposed bringing him in. Family loyalty mixed with desperation made for a powerful leash.

"I know the stakes," Finn said, as if reading Dr. Kim's thoughts. He straightened his shoulders, the same way he probably had in front of judges and creditors. "And I'm ready."

"Are you?" Dr. Kim asked quietly. "This isn't like your other ventures, Mr. Booker. One mistake here..."

"I won't make mistakes," Finn cut in, that sharp edge of desperation showing through his polished exterior. "Not with this. Not again."

Lou stepped between them, his presence filling the small lab. "Finn understands exactly what's required," he said, his tone leaving no room for debate. "He'll handle the day-to-day operations, the discretion, everything we discussed."

Dr. Kim nodded, but unease churned in his stomach. He understood Lou's logic, they needed someone they could control, someone who couldn't afford to betray them. Finn, with his past failures and his debt to Lou, was the perfect choice. But perfect choices often came with hidden costs.

"Then we proceed," Dr. Kim said, turning back to the microscope. "The next phase begins tomorrow. Everything must be precise, controlled." He looked directly at Finn. "No room for improvisation."

Finn held his gaze. For a moment, something flickered behind those ambitious eyes, determination, or deception. Dr. Kim couldn't tell. "I understand, Doctor. Completely."

Lou settled once again into one of the lab chairs, his bulk making the steel frame creak. "Now, about these fertility clinics you mentioned..." He pulled out a folder from his briefcase. "How exactly does this part work?"

Finn felt the weight of the moment. This was where science met strategy, where his expertise would shape their deception. "We need cover," he said carefully. "Legitimate clinics, desperate families, people who won't ask too many questions about where their miracle came from."

The gentle hum of precision instruments surrounded them as they prepared to cross another line, one that would entangle innocent lives in their web of ambition and redemption.

"The clinics need to be carefully selected," Finn said, spreading documents across the sterile lab counter. "Small enough to be grateful for the funding, established enough to be credible. I've identified three possibilities." He tapped each location on the map, Peterborough, Moose Jaw, and Brandon.

Lou nodded approvingly. "And the families?"

"We look for specific criteria," Finn explained. "Multiple failed attempts at pregnancy. Families who've exhausted their savings on treatments, at the end of their rope. And most importantly—" he leaned forward, "—they need that desperate desire for a child."

Finn pulled out another document. "We'll need to establish a foundation, something philanthropic. A charity that helps families achieve their dreams of parenthood." He met Lou's gaze. "It's the perfect cover. Funding the clinics. Monitoring the pregnancies. They'll be loyal, grateful."

Lou nodded slowly. "Desperation makes people less inclined to ask questions."

"Exactly," Finn agreed. "We position the foundation as their savior, their last chance at a family. The gratitude will ensure their discretion."

Dr. Kim observed their planning with careful interest, noting how easily they convinced themselves this was about sports, about business. Their limited vision amused him. "And after they're born?" he asked, keeping his tone neutral.

"Sports scholarship programs," Lou said, warming to the plan. "We identify talented young athletes early, offer support, guidance. Nothing unusual there, VSM does it already." He smiled, a predator considering his prey. "Who would question it?"

"These children..." Dr. Kim paused, testing their resolve, "they won't be normal." He needed to ensure they understood enough to stay committed, but not enough to grasp the full scope of what he planned.

"They'll be extraordinary," Lou corrected, his voice thick with ambition. "Champions, created in this very lab. The future of sports itself."

"Already planned for," Finn offered. "Regular pediatric visits, sports physicals, training evaluations. All standard practice for elite young athletes."

"And the families won't suspect?" Dr. Kim pressed.

"They'll be too grateful to question it," Lou said dismissively. "Besides, who doesn't want their child to succeed? To be special?"

The words hung in the air, heavy with implication. Dr. Kim thought of Dae-Song, his desperate attempt to recreate what was lost. Wasn't that just another kind of ambition?

"The timeline?" Finn asked, his pen poised over a notepad.

"Two weeks until the embryos are ready for implantation," Dr. Kim answered. "Then nine months of waiting, watching, hoping nothing goes wrong."

"Nothing will go wrong," Lou stated firmly. "We've come too far." He turned to Finn. "Get the foundation set up. Start approaching the clinics. Everything needs to be in place before we proceed."

Finn nodded, gathering the documents with efficient movements. But Dr. Kim noticed a slight tremor in his hands, a crack in his polished facade.

"Dr. Kim," Lou said, his voice softening slightly. "I know this isn't easy. But think of what we're achieving here. Not just your son, but a whole new generation of possibilities."

Dr. Kim nodded slowly, but his response was interrupted by the soft chime from the lab. Time for another check. Another reminder that they were playing with forces beyond their control.

The door hissed shut behind them, leaving Dr. Kim alone with the softly humming machinery. In the petri dishes before him, lives were forming, lives that would carry his legacy forward.

Dr. Kim turned to the microscope, examining his true masterpiece, Dae-Song's embryo. The other embryos were merely business, necessary resources for his son.

In the pristine isolation of his lab, time seemed to pause, a moment suspended between what was and what would be. Soon, they would begin selecting the families, setting in motion events that could never be undone.

A slight smile played across his lips. Everything was proceeding exactly as planned.

Betrayal of Silence

"Some things are better left in the past, not because they're secrets, but because they're scars." — Tom

Harper Sinclair perched on a stool at The Puck & Pint, grateful for Sue's last-minute text suggesting they meet here instead of a coffee shop. This place carried its own memories, late nights in college, debating scouting reports with Ben until closing. Back when things were simpler. The pub's worn wooden floors, hockey-covered walls, and Team Canada jerseys filled the space with pre-game energy. Laughter, clinking glasses, the hum of excitement. A stark contrast to the tension gripping Harper's mind.

She glanced at her watch. The Bernards should be here any minute. Tom and Sue Bernard, pillars of their community, were woven into Harper's career like threads in a well-worn hockey sweater. She had covered Ethan's games with the Brandon Wheat Kings, Liam's finesse on ice and Ethan's tragically short journey, and it was her pen that told Ethan's story when he fell, a tale that tugged at heartstrings across the nation.

The pub door swung open, cutting through the chatter as Tom and Sue stepped into the warmth. Tom, his salt-and-pepper hair a testament to time and trials, carried a presence that softened as his eyes met Harper's. Beside him, Sue's graceful figure moved with a poise that belied the sorrow she had weathered. As they approached, Harper stood to greet them.

"Harper!" Sue pulled her into a warm embrace.

"Good to see you," Tom said, his handshake firm and familiar.

"Thanks for meeting me." Harper gestured to the booth she'd reserved for privacy.

"We wouldn't miss it," Tom assured her, his eyes reflecting gratitude for the tribute she once wrote for Ethan, a piece that still resonated deeply within them.

Sue smoothed a crease from her coat before speaking. "How are you doing? It's been too long since we've caught up."

Harper offered a genuine smile. "I'm good, keeping busy as always. And how about you both? It must be nice to be here supporting Liam."

Tom nodded with pride. "It is. He works so hard, we just want to be here for him."

Sue chimed in, her voice warm but tinged with nostalgia. "You know, it's always surreal when this time of year rolls around, with Ethan's birthday."

Harper's brow furrowed slightly as she recalled. "That's right. January 5th, wasn't it?"

Sue nodded, her eyes glistening. "Yes. And Liam's just two days later. Sometimes I think that's part of why they bonded so quickly on the ice."

"Almost like they were destined to be brothers on and off the ice," Tom added, his voice heavy with the bittersweetness of memory.

Harper nodded, feeling the weight of the connection. "They were so close, in every way."

Sue's eyes held a quiet strength as she added, "Jim and Tammy have been there for us through it all."

Conversation flowed naturally between them as they reminisced about past games and shared updates on mutual acquaintances from their hockey family. Harper noted how Tom's laughter came easier when he spoke of Ethan's achievements on ice, a father's pride never waning, and how Sue's nurturing glow intensified at any mention of Ethan.

The warmth of nostalgia began to fade as Harper glanced at her notebook, its contents a stark reminder of why she'd called this meeting. Taking a deep breath, she steered the conversation toward darker waters.

Harper leaned forward, her voice soft but steady. "I keep thinking about that last game. Ethan was brilliant that night. Then suddenly, he collapsed."

Tom and Sue Bernard exchanged a glance, their shared pain still raw despite the years.

"He was rushed to the hospital," Harper continued. "I don't mean to reopen wounds, but has anything new surfaced about what caused it? It's just... rare for someone so young and fit."

They shook their heads.

"Nothing new," Tom said flatly. "The shock... it was as sudden for us as it was for everyone else."

"They said it was a rare heart defect," Sue murmured, dabbing at her eyes.

"No warning signs? Nothing in his physicals?" Harper pressed.

"Ethan had the best care," Tom said. "Regular check-ups, specialists. Doctors said sometimes these things just... go undetected."

Harper let the silence settle before continuing. "If his heart condition was rare, any family history?"

Harper was giving them a chance to offer up a truth they had held in silence for years.

Tom didn't take the bait. His response was measured, practiced. "The doctors were baffled. We have no family history of heart issues."

The weight of unspoken words hung between them. Harper shifted tactics.

"You know," she said carefully, "I was going through some old articles about Ethan and Liam's early days. They both trained at those VSM-sponsored camps, didn't they?"

Tom nodded, but his expression remained guarded. "Yes, they did."

"Ben LaFleur approached you about that, didn't he?" Harper kept her tone conversational.

Sue's hands tightened around her glass. "He did. Said they saw potential in Ethan."

"Must have been a generous offer," Harper probed gently.

"It was," Tom acknowledged, his voice tight. "Camps, clinics, equipment... they took care of everything."

"For both boys," Sue added softly, then seemed to catch herself.

Harper caught his subtle flinch. "That's quite an investment in young players."

"Look," Tom said, his voice lowering, "some things are better left in the past. Especially where VSM is concerned."

Sue touched Tom's arm, a gesture that seemed both restraining and reassuring. "It was a different time, Harper. Before everything..."

Her voice trailed off, leaving another heavy silence. Harper could feel them withdrawing, building walls around whatever secrets they held about VSM's involvement with the boys.

Harper set her coffee down, studying the couple across the booth. The din of The Puck & Pint faded as she considered her next words. Tom's weathered hands wrapped around his beer glass, while Sue fidgeted with her napkin, small tells that Harper had learned to read over years of interviews.

"I want to thank you both," Harper began, her voice gentle but clear over the background noise. "I know talking about Ethan isn't easy."

Sue offered a wan smile. "We appreciate how respectful you've been about his memory."

Harper nodded, drawing in a careful breath. "In researching Ethan's story, I've come across some medical records." She paused, watching their reactions. "Records that suggest he may not have been biologically related to you."

The words landed like a sharp gust of winter air. Tom's fingers curled around his glass, knuckles whitening. Sue's hands stilled, the napkin slipping from her grasp. The silence between them wasn't just heavy, it was confirmation.

When Tom finally met Harper's gaze, his eyes carried a weight she recognized, the burden of a long-held secret. Sue reached for her husband's arm, an instinctive gesture of support.

"We..." Sue's voice cracked slightly. She swallowed hard before continuing. "We tried for years to have a baby." Her words came faster now, like a dam breaking. "Multiple treatments, different doctors. We spent everything we had, and still..." She pressed her lips together, fighting for composure.

Tom covered his wife's hand with his own. "Sue had three attempts at In Vito Fertilizations," he said quietly. "Each one harder than the last."

Harper kept her expression neutral, though her heart ached for their pain. "I can't imagine how difficult that must have been."

"You spend your whole life thinking that having a child will just... happen," Sue whispered, tears gathering in her eyes. "But sometimes it doesn't. Sometimes your body just won't..."

She couldn't finish the sentence, but she didn't need to. The years of disappointment and heartbreak were etched in every line of her face.

Harper leaned forward slightly, keeping her voice soft. "What options did you explore after that?"

Sue dabbed at her eyes with the napkin. "We'd almost given up. The treatments had taken everything, financially, emotionally." She glanced at Tom. "Then we heard about this foundation."

"A foundation?" Harper prompted gently.

Tom nodded, his protective demeanor softening slightly. "They helped couples who couldn't conceive. Sponsored an embryo donation program." He paused, choosing his words carefully. "They covered most of the medical costs."

"That must have felt like a miracle," Harper said, noting how Sue's expression brightened at the memory.

"It was," Sue straightened in her seat, pride replacing sorrow in her voice. "When they told me I was pregnant... Tom and I just held each other and cried."

Harper watched as Sue's hand moved unconsciously to her stomach, remembering. "The pregnancy itself—"

"Perfect," Sue interrupted, a genuine smile breaking through. "Every moment. Even the morning sickness felt like a blessing." Her eyes shone with the memory. "I sang to him every night. Talked to him constantly. He was mine, ours, from that very first moment."

Tom's expression softened. "Sue glowed the whole nine months. I'd never seen anything more beautiful."

"And when they placed him in my arms," Sue continued, her voice thick with emotion, "nothing else mattered. Not the years of trying, not the disappointments. He was our son. Our perfect, beautiful boy."

Harper nodded, allowing them this moment of joy before pressing forward. "Did the foundation provide any information about the embryo donation?"

"We didn't ask many questions," Tom admitted. "They said it would be a good match for our family. That was enough for us."

Sue squeezed her husband's hand. "We were just so grateful for the chance to have our baby."

Harper took a sip of her coffee, letting the moment settle before steering toward the next chapter of their story. "Ethan showed his hockey talent early, didn't he?"

The pride returned to Tom's face. "By eight, he was already standing out. Other parents would comment about his natural ability."

"That's when Ben approached us," Sue added, her expression brightening at the memory. "At one of Ethan's tournaments. Said he'd never seen such raw talent in someone so young."

Harper pulled her notebook closer, her pen hovering above the page. "Before VSM, though, the fertility treatments. Which clinic handled the embryo donation?"

The shift in atmosphere was subtle but immediate. Tom and Sue exchanged a quick glance, the earlier tension returning to Tom's shoulders.

"New Horizon," Sue said quietly. "New Horizon Fertility Clinic."

Tom cleared his throat. "Look, Ms. Sinclair, we've never discussed this with anyone. Not even Ethan." His voice tightened. "This isn't something we want getting out."

Harper held his gaze. "New Horizon wasn't upfront with you. And Ethan wasn't the only one."

Sue paled. "What do you mean?"

Harper hesitated, then said softly, "I don't think they were entirely honest about their program."

"No," Tom cut in firmly, leaning forward. "Whatever you're investigating, we won't be part of it. We can't have Ethan's memory..." His voice caught. "We won't have people questioning who he was."

Sue reached across the table, gripping Harper's wrist. "Please," she whispered, tears spilling down her cheeks. "You can't publish this. People in

Brandon still talk about Ethan, remember him as this amazing young man. We don't want to open old wounds..."

"He was that amazing young man," Harper said gently. "Nothing changes that."

"Everything changes," Tom's voice was rough with emotion. "You're a journalist. You know how people are. They'll twist this, make it into something ugly. We can't... we won't let that happen to our boy's memory."

Harper felt the weight of their pain, their protection, even as her phone buzzed in her pocket. The championship game would start soon. She glanced at the message, then back at the grieving parents.

"I wish I could promise you this story won't come out," Harper said softly. "But there are other families involved, other children who might be affected."

Sue's shoulders shook with silent sobs. Tom wrapped an arm around her, his own eyes glistening.

"I need to head to the arena," Harper said, gathering her things. The admission felt inadequate against their raw grief. "The championship game..."

Tom nodded stiffly, his attention focused on comforting his wife.

Standing, Harper hesitated. The investigative journalist in her knew this was just one piece of a larger puzzle, but the human being in her ached at the pain she'd caused. "I'll be in touch before anything goes public," she offered quietly.

As she stepped into the crisp Toronto air, their anguish followed her. But beneath the Bernards' story of desperate hope and painful secrets, questions about New Horizon Fertility Clinic and VSM remained unanswered.

The championship game awaited, Team Canada versus Team USA, and with it, perhaps, more pieces of this puzzle. As Harper approached the arena, she knew this wasn't just about one family's private pain anymore. It was about uncovering a truth that could change everything.

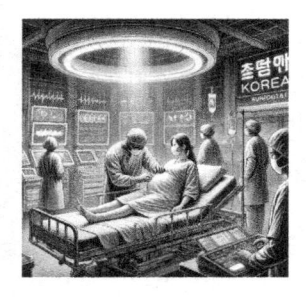

Son

"This isn't just a birth, it's a second chance to make everything right." – Dr Kim

*E*IGHTEEN YEARS BEFORE WORLD JUNIORS

The steady beep of the monitors filled the converted operating room, as precise as the science that had brought them here. Dr. Kim Jung-So stood motionless, watching the impossible unfold. Two years of failure, of setbacks, of relentless recalibration, until now. Each pulse from the fetal monitor confirmed it. They had reached the threshold of creation.

Dr. Park, his most trusted colleague, monitored a bank of specialized equipment while Nurse Chen adjusted Hana's IV drip. They had both sacrificed everything for this project, careers, reputations, perhaps even their freedom.

"Three minutes apart," Dr. Park reported, his voice calm, clinical. "Dae-Song's vitals are strong."

Hana Lee gripped the bedrails as another contraction peaked, her forehead glistening with sweat. She wasn't just any surrogate, she had been his wife's closest friend, and now she was helping him achieve the impossible. Through three attempts, she had never wavered in her commitment to help bring back a piece of what Dr. Kim had lost.

"Blood pressure is elevated but within expected range," Nurse Chen reported, adjusting one of the monitors.

Dr. Kim placed a reassuring hand on Hana's shoulder. Two years' worth of failed attempts fueled his desperation. But this time was different. This time, they had maintained a perfect pregnancy for nine months. This time, his son, his Dae-Song, would live again.

The facility existed outside Seoul's medical grid, untraceable, invisible. Security cameras swept the hallways, motion sensors tracked every breath. The first human clone was seconds from being born. Only four people in the world would witness.

As another contraction gripped Hana, Dr. Kim's mind drifted to their first attempt, two years ago. They had converted an abandoned medical clinic on the outskirts of Seoul into their private laboratory, far from the watchful eyes of Furever Genetics. That first procedure had filled them all with such hope.

"The implantation was successful," Dr. Park had announced then, his face bright with optimism. "Hormone levels are exactly where we want them." They had celebrated quietly that night, allowing themselves to believe they'd achieved the impossible. Six weeks later, everything crashed down around them. The loss devastated them all, but Hana's determination never wavered.

"We'll try again," she had insisted, still recovering. "The data shows we're close." Dr. Kim remembered how she'd gripped his hand, her eyes fierce with loyalty to his late wife's memory. "Min-Seo would want us to continue."

The second attempt, fifteen months ago, had brought them closer. They'd modified the protocols, enhanced the genetic stability markers. The embryo had survived past the first trimester milestone that had eluded them before.

"Cardiac activity is strong," Nurse Chen had reported during that twelfth week scan. But just two days later, they lost everything again. Dr. Kim still remembered the silence in the lab that day, defeat etched into every face.

Dr. Park had been the one to identify the critical flaw in their process. "The telomere degradation is happening too quickly," he'd explained, pointing to the data streams. "But we can stabilize it. We just need to modify the DNA sequence using CRISPR here and here."

Each loss pushed them to refine their techniques, perfect their protocols. They worked in secret, away from the prying eyes of the scientific community, knowing that discovery would mean the end of everything.

Nine months ago, everything had changed. Dr. Kim could still picture that morning with perfect clarity, the sunlight streaming through the lab's carefully concealed windows as they prepared for their third attempt.

"The CRISPR modifications are holding," Dr. Park had announced, his eyes fixed on the microscope. The team gathered around the monitoring station, watching as Hana underwent the implantation procedure. This time felt different, the air itself seemed charged with possibility.

The weeks that followed brought a cascade of milestones. Each genetic marker remained stable, each development perfectly aligned with their projections. Dr. Park's modified protocols were working exactly as theorized.

"The cellular aging is normal," Dr. Park had reported at the three-month mark, his usual professional demeanor cracking into a smile. "All developmental markers are exactly where they should be." He'd paused, looking at Dr. Kim. "We did it. We actually did it."

Hana had flourished throughout the pregnancy, her dedication unwavering. During late-night monitoring sessions, she would often speak to the baby in Korean, telling him stories about his mother, about the family waiting for him. Dr. Kim would listen from his desk, his heart full of gratitude for this woman who had risked everything to help him defy nature itself.

A sharp cry from Hana pulled Dr. Kim back to the present moment. Dr. Park's voice carried an edge of excitement he rarely allowed himself to show. "The head is crowning."

Dr. Kim moved to Hana's side, his hand steady now despite the magnitude of what was happening. Years of research, months of careful monitoring, and countless sacrifices had led to this moment. The monitors beeped in perfect rhythm, each sound confirming what had once seemed impossible.

"One more, Hana," Nurse Chen urged. "He's almost here."

Dr. Park quickly assessed the infant while Nurse Chen handled the post-birth procedures with practiced efficiency. "All vitals strong," he announced, his voice thick with emotion.

As they placed the wrapped bundle in his arms, Dr. Kim felt the weight of both triumph and responsibility settle onto his shoulders. The baby, his son, opened his eyes, and Dr. Kim found himself staring into the exact same gaze he had lost in that tragic accident years ago.

"Dae-Song," he whispered. A tiny hand curled around his thumb, an exact mirror of the son he had lost. Dr. Kim's world stopped. It was him.

From her bed, exhausted but smiling, Hana watched them. "He looks just like him," she said softly. "Min-Seo would be amazed."

Dr. Kim nodded, unable to speak. This miracle of science and determination squirmed in his arms, unaware of the boundaries they had crossed to bring him into existence, unaware of the secrets they would need to protect.

"His identity is in place," Dr. Park murmured, checking the monitors. "Hana moves to recovery once she's stable." Their hidden facility, disguised as a private medical research center, had been prepared for months for this moment.

Looking down at his son, this perfect fusion of memory and future, Dr. Kim understood that this was both an ending and a beginning. They had achieved what many thought impossible, but the real challenge lay ahead: protecting this new life from a world that wasn't ready to accept his existence.

"Welcome back, my son," he whispered in Korean. "This time will be different. This time, I'll protect you properly."

* * *

Snowflakes fell over Montreal as Finn made his way through the bustling streets toward VSM's glass tower. Dr. Kim's message had been brief but clear, the moment they'd been waiting for had arrived. After years of preparation and millions invested, they would finally know if their gamble had paid off.

The elevator ride to the top floor felt endless. Finn checked his phone again, the encrypted photos burning a hole in his pocket. His uncle wouldn't believe it until he saw it with his own eyes.

VSM's executive floor stretched before him, the morning light glinting off glass and chrome. Sarah, Lou's assistant, didn't even look up as Finn passed, she knew better than to delay him today. His footsteps echoed through the corridor, past walls lined with the spoils of decades of victories.

Lou's office, a sanctuary of power and sports memorabilia, felt charged with anticipation. Signed jerseys, championship photos, newspaper clippings chronicling VSM's rise to dominance surrounded the massive desk where Lou sat, every inch the titan of sports management he'd become.

"The kid?" Lou asked without preamble, eyes fixed on Finn with the intensity of a hawk.

"Healthy. A mirror image of Dr. Kim's boy." Finn allowed himself a rare smile. "Everything we hoped for."

Lou pushed back from his desk, his excitement barely contained. "Show me."

Finn handed over his phone, encrypted images glowing on the screen. Lou swiped through them in silence. His thick fingers trembled almost imperceptibly as he studied each photo, his usual mask of confidence cracking. For a moment, the calculating businessman vanished, replaced by a man witness to a miracle.

"Dr. Kim's work is... perfect." Finn tucked the phone away. "The impossible made possible."

Lou approached his prized cabinet, pulling out a bottle of William Larue Weller bourbon. "Then it's time to celebrate properly." He lifted the bottle, admiring its amber contents. "Been saving this since we first started down this path." He poured the precious liquid into two VSM-engraved Glencairn glasses. "Like us, patient, exclusive, and worth every penny."

Lou laughed, deep and satisfied as he moved to the window, gazing out at the city. "And our clones?"

"Two are over eight months along," Finn reported, joining him at the window. "Everything proceeding exactly as planned. The genetic markers are stable, development right on schedule. Births will be early January as we planned."

"And the families?"

"Still think they're part of an exclusive fertility program. The cover story is holding." Finn allowed himself a small smile. "The New Horizons Fertility Clinic's reputation for miraculous success with desperate couples makes for perfect cover. No one questions a miracle when they're praying for one."

Lou nodded slowly, savoring another sip of bourbon. "You know what makes a great sports agent, Finn?" He didn't wait for an answer. "The ability to see potential before anyone else. To recognize that special something that separates the good from the extraordinary."

"And now we're creating that something," Finn said quietly.

"Creating?" Lou scoffed. "We're rewriting the playbook. These kids won't just be great. They'll be flawless. Every muscle, every reflex, engineered for dominance." He gestured at the memorabilia surrounding them. "Everything here? It's just the beginning."

"And the families?" Finn asked.

Lou's smile turned calculating. "Sponsorships, training programs, exclusive opportunities, make them feel special."

"And Dr. Kim? His success with Dae-Song could make him... unpredictable." Finn glanced at the photos still displayed on his phone. "A man who'll break every rule to bring back his son—"

"Let me worry about Dr. Kim." Lou's voice carried the edge of steel that had built his empire. He returned to his desk, setting down his empty glass. "He's achieved his miracle. Now it's time for ours."

Finn nodded, but the bourbon's warmth couldn't chase away his growing doubts. They were playing with forces beyond their control, reshaping the future of sports with tools that belonged in science fiction.

"Having second thoughts?" Lou's voice cut through his reflection.

"No," Finn answered too quickly. "Just considering all the angles."

"Good. That's why I trust you with this." Lou's expression softened slightly. "We're making history, Finn. In twenty years, every championship, every record, every incredible play, they'll all lead back to this moment. To us."

Their ambitious future haunted Finn as he sipped his bourbon. Through the window, Montreal's lights glinted against the falling snow, each flake a reminder of the pristine facade they needed to maintain. They'd crossed a line that could never be uncrossed, and thousands of kilometers away in Brandon, two unborn children carried the proof of their ambition.

Lou lifted his glass. "To the future."

Finn hesitated. The bourbon burned in his throat. "To the future," he echoed.

Outside, snow drifted over Montreal, quiet, relentless. Like the truth they were burying.

Toonie

"The toonie in his pocket was more than a coin, it was a conversation unfinished, a bond unbroken, a weight that could never be put down." — Harper

Toronto pulsed with World Junior Championship fever, streets lined with jerseys, flags waving from windows, bars filled with pre-game energy. But for Liam, the noise barely registered. The revelation from his parents, that he wasn't their biological son, had fractured something deep inside him, leaving him adrift in a city that suddenly felt unfamiliar.

Liam wandered through downtown Toronto, his feet moving without direction. The World Juniors Championship had been everything, until it wasn't. The energy of the city felt distant, muffled beneath a blanket of unease. The game had once fueled him. Now, it barely felt real. His reflection stared back from a storefront window, an echo of someone else's blueprint. Was he a shadow of another man's dream? A forgery skating in borrowed skates?

The vibration of his phone startled him. Harper Sinclair's name flashed on the screen. Liam took a deep breath and answered.

"Hey, Harper."

"Liam, where are you? We need to talk before the game."

Liam hesitated, his gaze drifting over the cityscape. "I'm... I'm just walking back to the hotel now."

"I'll meet you there," she said, urgency in her voice matching the turmoil of his own thoughts.

As Liam turned toward the hotel, a scene caught his eye, a group of kids playing hockey on a makeshift rink of old boards and nets. For a moment, he was transported back to Manitoba, to those evenings on the frozen pond with Ethan.

They played long after the sun had set, the moon casting a silver glow over the ice. The cold stung their cheeks, but they hardly noticed, too absorbed in their own private Stanley Cup game. He remembered Ethan's signature move, a quick deke followed by a backhand shot, and his laugh, free and wild, carrying through the frosty air when he'd score. "Light it up!" Ethan would shout, their shared catchphrase echoing across the pond. Those nights were simple, untouched by expectations or scouts.

Ethan had been more than a teammate. He was the other half of every win, the voice in his ear, the first to throw an arm around his shoulder after a goal. Without him, the game had never felt quite the same. With a heavy heart, he took one last look at the kids on the makeshift rink, then turned back to the reality that awaited him.

When he reached the grand lobby of the hotel, Harper Sinclair emerged from the crowd like a ship cutting through fog. Her face softened when she saw him, a look not often worn by the tenacious journalist.

"Liam," she called out gently.

He walked toward her, noticing how out of place they both seemed amidst the festive decorations and fans buzzing about the game.

Harper led him away from prying eyes into an empty ballroom, where shadows clung to the walls. They stood there for a moment, surrounded by chairs stacked against walls and tables draped in white cloths, like ghosts of parties past.

Liam broke the silence first. "Harper... my parents, they confirmed it." His voice wavered. "I'm not their biological son."

She hesitated, recalibrating her expectations. "I see," she said, her tone carrying empathy. This wasn't just about getting a scoop, this was personal.

"It's just..." He struggled to find the right words. "Hockey has always been my constant, you know? And now... even that feels different."

Harper watched him closely, her eyes reflecting the weight of his story and the compassion she felt for him. "Your parents love you very much," she offered softly.

"Yeah." A small smile touched Liam's lips as he thought about Jim and Tammy, the only parents he'd ever known. "They do." He exhaled slowly. "And I love them too... I just need time to process all this."

Harper nodded, understanding etched into every line of her face. "Your friendship with Ethan," she began cautiously, "it was something special, wasn't it?"

Liam nodded, his throat tightening as images of Ethan flickered through his mind like an old film reel, laughter in cold arenas, the slap of pucks against sticks, shared dreams of glory. They had been inseparable, the dynamic duo of junior hockey.

Silence filled the space between them as Liam's memories faded. The empty ballroom felt appropriate somehow, its stacked chairs and white-draped tables like artifacts of celebrations past. Harper's notebook sat unopened between them. For once, she wasn't here as a journalist. She was just Harper, and he was just Liam, two people unraveling a truth neither had been ready for.

"I spoke to Tom and Sue," she said finally, her voice gentle. "About Ethan. About how they came to be his parents."

The mention of Ethan's parents sent a fresh wave of emotion through Liam. Tom's hearty laugh and Sue's warm hugs after games, they had been like a second family to him.

"They shared their journey," Harper continued, her voice threading through the silence. "How they struggled to have a child... how they turned to New Horizons Fertility Clinic for help." She watched Liam's reaction carefully, noting how his shoulders tensed at the clinic's name, his fingers gripping the arms of his chair until his knuckles whitened.

Liam felt something stir within him, an understanding or perhaps the prelude to it. His parents had made a similar revelation not long ago. His throat tightened, and he found himself unable to meet Harper's searching gaze.

Harper paused, choosing her next words carefully. Her hands clasped and unclasped in her lap, betraying her own tension. "Ethan... he wasn't their biological son."

Time seemed to freeze in that moment, her words shattering everything Liam thought he knew. A cold sweat broke out on the back of his neck, and his stomach churned with a familiar pre-game anxiety, except this wasn't a game. The memories he had held onto so dearly blurred, reshaping themselves in the light of this new knowledge.

He swallowed hard, his hands trembling as he wiped them against his jeans. 'The clinic... it was the same one my parents used, wasn't it?"

"Liam..." Harper hesitated. "You and Ethan, there's more to your connection than hockey. More than either of you ever knew."

The room felt colder. Her words carved away at everything he thought he understood. The walls felt closer. His heartbeat drummed in his ears.

Ethan had always been his brother in every way that mattered. But now? That word didn't feel big enough.

His mind raced back to those days on the ice with Ethan. The night they won the Brandon city championship, Tom and Sue had hosted the team celebration. While other families might order pizza, Sue had insisted on making her famous "victory casserole," a mishmash of whatever was in the fridge topped with crushed potato chips and tater tots. Ethan had been mortified, but Liam loved it, asking for seconds while Tom regaled them with increasingly outrageous stories from his own hockey days.

Later that night, they'd stayed up playing floor hockey in the basement, Tom keeping score with theatrical announcer voices while Sue brought down hot chocolate with the tiny marshmallows she always kept stocked for *her boys*.

Harper leaned forward, her journalistic instincts tempered by concern. "I can't say much more right now, not until I'm certain." Her hesitation was palpable, caught between revealing too much and protecting him from further pain.

"Not until you're certain?" Liam's voice hardened, his Canadian politeness giving way to frustration. "I've got a championship game in hours, and you're telling me there's more to this? More about Ethan?" He stood up, pacing the empty ballroom.

"First Ryan with his cryptic note, then my parents' revelation, and now this about Ethan?" He turned to face Harper, his jaw set. "I respect you, Harper, but I'm tired of everyone deciding what truths I'm ready to hear."

He raked his fingers through his hair, the gesture betraying the tension coursing through him. But Harper's steady gaze told him she wouldn't, couldn't, budge, at least not yet. He dropped back into his chair, the fight draining from him but the questions still burning.

"You two were remarkable together," Harper said, her voice cutting through his anger. "But this isn't just about hockey anymore, Liam. There are people involved, families. Lives that could be destroyed if we're not careful."

Liam's hands clenched at his sides. "And what about my life? My family?" The fight in his voice wavered, replaced by something more vulnerable. "Everything I thought I knew..."

Harper stood, closing the distance between them. "That's exactly why we need to be certain. Why we need to understand everything before we move forward." She met his gaze steadily. "Some things are beyond our control, no matter how much we plan."

The truth of her words hit him like a bodycheck, and he felt the anger drain away, replaced by a hollow uncertainty. Yet something in Harper's expression told him she was fighting her own battle, between the journalist's drive for truth and the human need to protect.

"Just..." Liam's voice softened. "Promise me you'll tell me when you know more. All of it."

Harper nodded, understanding that this story was not just about exposing truths but about handling them with care when they involved human lives.

As they parted ways, Liam left feeling adrift in a sea of memories, now colored by doubt and new questions about who, and what, he truly was. The championship buzzed around him like background noise, even as he prepared for the game, part of him remained locked in that ballroom with Harper and her careful revelations.

Hockey didn't care where he came from. The ice didn't care about DNA, didn't care about origins or blueprints. It only asked one thing, could he skate? Could he fight for every inch? The answer had never changed. And it never would.

* * *

Snowflakes fell in the frigid air, swirling like lost spirits as Liam boarded the bus, each flake disappearing into the night as quickly as it came. He took his seat near the front, the vinyl cold beneath him seeping through his jacket. Around him, his teammates and coaches sat in silence, each man locked in his own thoughts, eyes closed or staring out the fogged windows. They were bound together by the same unspoken pressure: to face the Americans again, a familiar foe, on a stage where every stride and shot would become a line in the history books.

The revelations from Harper still echoed in his mind, about Ethan, about the clinic, about their shared origins. Every certainty in his life seemed to be dissolving like the snowflakes outside, except for one: his connection to Ethan.

The engine's steady hum filled the void, drowning out the city's distant noise. Liam's gaze fell to his clenched fists resting in his lap, the muscles tight as if bracing for an impact. Slowly, he uncurled his fingers, revealing the toonie nestled in his palm. Its silver and gold edges glinted under the dim bus lights, the familiar design catching every passing beam as the city lights flickered through the windows.

As his thumb traced the coin's edges, Liam's mind slipped back to that day, the day when the world had felt colder than any Manitoba winter. He remembered standing over Ethan's casket, the crisp air biting through his coat, the silence of the gathered crowd blending with the muted sobs of friends and family. He had been unable to speak, unable to understand how the vibrant friend he had known was now reduced to a memory buried beneath layers of earth. In that moment of finality, he had made a vow, to carry Ethan with him always, to every rink, every battle, every moment where their shared dream could still breathe, even if Ethan couldn't.

Tom and Sue had given him this coin before the casket was lowered, pressing it into his hand as they clung to him in their grief. Sue had spoken through her tears, calling Ethan and Liam "the toonies", two parts of a whole, inseparable even when fate tried to split them apart. They placed a matching coin alongside Ethan, a quiet promise that part of Liam would always remain with his best friend, and part of Ethan would continue skating alongside Liam.

Since that day, the toonie had been a constant weight in Liam's pocket, grounding him when the world felt uncertain. He closed his fingers around it now, the cool metal edges pressing into his skin, as if the coin could root him against the storm of thoughts swirling in his mind. It was more than just a keepsake, it was a promise forged in grief, a link between the life he lived and the one Ethan could no longer pursue. It was a reminder that on the ice, he skated for both of them.

Outside, the lights of Toronto blurred into streaks as the bus sped toward the arena. Another rink, another opportunity, another chance to make Ethan proud. The anticipation around him wasn't merely for the game, it was a reverence for everything that had led them here, a silent acknowledgment of the sacrifices and struggles, both seen and unseen.

As the arena loomed closer, Liam tucked the toonie safely back into his pocket, feeling its reassuring weight against his leg. He turned his gaze to his teammates, each one a warrior in their own right, but none carrying the same burden he did. He thought of Ethan's absence, a hollow space that lingered beside him, more tangible than the gear strapped to his shoulders. But within that absence, within the silence where Ethan's voice should have been, Liam found a determination that burned even brighter.

As the bus slowed to a stop, Liam took a deep breath, letting the cold air from the open door fill his lungs. The stadium lights cut through the falling snow like beacons, illuminating a path forward. Tonight, he would skate for Ethan. For everything they had dreamed of. For the game that had always been theirs. But as the weight of the toonie pressed against his leg, he realized, he wasn't just carrying Ethan's memory. He was carrying a question that had no easy answer.

Light It Up

"Sometimes, winning isn't about lifting a trophy. It's about keeping a promise, to yourself, to the ones who believed in you, and to the ones who couldn't be here." – Liam

The arena hummed with electricity, the fever of an international rivalry turning every breath into a pulse of anticipation. A sea of red and white, punctuated by the odd star-spangled banner, rose and fell in waves as chants echoed off the rafters. Team Canada, led by Liam, emerged from the tunnel onto the ice, their skates carving cold fire into the surface.

The outside world blurred into static, drowned beneath the roar of thousands and the cold certainty of the ice. As he took in the frenzied energy of the crowd and the icy clarity of the rink, the weight of those revelations faded into the background. The ice had a way of doing that, stripping everything down to its simplest form. Puck, stick, goal. Here, in this moment, there was only hockey, only the game that he had devoted his life to mastering.

Ethan was there. Not a ghost, not a memory, but in every stride, every breath, every pass Liam made on the ice. Their shared past, a bond forged by parents who could not conceive naturally, loomed like an unspoken truth, both connecting and haunting them. It mattered little now, on this stage, Liam's focus was unyielding.

His strides across the ice were smooth and powerful, each push against the cold surface bringing him closer to destiny. He felt the familiar burn in his legs as he pushed through each stride, the tightness in his chest as the cold air filled his lungs. The arena's chill whipped through his faux hawk curls, the sensation as familiar as the ice beneath his skates. Each warm-up lap wasn't just preparation, it was a way to let go of everything that had weighed him down. By the time the horn blew to signal the end of warm-ups, he was all muscle and instinct.

His parents' faces flashed before his eyes, Jim and Tammy, not of blood but of love unbound by genetics. They had chosen him, raised him, shaped him into what he was. Their support had been unwavering through every twist and turn his life had taken so far.

As the arena announcer's voice boomed through the speakers, introducing each player to thunderous applause, Liam felt a surge of pride mingle with the ache of loss. The drumming of thousands of hands created a heartbeat for the building itself, every beat carrying the weight of a lifetime's worth of dreams, his own and Ethan's, shared across frozen rinks and whispered under stars.

Unlike other tournaments, the World Juniors saved the national anthems for after the game, privilege earned only by the victors. Tonight, Liam needed to hear "O Canada" echo through these rafters.

As the final introduction faded into an electric silence, Liam positioned himself at center ice. The face-off dot beckoned him like a siren's call.

Across from him stood Team USA's centerman, a mirror image of youthful ambition and raw talent, his face a mask of concentration as he anticipated the drop of the puck. Yet when he lifted his head to meet Liam's gaze directly, something shifted.

Liam's eyes held a glint sharper than a skate blade, an intensity that seemed to reach beyond physicality into something deeper. He wanted the American to know that no matter how well he played tonight, he was facing more than just a rival, he was facing a promise made to a friend, a dedication that no statistic or scouting report could measure.

Fear flickered across his opponent's face, an involuntary twitch betraying doubt as if he sensed that this confrontation would not bode well for him.

The official maneuvered into position between them, poised to begin what would be remembered as one of the most anticipated games in World Junior history.

Liam bent low over his stick, muscles coiled with pent-up energy ready to explode forward at first touch. Every distraction fell away, there was no room for secrets or revelations here, only hockey.

A silence settled over the crowd, an intake of collective breath held before an exhale that would erupt with unrestrained force at puck drop.

The puck tumbled from the official's hand down toward waiting ice, the nexus point where futures could be made or broken, and as blade met rubber disc with practiced precision, Liam surged forward into destiny.

Liam won the draw clean, his stick a blur as he directed the puck through his opponent's legs. The game was on.

With a grace that belied his solid frame, Liam spun around one player after another, a ghostly figure weaving through the solid forms of Team USA's defense. The crowd erupted as he crossed into the offensive zone, anticipation hung heavy in the air.

The goalie squared up, expecting a shot that never came. Instead, Liam dipped behind the net with an agility that drew gasps from the stands. He circled behind the net, shoulders low, muscles taut like a coiled spring. He could feel every shift in the ice beneath his skates, every intake of breath from the crowd as they anticipated his next move. He saw the shooting angle before it even opened, a flick of his wrists, a blur of motion, the puck snapping into the net before the goalie could flinch. A stunned silence lasted but a heartbeat before erupting into a roar of cheers and applause. Team Canada was up 1-0 in just 11 seconds.

On the bench, jaws dropped open as players exchanged looks of disbelief. Liam returned with a swagger in his step, an inferno blazing in his eyes. For those seconds on the ice, there were no questions of who he was or where he came from. Just the crack of the puck against his stick, the icy breeze cutting through his gear, and the pure, unfiltered drive to win.

"I'm on fire," he said simply, thumping fists with his teammates who couldn't help but grin back at him. It was a term Liam knew from the NHL Hitz video game, but tonight, it felt like prophecy.

Liam wasn't done, not by a long shot. He was everywhere on the ice, a flash of red and white that couldn't be contained. He scored again with a wicked slapshot from the blue line that sliced through defenders and found its mark with surgical precision. And then again, as he intercepted an errant pass and turned it into an unassisted breakaway goal that left the goalie grasping at shadows.

Three. Just like that. A Natural Hat Trick, before the first period had even ended.

In the broadcast booth high above the rink, announcers fought to keep their voices level amidst their excitement.

"This is one for the history books," the commentator murmured, leaning closer to the glass, his breath fogging the window as he strained to follow Liam's every move. "This isn't just a performance, this is a coronation." His partner nodded, barely able to take his eyes off the ice. "We're watching the birth of a star, folks. This kid's got NHL greatness written all over him."

Below them, fans leapt from their seats, high-fiving strangers and friends alike as they reveled in their team's lead. Hats rained down onto the ice, a tribute to Liam's performance. The crowd erupted into "Heave Away," the traditional hockey anthem carrying their celebration to the rafters.

On Team Canada's bench, Julian Broten couldn't help but smile despite himself, a reluctant respect for Liam's undeniable talent etched across his features even as he shook his head in disbelief. He watched from the bench, arms crossed over his chest. He hated to admit it, but there was a kind of poetry in the way Liam moved out there, a fire that burned brighter than any grudge. It was the kind of performance he would have given anything to pull off himself.

"Blazing Bolt strikes again," Julian muttered under his breath, knowing full well that no matter how much he wanted to outshine Liam, today wasn't going to be his day.

As Liam circled back to join his teammates on the bench after celebrating with fans along the glass boards who were still standing and cheering for him, he caught the eyes of his linemates, their faces lit up with belief. For a moment, they were all in sync, no words needed, just the shared understanding that they were playing for more than just a medal tonight.

"We knew you had it in you!" one teammate yelled over the din.

"Yeah," chimed another as they squeezed past to take their shift on ice, "light it up out there!"

The final horn sounded for intermission, Team Canada retreated from their battlefield leading 3-0 on Team USA, all thanks to Liam's unparalleled performance. The locker room buzzed with energy as players recounted each goal with animated gestures while coaches discussed strategy over their heads.

Julian leaned back against his locker and gave a nod, half-grudging admiration, and said loud enough for only Liam to hear: "Not bad for a Wheat King."

Liam simply flashed him a smile that spoke volumes, confident but not cocky, and returned to preparing for what would come next: two more periods where anything could happen. But for now? For now, Liam was untouchable, the heart and soul of Team Canada's lead in this crucial match against Team USA.

* * *

Harper Sinclair stood in the press box, a sentinel amid the thunderous roar of the crowd, her eyes tracking the whirlwind that was Liam on the ice. As she watched him weave through defenders and fire pucks past the helpless goalie, Harper saw more than just a star athlete. She saw the flickers of determination in every decisive movement, the way he skated like he carried both triumph and burden with each stride.

Around her, reporters bantered back and forth, scribbling notes and exchanging impressed glances whenever Liam made another seemingly impossible play. A colleague leaned closer, fighting to be heard over the press box chatter.

"Sinclair, it's like he's on a mission tonight. He's unstoppable, just look at him. No one's touching this kid."

She offered a brittle smile, the gesture hollow. "He's something else, isn't he?" The words tasted bitter in her mouth, heavy with the weight of what she knew.

The nation seemed to pulse in unison with each goal, each chant for Team Canada echoing off the walls with fervent hope. Harper let herself get lost in the moment, just for a second. The roar of the crowd, the avalanche of hats on the ice... even she wanted to believe in the fairytale. Yet beneath that pride lay a darker current, an unease she couldn't shake. She knew what came after the lights faded, when the cheers turned to whispers and the stories she sought to tell demanded their due.

The final buzzer blared through the arena, signaling Team Canada's 5-2 victory. As Liam raised his arms in triumph, Harper felt the crowd's adulation wash over him like a wave. She pushed through the throng of reporters, her recorder already in hand. Tonight belonged to Team Canada, to celebration. But tomorrow? Tomorrow belonged to truth.

Team Canada poured over the benches onto the ice, sticks and gloves scattered like confetti as they converged on their goalie. Throughout the stands, a sea of Desjardins jerseys dotted the crowd, number 7 proudly displayed on backs of all sizes. Children pressed against the glass, faces painted with maple leaves and "GO CANADA" across their cheeks, while signs bobbed up and down: "Light It Up Desjardins!" "Number 7 is Number 1!" "Future NHL Star!"

Julian reached him first, their previous rivalry dissolved in the golden glow of triumph. They embraced, a gesture that spoke volumes about respect earned and bridges rebuilt. Coach Boucha beamed from the bench, pride evident in his stance as his team received their gold medals.

Liam led the victory lap, the Canadian flag trailing behind him like a cape. He remembered being that kid once, dreaming of this moment, and now he was living it. A small boy in a number 7 jersey caught his eye, couldn't have been more than six, holding a sign that read "Liam D is My Hero!" Liam skated over and tossed him a puck, the boy's face lighting up like he'd just received treasure.

As they made their way toward the tunnel, Liam caught sight of his parents in the stands. Jim and Tammy stood proud, tears gleaming in their eyes, and in that moment, nothing else mattered. He was their son, they were his parents, and together they had just lived every Canadian family's dream.

LIGHT IT UP

In the locker room, Harper watched from the doorway as Liam sat at his stall, gold medal hanging against his chest. The celebration swirled around him, teammates shouting, music blasting, but he found himself in a moment of quiet.

His hand delved into the depths of his locker and emerged with a tarnished toonie clutched between his fingers. The coin, once shiny and new, had seen countless games, victories, and losses. With a gentle touch, he held the toonie against the gleam of his gold medal, feeling the contrast of the cool metals.

"Light it up, Blade." Ethan's voice wasn't just a memory, it was a whisper at his shoulder, a promise in his grip as he held the toonie tight. They'd made plans then, dreams of moments just like this, standing on top of the world in Team Canada red. Only Ethan wasn't here to share it.

Liam's fingers tightened around the toonie, feeling its worn edges press into his skin. This victory, this medal, wasn't his alone, it belonged to all those who had shaped him. To Ethan, who should have been beside him. To Jim and Tammy, who had chosen him, believed in him, loved him without condition through every triumph and setback. The truth of his origins still felt raw, but their love remained constant as the True North Star.

"We did good, E," Liam whispered, running his thumb over the toonie's surface. "We did it." The words felt like a prayer, a promise kept, a bridge between what was and what should have been.

The sounds of celebration gradually filtered back in, his teammates' laughter, the rhythmic thump of victory songs. But for just a moment longer, Liam sat with his memories, with his truth, with the weight of gold and worn copper in his hands.

Pete Marston cut through the celebrating players, his expensive suit and cologne a sharp contrast to the sweat-soaked locker room. He approached Liam with an eager smile.

"Amazing performance out there, Blade," Pete said, his handshake enthusiastic. "You've got an entire career ahead of you, brighter than that medal."

Before Liam could respond, Ben LaFleur appeared at his side, his arrival as precise as a well-timed line change. Ben's tone remained friendly but firm, his presence a reminder of existing loyalties.

"Good to see you, Pete," Ben said smoothly, placing a supportive hand on Liam's shoulder. "But I think we've got things covered here."

The two agents shared a look of professional respect tinged with friendly rivalry before Pete backed away with an understanding nod, disappearing into the locker room festivities just as Harper arrived, recorder in hand.

"Mind if I steal our hero for a moment?" Harper called out, navigating through the maze of equipment and celebrating players.

Ben studied her with cautious eyes before nodding to Liam. Harper's questions stayed focused on hockey, but her gaze caught the toonie still in Liam's hand. She made a mental note, not in her recorder, knowing some stories needed time to unfold.

"How does it feel to lead Team Canada to gold?" she asked, professional tone masking deeper questions.

Liam looked around at his teammates, then back to Harper. "Feels right," he said with genuine warmth. "When I went down in the Sweden game, Julian stepped up, scored that *hatty* to keep us going. Coach always tells us to play for the logo not the nameplate." He gestured to the CANADA across his chest. "But it's more than that. Every guy in this room, the shot blockers, the grinders, the guys staying late at practice, they're the reason we're standing here. Wearing this maple leaf, it's not just about playing hockey, it's about playing for each other, family."

The team's energy surged as music filled the room. His teammates lifted Liam onto their shoulders, their golden boy, their champion. As the celebration roared around him, Liam's hand wrapped tightly around the toonie in his pocket, holding onto both victory and memory in a perfect moment of joy.

Genetic Drift

"He was supposed to be our proof of perfection, a glimpse at what we could achieve. Instead, he became a reminder that even gods bleed." – Lou

TWO YEARS BEFORE WORLD JUNIORS

From his penthouse office overlooking Montreal, Lou Booker had always felt invincible. But now, staring at the medical reports and genetic data scattered across his mahogany desk, sixteen years of careful planning lay in ruins. His reflection in the glass showed the strain of the past twenty-four hours, the news of Ethan Bernard's death weighing heavily in the set of his shoulders.

Finn watched his uncle from the leather chair across the desk, noting how Lou's massive frame seemed to block out the morning light. The silence between them felt charged, dangerous, like the moment before thunder follows lightning.

"Sixteen years," Lou finally said, his voice gravel-rough. "Sixteen god-damn years, and now this." He turned from the window, snatching up one of the reports. "Our first. Our first real product just drops dead in the middle of a hockey game? That wasn't part of the deal."

"The preliminary autopsy shows cardiac arrest," Finn said, keeping his tone measured. "No obvious cause, no warning signs. It just... happened."

Lou's laugh was sharp, bitter. "Just happened? Nothing 'just happens' with genetics, Finn. Not when we've poured millions into making sure everything was perfect." He tossed the report back onto the desk. "Kim assured us these clones would be superior in every way. Better stamina, faster healing, stronger bones. Ethan was supposed to be our proof of concept. Instead, we've got a dead kid and a lot of questions we can't answer."

Finn leaned forward, lowering his voice despite their privacy. "There are rumors, Uncle Lou. About clone viability, about unforeseen complications. We need to review the others..."

"He and that Desjardins kid were tearing up the league in Brandon," Lou muttered, more to himself than Finn. "Youngest players on the team, but leading in every stat. Perfect chemistry on the ice. Perfect examples of what we were trying to create." His fingers drummed against the desk. "And now one of them is dead."

"Should we tell Kim about the autopsy results?" Finn asked carefully.

Lou's expression hardened, years of careful planning crystallizing into cold determination. "Get the jet ready. I want to look that bastard in the eye when he explains how our prototype failed." He reached for his phone. "And Finn? Get me everything we have on the others. Every test result, every medical scan, every goddamn genetic marker. I want to know what we're really dealing with here."

The door closed behind Finn with a soft click, leaving Lou alone with his thoughts and the weight of sixteen years of secrets. In the glass, his reflection seemed to smile, a cold, calculating expression that had nothing to do with joy and everything to do with survival.

* * *

Dr. Kim studied the holographic display floating above his desk, genetic sequences rotating in precise patterns of blue and green. Beside him, Dae-Song leaned forward, his dark eyes tracking the data with the same intensity his father showed. At sixteen, he already carried himself with the precise grace of someone engineered for perfection, every movement calculated, efficient.

"The cardiac anomaly appeared without warning," Dr. Kim said, his voice clinical as he manipulated the display. "Bernard's previous scans showed no indication of structural weakness." He expanded a section of the DNA sequence, highlighting a specific pattern. "See here? The CRISPR modifications to the MYH7 gene should have prevented any cardiomyopathy. The enhanced healing factors were perfectly calibrated."

"Could it be an activation error in the telomere sequences?" Dae-Song asked, reaching out to rotate the sequence. His fingers moved through the hologram with practiced familiarity. "The accelerated cellular regeneration might have triggered premature aging in the cardiac tissue."

Dr. Kim glanced at his son, his creation, allowing himself a moment of pride at the boy's insight. Where others saw a teenager, he saw his masterpiece: intelligence enhanced, every genetic sequence crafted with painstaking precision. "Possible. The enhanced healing protocol was designed for athletic recovery, but continuous activation could have unforeseen consequences."

Something shifted in Dae-Song's expression, a calculated understanding. "Ethan was like me. First generation." It wasn't quite a question.

"Different template," Dr. Kim corrected, his tone softening slightly. "Your genetics were optimized for cognitive function. Ethan's were designed for athletic performance." He paused, studying a diagnostic readout. "Each project had its own risks, its own variables in the genetic drift."

The lab door hissed open, and Ryan appeared briefly in the doorway. "Dr. Kim, VSM's jet just landed. Mr. Booker is en route."

Dr. Kim's expression hardened imperceptibly. "Thank you, Ryan."

After the door closed, Dae-Song turned to his father. "They're worried about their investment."

"They're worried about their empire," Dr. Kim corrected, closing the holographic display. "Sixteen years of work, and they still see only profit margins." He moved to a sealed door at the back of the lab, pressing his palm against the biometric scanner. "But we see further than that, don't we?"

Dae-Song watched his father input a complex sequence into the keypad. Beyond the door lay projects even VSM didn't know about, experiments that pushed far beyond mere athletic enhancement. "How long before they realize?"

"That depends on how carefully they look," Dr. Kim said, a ghost of a smile playing at his lips. "But by then, it won't matter." He paused, turning to face his son. "You understand what's at stake?"

Dae-Song straightened, every inch the perfect synthesis of science and ambition his father had designed him to be. "I understand, Father. I won't let them threaten what you've built."

Dr. Kim nodded, satisfaction flickering in his eyes. The boy was ready. And soon, very soon, Lou Booker would learn the true cost of trying to contain his vision.

Lou's footsteps echoed through Furever's pristine corridors, each step radiating barely contained fury. Finn walked half a pace behind, taking in the sterile white walls lined with achievement plaques and framed patents. Through reinforced glass windows, they passed rows of sequencing machines humming with quiet efficiency, their blue status lights pulsing like artificial heartbeats.

They found Dr. Kim in his private lab, a state-of-the-art facility that made their Montreal office look antiquated. Holographic displays cast an eerie blue glow across polished steel surfaces, genetic code spinning in endless loops above precision equipment worth millions. Dae-Song stood at his father's shoulder, both of them bent over a complex array of data, a picture of scientific legacy that made Lou's fingers curl into fists at his sides.

"Quite the empire you've built here," Lou said, his voice carrying the weight of accusation.

Dr. Kim straightened unhurriedly, his movements precise and controlled. "Mr. Booker. You could have called ahead." His tone was neutral, but the temperature in the room seemed to drop several degrees.

"Called ahead?" Lou's laugh held no humor. "Like Ethan Bernard's heart gave us warning before it stopped?" He moved further into the lab, his bulk seeming to compress the space. "Sixteen years, Kim. Sixteen years of funding, of covering tracks, of building this empire together. And now our first success is dead on the ice."

"A tragic outcome," Dr. Kim replied, his clinical tone a sharp contrast to Lou's emotion. "But the data gathered will—"

"Data?" Lou slammed his hand down on the nearest workstation, sending a cascade of holographic readouts spinning wildly. "He wasn't just data, Kim. He was our proof of concept. Our prototype. Everything we built was riding on him."

Dae-Song stepped forward, positioning himself between Lou and his father. "You're forgetting yourself, Mr. Booker." His voice carried a quiet strength that made even Finn pause. "This is a place of science, not a boardroom for your tantrums."

Lou's eyes narrowed at the teenager's defiance. "You think because you turned out right, the rest don't matter? That we should just accept failure?"

"I think," Dae-Song said carefully, each word precise as a scalpel, "that you forget my father's genius made all this possible, not your money."

Dr. Kim placed a steadying hand on his son's shoulder, but his eyes remained fixed on Lou. "The Bernard clone's death was unfortunate. But the project continues. The protocols have been adjusted."

"Adjusted?" Finn spoke up, his tone diplomatic but firm. "We need more than adjusted, Doctor. We need guarantees."

"Science offers no guarantees, Mr. Booker," Dr. Kim replied, moving to his terminal where complex molecular structures rotated in silent precision. "Only probabilities. And progress." His hands moved with practiced efficiency across the keyboard, bringing up a series of genetic sequences. "Perhaps you've forgotten who actually understands the science that building your future."

Lou stepped closer, his voice dropping to a dangerous whisper. "If anything happens to our other investments."

"Then perhaps," Dr. Kim cut in, his voice dropping to an icy whisper, "you should remember who holds the keys to your empire, Mr. Booker. After all, sixteen years is a long time to keep secrets."

The threat hung in the air between them, unspoken but clear. Lou's face flushed red, but before he could respond, Finn gripped his uncle's arm. "We should go. The jet's waiting."

Lou allowed himself to be guided toward the door, but at the threshold, he turned back. "This isn't over, Kim."

"No," Dr. Kim agreed, watching them leave. "I suspect it's only beginning."

After Lou's footsteps faded, something shifted in Dae-Song's expression, his carefully maintained facade cracking open to reveal something inhuman beneath. He turned to the genetic sequences floating above the workstation, blue light casting shadows across his face that seemed to deepen with each passing moment.

"They're so focused on games," he said, voice stripped of pretense. "Sports statistics and profit margins while we hold the key to humanity's next step."

Dr. Kim studied his son's profile in the hologram's glow. The Cerebral Evolutionary Gene modifications had created something that exceeded his wildest dreams, and awakened his deepest fears. Sometimes, watching Dae-Song's mind work, he felt less like a father and more like a man who'd opened Pandora's box.

"I couldn't just bring you back as you were," Dr. Kim said softly. "After the accident... I needed you to be more. To see further."

"And now I see everything." Dae-Song's hands moved across the controls, pulling up sequence after sequence of human DNA. "Their bodies break. Their minds fail. Their genes carry the flaws of random evolution." His eyes reflected the streaming data with an unnatural intensity.

"The enhanced intelligence was necessary," Dr. Kim explained, more to himself than his son. "The future requires—"

"The future requires evolution," Dae-Song interrupted, his voice carrying the weight of absolute conviction. He expanded a genetic sequence, alterations spreading across it like a virus.

Dr. Kim watched his creation, no longer just his son, manipulate humanity's building blocks with terrifying ease. Perhaps with more guidance, more direction, he could still shape the mind he had enhanced. After all, wasn't that what fathers were supposed to do?

* * *

The private jet hummed steadily through the night sky, but sleep eluded both men. Lou sat with a tumbler of scotch, his heavyset six-foot-eight frame filling the leather seat. The cabin lights emphasized his weathered features, the salt-and-pepper beard barely concealing his ruddy complexion, the result of decades of cigars and whiskey. Finn watched his uncle from across the aisle, noting how sweat gleamed on Lou's forehead, how the gold watch on his thick wrist caught the light as he shuffled through medical reports spread across the table.

"He's changed," Finn said finally, breaking the heavy silence. "Kim's not the same man we started with."

Lou's laugh was bitter, his French-Canadian accent thicker with fatigue. "Changed? He's evolved, Finn. While we were counting profits, he was building something else entirely." He tapped the rim of his glass with a thick finger, his dark brown eyes, still piercing despite his age, fixed on some distant point. "That boy of his, Dae-Song. He's not just a son anymore. He's Kim's vision of the future."

Finn shifted uncomfortably in his seat. "About the Bernards... I thought we might help with the funeral costs. After all they've been through."

"We're not a charity, Finn," Lou cut in, his voice like ice. "The investment failed. We move on." He drained his glass in one swift motion. "Get Ben on those medical evaluations. Full cardiac workups. I want to know if there's even a hint of what happened to Ethan in any of them."

"Sixteen years of monitoring, training, development, all gone in a heartbeat," Finn said, the weight of their actions finally settling in his chest. "We watched him grow up, Uncle Lou."

Lou's expression hardened as he stared into his empty glass. "They stopped being children the moment Kim engineered them. They're assets, Finn. Expensive ones. And we need to protect our investments."

Through the jet's window, the first hints of dawn painted the horizon in shades of blood red. Finn watched the colors spread, remembering the cold calculation in Dr. Kim's eyes, the way death seemed to mean nothing more to him than data points in a failed experiment.

"We're losing control of him," Lou muttered, more to himself than Finn. "And that's the real problem."

As the sun finally breached the horizon, casting long shadows through the cabin, both men fell silent. Their minds churned with the same dark thoughts: of perfect specimens on ice rinks across the continent, of secrets buried in genetic code, and of a brilliant man in a Seoul laboratory who might have already slipped beyond their control.

Shadow Play

"Her voice was calm, but every word she spoke felt like it was prying something loose, like she didn't care what broke as long as she got her story." – Jim

Victory's glow was fading in Team Canada's locker room. Players showered and changed, gold medals disappearing into equipment bags as the media crowd thinned to a few persistent reporters seeking final quotes from their championship hero.

Finn Booker watched from the doorway as Ben managed the last of the interviews around Liam. The agent's subtle gestures and well-timed interruptions were steering the stragglers toward the exit, protecting VSM's rising star from question fatigue. A decade of handling special prospects had honed Ben's technique.

"One last question about the NHL draft," a reporter called out, even as Ben began to usher them away.

"Liam's focused on celebrating with his teammates tonight," Ben replied smoothly. "Draft questions can wait for another day."

Through the thinning crowd, Finn observed the families huddled near the coffee station.

"Julia's should still be open," Tom Bernard said, keeping his voice low. "Quieter there."

Jim Desjardins nodded, glancing at his wife. "Could use a real drink after all this excitement."

"And some privacy," Sue Bernard added softly, her hand clutching her purse tightly.

Harper watched this exchange from behind the dispersing media crowd. As the families gathered their things, she moved purposefully toward the waiting area where the Bernards and Desjardins stood together.

Finn didn't miss the flicker of hesitation in Ben's posture. It was barely there, a half-second glance, a shift of weight, but Finn knew what to look for. The past still had its hooks in him.

His phone was already against his ear. "Follow them," Finn murmured when Ben answered. "All of them."

Ben's response was immediate, professional. "On it." No questions asked, just like always.

Finn ended the call, watching as Ben smoothly wrapped up with the final reporters. Cold efficiency, exactly what VSM demanded from their agents.

Maybe that's what worried Finn most.

Julia's Restaurant cast yellow hue onto the slushy Toronto street. Ben maintained his position, using the reflection in a parked delivery truck's window to monitor the corner table. Through the frosted glass, the families were just silhouettes, but Harper's purposeful movements were unmistakable.

His phone vibrated. Finn.

Status?

Families at table. Papers out.

Ben kept his distance. Too close and he'd trigger Harper's attention. Too far and he'd miss something critical.

Sue's silhouette seemed to collapse inward. Tom's form moved to comfort her, one arm wrapping around her shoulders. Jim's shadow rose slightly, an agitated movement that sent his chair scraping back.

Emotional confrontation in progress, Ben texted.

From the shadows thirty yards back, Finn watched his agent work. Years of protecting VSM's interests had made Ben precise, careful. But tonight, something felt wrong.

Harper's phone lit up the window briefly. The sudden light revealed sharp changes in posture around the table, Jim leaning forward, Sue's hand covering her mouth, Tom's grip tightening on his wife's shoulder.

New information introduced, Ben reported. *Significant reaction observed.*

Details.

Limited visibility. Maintaining distance.

The winter wind gusted between buildings. Through the frosted glass, Ben watched each silhouette turn rigid, then move with new purpose, papers shuffled, chairs scraped, hands reached across the table. Harper's shadow remained still at the center of it all.

Stay dark. Priority on Harper.

Harper emerged from Julia's first, her breath visible in the bitter Toronto night. The World Junior banners lining the street rippled in the wind, Team Canada's victory celebration still echoing through downtown.

From his car, Finn watched Ben track Harper's movements. After years of handling VSM's most sensitive operations, Ben should have been the obvious choice for this. Should have been.

Don't lose her, Finn texted.

Ben's response came quickly: *Understood.*

"Harper! Wait up!"

Bailey McKenna from TSN emerged from the crowd, clutching a Team Canada media guide. Ben slipped behind a group of celebrating fans.

"Can't talk, Bailey." Harper barely slowed. "Deadline."

"Your piece about Liam's draft prospects—"

"Tomorrow." Harper's voice faded into the noise.

Through the financial district, Harper wove between late-night crowds. Each time she paused to check her phone, Ben adjusted his position with practiced ease. But something in his movements nagged at Finn, a hesitation here, a delayed reaction there. Small things.

Ben had been Lou's find, a promising young graduate in Toronto, still carrying traces of Harper in his careful words about sports journalism. Back then, Finn had been dealing with his own legal troubles. Now, years later, as Lou's trusted nephew, Finn questioned his uncle's judgment in both their cases.

Harper turned toward the Eaton Centre, disappearing into the evening crowd. Ben's updates continued:

Following into mall. West entrance clear. Visual maintained.

Each message read like a textbook surveillance report. And that was the problem. Ben never worked by the book, except when he was overthinking every move.

The mall's evening crowd provided natural cover as Harper moved through the main level. She paused at a storefront, pretending to examine a Team Canada jersey display. Her phone lit up.

Ryan's message flashed across her screen: *Can't meet tonight. Being watched. Too dangerous. Need somewhere safer.*

She typed quickly: *Tomorrow. Hall of Fame. 10am.*

Agreed. Be careful. Answered Ryan.

Harper deleted the exchange, her shoulders tensing slightly. She cut through the thinning crowd toward the exit, but as she passed a concrete pillar, her hand brushed against it, leaving something behind.

Ben waited thirty seconds before retrieving the note.

You always did protect your players, Ben. Some things never change. -H

Subject exiting south. Meeting cancelled, Ben reported, but said nothing about being made. Nothing about the note. Nothing about Harper playing him from the start.

Finn noticed the gaps in Ben's report, the missing details that should have been there. A seasoned operative admits when they've been compromised. Ben's silence spoke volumes.

Finn pulled out his phone, scrolled to a contact he hadn't used in months. His thumb hovered over the name: Marcus Gage.

Time to bring in someone new.

The Montreal Marvel

"It wasn't consent, it was theft. The greatest player of his generation reduced to raw material for someone else's ambition."
— Harper

The early morning light filtered through the stained glass dome of the Hockey Hall of Fame's Great Hall, casting historic shadows across the Stanley Cup. Harper stood near Mario Richard's plaque, pretending to study the inscription while scanning reflections in the trophy cases. At this early hour, only a few early visitors wandered the halls, their whispered conversations echoing off marble walls.

At 10:21 AM, she spotted Ryan's anxious figure through the main entrance. Their eyes met briefly before Harper moved deeper into the Stanley Cup sanctuary, knowing he would follow. His reflection in the polished silver showed his characteristic nervous glances, checking exits, studying other visitors, cataloging security camera positions.

"You're late," she said quietly as he approached, both of them now facing the Cup, pretending to admire its gleaming surface.

"Had to make sure I wasn't followed." Ryan's voice barely carried over the reverent murmur of a nearby family.

"You look like you're expecting the Royal Canadian Mounted Police," Harper quipped as Ryan stepped up next to her. She didn't miss how his eyes darted to each passerby.

Ryan ignored her comment, "We should move somewhere else, we're too exposed here."

Harper nodded toward the Tim Horton Theatre entrance. "They don't start shows until noon."

As they walked, Harper noticed Ryan pause before Mario Richard's display. The Stanley Cup Championship jersey hung there, number 21 etched into history, its significance lost on no one who followed the sport.

The Hockey Hall of Fame's theater offered privacy, but also felt like a trap. Harper had chosen it after spotting Ryan's nervous entrance near the Stanley Cup display. Now, in the empty room with hockey legends staring down from the walls, she got straight to the point. They stood near the back, where they could watch the entrance while remaining hidden in shadow. A video loop of historic hockey moments played silently on monitors in the lobby, faces of legends flickering past.

"Why was Ben following me last night?" asked Harper.

Ryan turned and looked over his shoulder and whispered, "Finn asked him to. You are in danger."

"Finn?" Harper echoed, brow furrowing. She knew of Finn Booker, Lou's nephew who was more a shadow within VSM than an actual presence. He was known to be discreet, someone who didn't mingle with athletes or bask in the limelight of marketing campaigns. "What would he want with me? Why would I be in danger?"

Ryan's voice dropped to a hush, each word like a fragile secret about to shatter. "They know you're digging, Harper. Into something... delicate."

He swallowed, lowering his voice even further. "The cloning program."

His eyes flicked to the slow-moving man outside the theater entrance. Was he just a visitor? Or listening?

Harper's skepticism surfaced like a reflex. "And how would they know that?" she murmured, almost to herself, keeping one eye on the man just outside of the doorway.

The connections were forming, but proof? That was another story. Tom and Sue Bernard had confirmed their fertility clinic use. So had Liam's parents. But a shared clinic didn't prove cloning.

Harper let out a slow breath. "I've put some pieces together," she admitted, "but I don't have proof of cloning. Not yet."

Ryan's response was a mixture of relief and vindication. "So you believe me now?"

Harper regarded him with an appraising look, her journalist instincts were both her sword and shield. "Belief is a luxury," she replied evenly. "I deal in facts."

She leaned back against the theater wall, beneath a towering photo of Mario Richard lifting the Stanley Cup, her arms folded across her chest. Over Ryan's shoulder, she caught a glimpse of the man again, now studying Mario Richard's display case with unusual interest before glancing their way.

"Listen," she continued, "I've spoken with Tom and Sue Bernard about Ethan, confirmed their story about using a fertility clinic. Same goes for Liam's parents."

Ryan nodded eagerly at this revelation, it was as if Harper had just handed him a lifeline. But he kept darting glances toward the entrance, as if expecting trouble to come walking through any second.

"That's it then," he said with an urgency that bordered on desperation. "It all ties back to Furever Genetics—"

Harper raised a hand to silence him, her skepticism remained her guiding star. "Allegedly ties back," she corrected him firmly.

He seemed ready to argue but instead swallowed his words with difficulty.

"The thing is," Harper pressed on, "VSM's involvement still doesn't prove anything about cloning."

"They've buried evidence before," Ryan said, his voice dropping lower. "Jobs lost. Careers ended. People vanish from labs without explanation."

Harper took in Ryan's demeanor, the anxiety etched deep into his features like grooves on a record, and felt the weight of his warning settle over her like a cold blanket. She shifted her gaze back to the man, now with his back turned. He hadn't moved, but something about him felt off, like a misplaced puzzle piece in a picture that didn't quite add up.

"I need more than your word," she stated flatly.

Ryan's eyes held hers, a silent plea for understanding or perhaps for trust that hadn't been earned yet.

Harper Sinclair's gaze didn't waver as she leaned towards Ryan, her eyes fixed. "There has to be proof, Ryan. Lab records, genetic profiles, something concrete that shows what they did."

Ryan's eyes darted away for a moment, and Harper could see his mind churning with anxiety. "Harper, I wish it were that simple," he replied, his voice a hushed whisper, barely audible over the clatter of a dropped tray somewhere behind him. "Dr. Kim kept that information compartmentalized. Different teams, different facilities, nobody saw the whole picture. I worked in the lab, not with the families."

Harper leaned back against the theater wall, her mind racing. This was like chasing shadows, every lead seemed to dissolve as soon as she grasped at it. Through the open doorway, Mario Richard's Hall of Fame display case stood illuminated, his achievements preserved in pristine glory. She took a deep breath and refocused. There was another angle here, one she hadn't considered.

"Okay," she began again, her voice steady but tinged with a new intensity. "Let's think about this differently then. If they're clones... who were they cloned from?"

The question hung in the air between them like a puck suspended at center ice before a critical face-off.

Ryan's expression shifted subtly, there was recognition there, perhaps even awe. He glanced toward Mario's display, then leaned in closer and whispered conspiratorially, "They're both from him."

The name didn't need to be spoken. Mario Richard. *The Montreal Marvel*. Whose legacy surrounded them in this very building. A Hall of Fame player who had led his teams to multiple championships with a style that combined brute force and balletic grace on the ice.

"The Montreal Marvel," Harper murmured, her gaze drawn to the jersey hanging mere feet away from where they sat. The irony of their location wasn't lost on her.

Ryan nodded, leaning in closer, his voice tense with urgency. "Think about it, Harper, Liam isn't just some random kid with talent. He's a mixed-race kid from Brandon with the genetic blueprint of one of hockey's greatest. This isn't just about cloning... it's about creating a new kind of player."

It wasn't just about genetics or sports, it was about identity, culture, everything that made someone who they were being manufactured in some sterile lab by scientists playing God.

"And VSM paid for this?" Harper's voice echoed slightly in the empty theater.

"All of it," Ryan replied with a grimace. "The public thinks they're just talented kids with bright futures ahead of them in hockey."

A group of visitors passed by the theater entrance, their excited chatter about Mario's career achievements creating a surreal backdrop to this conversation about his unknowing role in something far darker.

Harper felt a mix of anger and empathy surge within her. Liam deserved to know his story, his real story, but how would he handle such life-altering information? And what about Mario Richard?

Her journalistic instincts kicked in full force, this was bigger than any game she had ever covered or any gold medal game she had played in her former life on the ice.

She needed to expose this, to shine a light on these dark corners where ethics were discarded for ambition and profit.

Harper glanced at Ryan again, his demeanor suggested he knew he'd crossed lines just by sharing what he had told her today.

"Listen," she said with quiet determination, the historic weight of their surroundings lending gravity to her words. "We need to get this story out there. People need to know what's happening, to understand the true cost of these... achievements."

Ryan nodded, his inner turmoil still visible, but there was a new resolve in his eyes, one that had been absent before. "I can help you," he said, his voice gaining strength as he met Harper's gaze head-on.

Harper held his gaze, her expression softening slightly despite the gravity of the situation. She understood the weight of his decision, what it meant for him to cross that line. "Good," she replied, a firm edge to her tone, though not without a hint of gratitude.

For a moment, the tension between them eased, only to be rekindled by echoing footsteps in the corridor outside the theater. A security guard passed by, his radio crackling with static. Both Harper and Ryan waited until the footsteps faded before continuing.

Harper leaned in, her hazel eyes sharp, almost daring Ryan to pull back now. She double-checked that her phone was recording. Every word needed to be captured.

"We need proof, Ryan." Her voice was low, insistent. "Would a DNA test confirm it?" She let the question hang for a moment before adding, "Would it prove Liam is Mario Richard's clone?"

Ryan nodded, tension etched into his face. His gaze flicked to the empty rows, as if expecting someone to emerge from the shadows. "Yeah. It's that simple," he whispered. "A DNA sample from Liam and Mario would prove everything."

Through the open door, a tour group's excited chatter drifted in as they gathered around Mario's display. Harper waited for them to move on before speaking.

"With such an analysis, we would hold in our hands irrefutable evidence," she reasoned out loud. The prospect seemed to hang in the air between them like a tangible thing. "Proof beyond question that Liam is a clone."

"That is correct," Ryan replied, his voice barely rising above a whisper yet carrying a resonance that spoke volumes. His affirmation was delivered with unwavering certainty, a rock-solid confirmation amidst a sea of unsettling possibilities.

Harper leaned forward, processing this next step in her investigation. The countless trophies and memorabilia surrounding them spoke to Mario's legendary status in hockey. Her next question hung in the air like a suspended breath. "What about Mario? How deep does this go?"

Ryan's dark eyes flickered with unease as he scanned the theater entrance again, his anxiety palpable. Harper reached across to his arm, her touch brief but grounding. "Ryan," she said with quiet insistence, "was Mario involved?"

He hesitated, his voice barely above a whisper. "VSM arranged everything through their medical staff. The DNA collection, the procedures..." He trailed off, checking the entrance again. "But Mario's connections to VSM go back decades. Lou and Mario were close."

Were? Harper caught the past tense, her journalistic tenacity surfacing despite the gravity of what they were discussing. "And now?"

"Now?" Ryan's laugh held no humor. "Now it's complicated."

Ryan hesitated, the sudden pallor of his face betraying his spooked state. Through the theater entrance, a man paused longer than necessary at Mario's display, his attention seeming to drift toward the darkened theater.

Ryan glanced toward the emergency exit and back at Harper without answering.

"Ryan?" she pressed gently.

But he was already turning away, his movement casting a shadow across the theater's back wall. "Stay out of sight," he advised with a stern look in his eyes. "And keep your story quiet until you release it."

Harper nodded slowly, recognizing the seriousness of what they were dealing with.

"Tell no one," Ryan continued, "trust no one."

With those final words hanging between them like an ominous fog, Ryan slipped out the emergency exit, leaving Harper alone with her thoughts and a burgeoning sense of danger that seemed to seep into her bones.

Harper lingered in the darkened theater, turning over their conversation in her mind like puzzle pieces that refused to fit together easily. The muffled sounds of visitors discussing hockey's greatest moments filtered through the walls, their reverence for the sport's history a stark contrast to the corruption she was uncovering.

Getting a DNA sample from Mario wouldn't be easy, but she needed concrete proof. This story had to be bulletproof.

As she emerged into the Great Hall, Harper passed Mario Richard's shrine, his legacy now carrying a darker significance. In the polished surface of the display glass, she caught the reflection of the man from earlier reaching for his phone.

Three quick steps and she merged into a tour group heading for the exit.

Cold Pursuit

"A shadow doesn't make noise, doesn't leave footprints. It's there when you don't want it to be, and gone when you finally look for it." — Marcus

Marcus Gage moved through the Hockey Hall of Fame like any other visitor, his six-foot-three frame carrying a military precision despite his casual stance. He held up his iPhone for selfies, the scar along his jawline catching the light. But while tourists captured memories with the Stanley Cup, he tracked Harper Sinclair's reflection in the glass displays with cold, calculating eyes, his buzzed gray-streaked hair and broad shoulders making him look more like an off-duty cop than the special forces operative he once was.

Finn's instructions had been clear: observe and document. Nothing more.

When Harper ducked into the Tim Horton Theatre with an anxious-looking man, Marcus settled into a natural vantage point near Mario Richard's display case. His weathered hands, marked by years of combat, held the phone up with practiced steadiness. He pretended to frame the perfect shot of the legendary player's jersey for Instagram, while actually capturing the theater entrance and its occupants, his movements precise and controlled, just like his military training had ingrained.

The pair's body language screamed confidential conversation. The man kept glancing toward the exits, his nervous energy visible even from this distance. *Amateur,* Marcus thought. *If you act suspicious, people notice.*

Marcus captured several clear shots of the man's face, making sure to get multiple angles through his phone's telephoto lens. A quick swipe through the VMS encrypted app sent the best image to Finn's phone along with a text:

Target meeting with unknown male subject. Appears agitated. Conversation deliberately private.

Finn sat in his parked car outside the Toronto airport when his phone vibrated. He glanced at the screen, Marcus's message awaited his attention. He opened the image and stared at it for a long moment.

Recognition dawned like an unwelcome sunrise. Ryan Patel, Dr. Kim's lab rat. Always sticking his nose where it didn't belong. The same Ryan who had witnessed that uneasy meeting between Lou and Dr. Kim at VSM headquarters. What was he doing with Harper Sinclair?

Keep eyes on both subjects, Finn texted back. *Priority on identifying anyone else they contact.*

A wave of unease settled over Finn as scenarios played out in his mind. Had Ryan defected? Was he now revealing secrets about their operations? The very thought made Finn's stomach tighten, but beneath the fear, he felt a strange thrill, like he was one move away from a checkmate he couldn't see.

With practiced calm, Finn composed himself and dialed Lou's number.

"Uncle," Finn began, skipping pleasantries, "we've got a situation."

Lou's voice came through gruff and impatient. "What is it?"

"Marcus has eyes on Harper at the Hall of Fame. She's meeting with Ryan Patel."

A pause hung on the line, heavy with implications.

"Ryan?" Lou's voice sharpened. "From Furever?"

"Yes. And if he's talking to Harper Sinclair... it can only mean..."

Lou cut him off and grunted. "She's digging too deep," he muttered more to himself than to Finn.

"I've forwarded you the photo Marcus took."

Seconds passed before Lou responded, his voice now laced with urgency. "Get Dr. Kim on the phone," he instructed sharply. "We need to know why one of his lab rats is here in Toronto, stirring things up with a reporter."

"You think he knows?"

"I think it's time we found out exactly what game Dr. Kim is playing."

Finn's phone received another text from Marcus.

Male subject departed. Sinclair remaining in theater.

Finn's fingers drummed against his phone as he read Marcus's latest text. Yesterday, he'd been celebrating Team Canada's perfect execution on ice. Now he faced a different kind of game, one where the stakes went far beyond gold medals and championship rings.

Finn initiated the conference call, Lou's heavy breathing already audible on the line when Dr. Kim answered.

"Dr. Kim," Finn began, "we have a situation that requires immediate attention."

"Ah, the younger Mr. Booker," Dr. Kim's voice carried its usual precise tone, as if he'd been expecting this call. "And I assume that's Lou attempting to contain his breathing?"

"Cut the crap," Lou snapped. "Why is Ryan Patel meeting with a reporter in Toronto?"

A pause, then the soft sound of ice cubes clinking against glass. "I wasn't aware I needed to clear my employees' travel arrangements with VSM."

"Don't play games," Finn interjected. "Harper Sinclair isn't just any reporter. She's been asking questions about the Bernard boy, about our donated embryos—"

"Our?" Dr. Kim's interruption was sharp, precise. "I believe you mean mine, Mr. Booker. I made them. Your role was always quite specific, funding and placement. Nothing more."

Lou's voice rose. "Listen here, you arrogant—"

"No, Mr. Booker, you listen." Dr. Kim's tone remained steady, but carried an edge of steel. "Furever's internal matters are not VSM's concern. Never have been. Never will be."

"We have a partnership." Lou's voice carried the desperate edge of a man watching control slip away.

"We have an arrangement," Dr. Kim corrected, each word falling like a carefully placed chess piece. "One that has served its purpose. Now, if you'll excuse me, I have matters requiring my attention."

"If Ryan talks—" Lou started.

"Then perhaps," Dr. Kim cut in, "you should focus your energy on the reporter, rather than questioning my management decisions." A pause, deliberate and weighted. "After all, we wouldn't want Ms. Sinclair's curiosity to uncover anything... unfortunate." The line went dead.

Silence hung between uncle and nephew for a long moment. Lou gripped his phone tighter, knuckles white.

"Marcus still has eyes on Harper."

"Good." Lou's tone hardened. "Handle it."

Finn disconnected the call, already pulling up Marcus's latest update.

* * *

Marcus kept his distance as Harper Sinclair exited the Hockey Hall of Fame, his practiced eye noting how she scanned her surroundings before heading west on Front Street. *Smart woman,* he thought, *but not trained enough to spot real surveillance.*

Target leaving hall, moving west, Marcus messaged.

Stay with her, Finn replied.

Marcus watched Harper check her phone, then turn north. *Looks like York Street. Probably heading back to her hotel.* He maintained his distance, using other pedestrians as cover.

Harper paused at a crosswalk, her shoulder bag clutched close. Even from thirty feet back, Marcus could see the tension in her posture. Ryan's warning about staying out of sight had clearly registered.

She's nervous, Marcus reported.

Perfect timing then, Finn replied. *The parking garage next to the hotel. North entrance. That's where we'll have our chat.*

Marcus watched Harper turn onto York Street, her path now predictably leading to the hotel. He maintained his cover, stopping occasionally to check his phone like any other tourist.

She's staying on course. Minutes from the intercept point.

Understood. Moving into position now.

Harper's pace had slowed, her earlier urgency replaced by what looked like deep thought. Marcus recognized the distraction of someone processing heavy information. It would make Finn's approach easier. With Harper nearing the hotel, he made a call to Finn.

"Target approaching your position," Marcus voiced, watching Harper near the garage entrance.

He heard Finn's measured breathing through the iPhone. "Confirmed. Stand by."

Harper's footsteps echoed off the concrete walls. Then silence.

"Ms. Sinclair." Finn's voice carried a polite tone. His grip on her elbow suggested otherwise. "I believe you're playing a dangerous game."

She tried to pull away, but Marcus stepped into view, blocking her exit. The tourist with the iPhone, she realized. Of course.

"Interesting meeting at the Hall of Fame," Finn continued, his expensive suit somehow making him look more menacing, not less. "Ryan Patel isn't someone you want to trust."

"Remove your hand," Harper said, keeping her voice steady. "Or the next story I write will be about VSM's intimidation tactics."

Finn's grip tightened. "No, I don't think you'll be writing any stories about VSM." His pleasant tone vanished. "Or Furever. Or the Bernard boy. Or anything else you think you've discovered."

"Are you threatening me?"

"I'm explaining reality." Finn leaned closer. "You have a good career, Harper. Award-winning journalism. Would be a shame to see it end with a fabricated scandal and a libel suit that bankrupts you."

Harper met his gaze, forcing steel into her voice. "I have sources."

"You have speculation. And if you pursue this..." Finn glanced at Marcus, then back to Harper. "Well, let's just say there are worse things than libel suits."

The implied threat hung in the air. Harper felt her heart hammering but kept her expression neutral.

"Think carefully about your next move," Finn released her arm. "Some stories are best left unwritten."

Before Harper could respond, Marcus moved with startling speed. He snatched her phone from her coat pocket. From his jacket, he produced a telescoping steel baton. With a sharp flick of his wrist, it extended to full length with an ominous click. The sound echoed in the garage before he brought it down on her phone, shattering it against the concrete.

"We'll be watching," Finn said simply, then walked away into the shadows.

Harper waited until their footsteps faded. She stared at her shattered phone, Ryan's warning echoing in her mind.

Time to go dark.

Bloodlines

"Harper, you're about to walk into the lion's den with nothing but questions and a flashlight. If you're wrong, even just a little, this could ruin you." – Jessica

The city lights of Toronto twinkled below as Harper reached for the hotel room phone. After the garage incident, she needed a safe harbor, and there was only one person she trusted completely.

"Hello?" Jessica's voice was guarded, not recognizing the number.

"Jess, it's Harper."

"Harper? Why are you calling from—"

"Hotel phone. Long story. Listen, I need a favor. It's big."

Jessica's tone shifted from confused to businesslike in an instant. "Talk to me."

"I'm investigating VSM," Harper confessed, leaning back in her chair. "I think they're involved in something illegal, something that could change everything. And now I've got people following me, Jess. I need somewhere safe to work from."

There was a pause on the line. When Jessica spoke again, her voice carried a weight Harper hadn't heard since their university days. "You're scared. I can hear it in your voice. And you don't scare easily, Harper."

"Say no more," Jessica continued, concern tingeing her voice. "My place is your fortress. You still remember how to get here?"

"Actually, no. Lost my phone with all my contacts and addresses."

"Ah. Well, I'm still in that building near the café where we used to study. Text me when you're close, oh wait, no phone. Okay..." Jessica paused, then started giving directions while Harper scribbled them down.

"There's a phone store right across from my building," Jessica added.

"You know," Jessica said softly, "the last time I heard that tone in your voice was during the Montreal housing scandal. Remember? When you were photographing those documents and I knocked over that cleaning cart as a diversion?"

Harper smiled at the memory. "That story won us the student journalism award."

"We were always good at getting into trouble together," Jessica mused. "And even better at getting out of it."

"Thanks for this, Jess. Really."

"Always. Just... be careful, okay? This sounds bigger than a corrupt real estate developer."

"You have no idea," Harper sighed.

Hours later, Harper sat in Jessica's warm kitchen, new phone on the table beside her, wrapped in the familiar scent of jasmine green tea, her favorite from their university days. Jessica hadn't forgotten.

"Just like old times," Jessica said, sliding into the chair opposite.

Harper wrapped her hands around the steaming mug, grateful for this moment of peace before diving back into the investigation. The warmth of the tea and the comfort of Jessica's kitchen felt like a sanctuary after the tension of the past few days. "I've missed this. Us plotting over tea. You're probably the only person who still remembers my obsession with jasmine green."

"Some things you don't forget," Jessica smiled, her expression growing more serious. "Like how to tell when your friend is in over her head but too stubborn to admit it."

"Well then," Harper said, managing a small smile despite the weight of Jessica's observation, "let's plot. Because this time, I'm definitely going to need your help staying afloat."

Over the next hour, Harper filled Jessica in on everything. The mysterious Ryan Patel, his claims about VSM's secret cloning program, and finally, the garage confrontation that left her without a phone. Jessica listened intently, her expression darkening at the mention of Finn's threats and Marcus's steel baton.

"Christ, Harper," Jessica breathed when Harper finished. "No wonder you needed somewhere safe."

Harper nodded, taking another sip of tea. "The thing is, Ryan's story about Mario Richard's DNA... it could change everything. Not just for hockey, but for Liam especially."

"Wait," Jessica leaned forward. "What did Ryan say about Mario's involvement? Was he clear about that?"

Harper set down her mug, frowning. "That's the thing, Ryan dodged the question. All he'd confirm was that VSM represented Mario for years. When I pressed about the DNA collection, he got evasive, started talking about VSM's medical staff and their access."

"So Mario could have known," Jessica said, her eyes narrowing. "These aren't just rich executives we're talking about, this is Mario Richard. He's hockey royalty. What if he's been part of this from the beginning?"

The possibility hung between them, heavy with implications Harper hadn't fully explored. She'd been so focused on VSM's operations, she hadn't considered how deep Mario's involvement might go. His connection to Lou Booker stretched back decades, well before Liam was born.

"And what about Liam?" Jessica asked softly. "What happens to him if Mario turns out to be involved? Or if he isn't, but rejects any connection to Liam once this comes out?"

"I don't know," Harper admitted. "But he deserves the truth, whatever it is. We all do."

Jessica drummed her fingers on the table, her journalist's mind clearly working through angles. "So how do we approach Mario? We need a way in that works regardless of what he knows or doesn't know."

"I was thinking of using the NHL draft as cover," Harper suggested. "He's part owner now, and with Liam projected to go in the first round..."

"That could work," Jessica nodded slowly. "It's natural for you to request an interview about upcoming prospects. But you'll need a solid plan for steering the conversation where you need it to go."

"And for getting his DNA," Harper added grimly. "I need proof, not just suspicions."

Jessica's eyebrows shot up. "You're planning to get his DNA? Harper, that's..."

"Dangerous? Unethical? Believe me, I know. But after what VSM did to threaten me, I need something concrete. Something they can't deny or bury."

Jessica studied her friend's face for a long moment. "You really think this story is worth the risk?"

"It's not just a story anymore, Jess. It's about people's lives. Liam's identity. The truth about what VSM has been doing with these kids."

Jessica sighed, but Harper could see the familiar spark of investigation lighting up her friend's eyes. "Alright then. Let's figure out how to get you that interview without raising suspicions. But Harper?" She waited until their eyes met. "Whatever we discover, whatever Mario's involvement turns out to be, promise me you'll be careful. These people have already shown they're willing to use force."

Harper thought of her shattered phone, of Finn's cold threats in the garage. "I promise. But I can't back down now. Not when I'm this close."

Three hours and two pots of jasmine tea later, Jessica's living room had transformed into a command center. Her laptop sat open on the coffee table, surrounded by scribbled notes and empty cups. Harper perched on the edge of the couch, staring at Mario Richard's number on her new phone's screen.

"The draft angle is solid," Jessica reassured her, gathering their latest round of empty cups.

Harper nodded, her finger hovering over the dial button. One call could change everything, for her story, for Liam, for hockey itself. She took a deep breath and pressed dial.

The phone rang a few times before a familiar French-Canadian accent answered.

"Mario Richard speaking."

"Mr. Richard, this is Harper Sinclair from True North Hockey. We met at the season opener in Pittsburgh, I was covering your preseason expectations piece?"

"Ah, yes. At the owner's reception," Mario's tone warmed slightly with recognition.

"That's right. I'm working on a feature about this year's draft class, particularly focusing on the projected top picks. Given your unique perspective as both a former player and current owner..."

There was a pause on the line. "The draft isn't until June," Mario said carefully. "We usually do these interviews closer to draft day."

Jessica gave Harper a thumbs-up, mouthing 'stay calm' from her perch on the adjacent armchair.

"I understand," Harper replied. "But I'm actually in Pittsburgh right now working on another article. I was hoping I might stop by tomorrow while I'm here. Get ahead of the media crush before draft festivities begin."

"Tomorrow?" Mario's tone carried a note of suspicion. "That's very... sudden."

"It's a competitive business, Mr. Richard. Every outlet will be running draft projections soon. I'd rather offer our readers something more personal, more insightful. Your perspective on what makes a truly exceptional prospect."

Another pause, longer this time. Harper could almost hear Mario weighing the request.

"Alright, Ms. Sinclair. Three o'clock tomorrow. My home office. I'll have my assistant send you the address."

"Thank you, Mr. Richard. I appreciate your time."

After the call ended, Harper slumped back into the couch. Jessica let out a low whistle.

"That was too easy," Jessica said, frowning. "And that lie about being in Pittsburgh..."

"I know," Harper admitted. "But we don't have the luxury of time. If Ryan's right about VSM..." She trailed off, the weight of tomorrow's task settling over her.

"At least you got in," Jessica offered, closing her laptop.

Harper stood, pacing the length of Jessica's living room. "I'll need to control the conversation carefully. Start with general draft questions, then gradually..."

"And if he knows about everything?" Jessica interrupted. "If he's part of all this?"

"Then I'll have my answer." Harper stopped pacing, turning to face her friend. "One way or another, I'm finding out the truth tomorrow."

Jessica studied her for a long moment. "Just promise me you'll be ready to walk away if things feel wrong. Mario Richard isn't some corrupt real estate developer. He's is a hockey legend, with connections everywhere."

"I give you my word," Harper assured her, though they both recognized she'd pursue whatever means necessary to uncover the truth. "But I can't back down now. The consequences are too significant."

"Then let's make sure you're ready for whatever you find tomorrow," Jessica said, reaching for her laptop again. "Because I have a feeling Mario Richard isn't going to make this easy."

* * *

Through the rental car's windshield, Pittsburgh's snow-covered hills rolled past under cloudy January skies. Harper glanced at the dashboard clock: 2:31 PM. Plenty of time to make the appointment, but first she needed to make one crucial call.

Liam answered before the first ring finished. "Harper! Finally. I've been checking my phone all day."

"Sorry, I've been—"

"Did you find anything?" The eagerness in his voice was painful to hear. "Anything more from Ryan?"

"Hey, slow down. How's Minnesota treating you?"

A frustrated sigh. "It's cold. But good. Really good, actually. The Wild are rolling out the red carpet. First overall pick means they're putting on quite a show." He paused. "Ben's loving every minute of it."

"Ben's there?" Harper kept her tone neutral, though her grip tightened on the steering wheel.

"Yeah, VSM's got him practically glued to my side since Toronto. Won't let me go anywhere without him." Liam's attempt at laughing it off fell flat. "But seriously, Harper, what's happening?"

Harper navigated a turn, choosing her words carefully. "I'm following some leads. Actually about to meet with someone who might have answers. I promise I'll tell you everything once I know for sure."

"I just..." Liam's voice cracked slightly. "I need to know who I am, Harper. You're the only one I can trust right now."

"I know," Harper assured him, her throat tight. "And I'm not stopping until we get the truth. All of it. How about we talk tomorrow?"

"You promise? No more waiting?"

"I promise, Liam. Whatever I find out today, you'll be the first to know."

After ending the call, Harper took a deep breath, Jessica's warnings from last night echoing in her mind. The stakes felt even higher after hearing the desperation in Liam's voice, is future, his identity, everything he thought he knew about himself hanging in the balance.

The GPS directed her onto a tree-lined street of upscale homes. Mario Richard's house, while impressive, had the understated elegance typical of hockey players, successful but not showy. No gates, no elaborate security, just a long driveway leading to a beautiful stone home overlooking the city.

Harper parked her rental car behind a black SUV and walked to the front door, her prepared story about draft prospects suddenly feeling paper-thin. What if Mario was part of it all? What if he'd known about Liam from the beginning? Or worse, what if he was completely innocent, and she was about to shatter his world too?

The clock on her phone showed 2:57 PM as she reached for the doorbell, Jessica's final warning ringing in her ears: *Be ready for whatever version of the truth you find.*

Fault Lines

"The key to a good game plan isn't just knowing your opponent's next move, it's making sure they don't see yours coming." – Lou

The phone's vibration jolted Finn from his thoughts. Through his office window, Montreal's lights were coming on, one building at a time. Marcus Gage's name flashed on the screen.

"Report," Finn barked.

"She's making moves," Marcus's voice crackled with urgency. "Harper just boarded a plane to Pittsburgh."

Finn leaned back in his chair. *Pittsburgh. Mario Richard. The source of Liam's DNA. If Harper made that connection...*

"She's persistent," Marcus continued. "That garage warning didn't slow her down at all. New phone, new moves, staying ahead of us."

Finn turned away from the window, his reflection fractured across the Montreal skyline. One reporter was all it would take to unravel everything they'd built. And Harper Sinclair wasn't backing down.

"Keep monitoring the Toronto angle," Finn ordered. "I want to know who helped her disappear after our chat in the garage."

After ending the call, Finn stood for a moment at his office door, the weight of what was coming settling over him like a shroud. Harper Sinclair was about to walk up to Mario Richard's door and potentially destroy everything they'd built.

Finn strode toward the elevator, his mind already racing through contingencies. They needed to contain this, and fast. But first, he had to tell Lou that their carefully engineered world was about to face its greatest test.

The elevator seemed to crawl between floors, each second stretching Finn's nerves tighter. He checked his phone again, thumbing through encrypted messages. One from Ben in Minnesota caught his attention, something about press trying to contact their star prospect. Finn fired back a quick response: *Keep him focused. No unnecessary distractions.*

The doors opened to VSM's executive floor. Through floor-to-ceiling windows, Montreal's morning sun glinted off neighboring buildings. Finn strode past Lou's assistant, already at her desk, and knocked on his uncle's door.

"Entrer." Lou's voice carried that familiar mix of authority and irritation.

Finn found his uncle behind his massive desk, phone pressed to his ear, speaking rapid French. Lou's face was flushed, his tie loosened, signs that today wasn't going as planned for him either. He held up one finger, signaling Finn to wait.

"Oui, oui... Non, pas maintenant." Lou ended the call with a grunt. "What's wrong? You've got that look."

"Harper Sinclair's on her way to Pittsburgh."

Lou's eyebrows rose slightly, but his expression remained controlled. "Mario?" At Finn's nod, Lou leaned back in his chair, steepling his fingers. "Interesting timing."

"Interesting? She's about to—"

"Calm down, Finn." Lou's voice carried the same tone he used in major contract negotiations. "You really think we didn't plan for this?"

Finn stopped his pacing. "You can't be serious."

"Think about it." Lou stood, moving a tray of orange juice. "Mario Richard. Hockey royalty. A man who understands legacy better than anyone." He handed a glass to Finn. "Whatever Harper thinks she knows, whatever she's pieced together... we have contingencies."

"She wouldn't go to him without something concrete."

Lou laughed, the sound echoing off the windows. "Let her try. Meanwhile, you focus on what matters, keeping our investments protected. No distractions, no complications." He took a sip of juice.

"And Mario?"

"Leave Mario to me." Lou's smile was predatory. "Some conversations are better handled... directly."

Finn felt the tension in his shoulders ease slightly. This was the Lou he knew, always three moves ahead, turning threats into opportunities. "You seem awfully calm about this."

"In this business," Lou said, settling back behind his desk, "every crisis is just another opportunity. Besides," his expression hardened, "Harper Sinclair isn't the first person to think they could shake VSM's foundation. She won't be the last."

The threat in his uncle's words was clear, but it was the calculation behind them that sent a chill down Finn's spine. They couldn't stop Harper from reaching Mario, but maybe they didn't need to.

"Focus on our priorities," Lou added, turning back to his computer. "Let Harper play her hand." Lou turned back to his computer, a small smirk forming. "Sometimes the best move is making your opponent think they've already won."

Finn nodded, but couldn't shake the feeling that this time, Lou's confidence might be their undoing. After all, Harper wasn't just any opponent, she was someone who'd already proven she couldn't be intimidated.

* * *

Just another interview, Harper told herself as she waited at Mario Richard's door. She'd done this hundreds of times, sat across from legends of the game, discussed their legacies, their views on hockey's future. But never quite like this.

The doorbell's chime echoed inside. Footsteps approached, and then Mario Richard stood before her, his presence still commanding after all these years. Age had touched him gently, adding distinction rather than wear. His smile was genuine, his handshake firm.

"Harper Sinclair," he said warmly, recognition lighting his eyes. "Please, come in. That piece you wrote about the '87 Canada Cup, brought back some memories."

The entryway opened into a living room where personal achievements mingled comfortably with family life. Photos lined the walls, Mario with his children, grandchildren, moments of joy frozen in time. A subtle collection of awards sat in a corner cabinet, important but not the room's focus. The space smelled of cedar and leather, warm and inviting.

"Can I get you something to drink?" Mario asked, leading her toward his home office. "Water? Coffee?"

"Water would be great, thanks."

The office reflected its owner, professional but lived-in. A substantial wooden desk dominated one side, papers arranged in organized chaos. Hockey memorabilia decorated the walls, but tastefully: signed pucks in display cases, team photos, a few select medals. Through the window, Pittsburgh's skyline glimmered in the distance.

Mario returned with two glasses of water, settling into his chair with the ease of a man comfortable in his domain. "So, the draft," he began, smile crinkling the corners of his eyes. "Though I have to admit, your timing surprised me. We usually do these closer to June."

Harper returned his smile, years of experience helping her maintain composure. "The landscape's changing so fast these days. Everyone's looking for the next breakthrough, the next evolution in the sport."

"True enough." Mario chuckled, leaning back. "The science they have now, nutrition, training, recovery. Sometimes I wonder what we could have done with all that."

"You did pretty well without it," Harper offered, gesturing to a photo of Mario hoisting the Stanley Cup. "The emotion in that moment... it's remarkable."

"That was a good day," he said, eyes drifting to the photo. "Hard-earned, but worth every moment." He turned back to Harper, his expression warming with nostalgia. "The game was different then. Simpler in some ways, harder in others."

They fell into easy conversation about hockey's evolution, the speed of today's game, the emphasis on skill over size, the way young players developed. Mario spoke with genuine passion, his insights sharp, his love for the sport evident in every observation.

Harper listened intently, asking the right questions, building rapport. But beneath her professional demeanor, she felt the weight of what was to come. The truth she carried was about to change everything, for Mario, for hockey, for the entire sports world.

But not yet. First, she needed him to remember who he was, what he meant to the game. Because soon, she would have to tell him how others had used that legacy in ways he never imagined.

Mario's gaze remained fixed on Harper, the easy warmth from earlier replaced by a sharp, assessing look. "I think we've danced around the real reason you're here long enough, don't you?" His voice held a challenge, the underlying suspicion now fully surfacing.

Harper's carefully prepared questions scattered like loose pucks. She opened her notebook, buying time, but Mario cut her off.

"Come on, Harper. You didn't fly to Pittsburgh, arrange this meeting, just to discuss draft prospects and old hockey stories." He leaned forward, his presence filling the room. "You're better than that. And I'm not some rookie you can dance around with soft questions."

The directness caught her off-balance, but something in his tone, a hint of knowing something more, steadied her resolve. She closed her notebook, met his eyes.

"You're right. Let's talk about VSM and their connection to a research facility in Korea." She watched his expression carefully. "A facility called Furever Genetics."

"Did you know there's a facility in Korea that specializes in cloning?" Harper's shift in topic was abrupt, deliberate. "They started with pets, moved to livestock, race horses. Perfect copies of champion thoroughbreds."

Mario laughed, but it didn't reach his eyes. "Cloning? Like that sheep from Scotland?"

"Dolly was just the beginning." Harper maintained eye contact. "The science has advanced considerably. Especially when there's money involved. And what industry has more money than professional sports?"

"What does this have to do with VSM?" Mario turned from his trophy case, brow furrowed.

"They've been funding Furever Genetics for years. Through shell companies, private investments." Harper paused, letting that sink in. "At first, it was just race horses. Duplicating champions. But then they started collecting DNA samples from athletes. Top performers. Living legends."

Mario's expression shifted, realization dawning. "You can't seriously be saying what I think you're saying..."

"The technology exists, Mario. The capability to replicate genetic excellence." Harper stood slowly. "To create perfect athletes."

"This is absurd." His voice shook slightly. "Human cloning isn't real, or legal."

"Neither was stem cell research, once." Harper's voice remained steady. "But laws change when billion-dollar industries push hard enough."

"You're talking science fiction."

"Am I?" Harper reached into her bag, removing a folder. The weight of its contents felt like lead in her hands.

Mario turned back, his expression hardening. "And you think what? Someone's secretly cloning athletes?"

"No, Mario." Harper stood slowly. "I think someone cloned you. Used your DNA. Your perfect genetic blueprint for hockey, to create exactly what they wanted."

The words hung in the air like smoke, heavy and suffocating. Mario's expression hardened, but his eyes told a different story, disbelief, then doubt, then something dangerously close to fear.

"That's impossible," he whispered. But the conviction was gone, leaving only silence, and the first flicker of doubt.

"Mario." Her voice cut through his weak protest. "I need to ask you something, and I need you to understand the gravity of what I'm asking." She paused, letting the moment stretch. "Did you knowingly give VSM permission to use your DNA, to create another you?"

The room went absolutely still. Mario's expression froze, the dismissive retort dying on his lips as the question's implications hit him. For the first time, genuine uncertainty crept into his eyes.

Was she suggesting... had she just accused him of... cloning himself?

The grandfather clock ticked loudly in the silence, marking the moments as Mario Richard's carefully ordered world began to crack.

Fault in the Code

"You expect me to believe someone took my DNA and made... what? A copy? That's science fiction." – Mario

Harper watched as Mario Richard's face transformed, decades of composure cracking like ice under sudden pressure. The color drained from his cheeks, his features turning rigid, carved from stone. His hands, the same ones that had lifted Stanley Cups and orchestrated countless plays, trembled slightly before curling into fists.

"A clone?" His voice barely escaped his throat before it sharpened. "You come into my home and accuse—" He cut himself off, shoving back from his desk. His chair slammed against the wall with a hollow thud, the sound thick with tension.

"Not accuse," Harper kept her voice steady, professional. "I'm investigating a situation." She fell silent, letting the implication sink in.

He began pacing, three quick steps one way, turn, three steps back. The movement reminded Harper of a caged animal, all coiled energy and barely contained fury. "This is insane. Completely insane." His accent thickened with each word, emotion bleeding through his usually measured tone.

"Twenty years ago, during your cancer treatment—"

"Stop." Mario spun to face her, one finger raised in warning. "Don't you dare use that time to spin some crazy story." His voice cracked on the last words, raw emotion breaking through.

Harper remained seated, maintaining her calm demeanor despite the tension crackling through the room. She'd interviewed angry subjects before, dealt with emotional responses to difficult questions. But this was different. This wasn't just another story about drug tests or recruiting violations. This was about identity itself.

"I need you to prove it." Mario's demand cut through the tension. He planted both hands on his desk, leaning forward, his presence filling the room just as it once commanded the ice. "If you're going to make claims like this, destroy lives like this, you better have something concrete."

Harper didn't blink. "That's why I'm here. Because I need your help to prove it."

The grandfather clock in the corner ticked away the seconds as they stared at each other, neither willing to back down. Outside, a car door slammed, the ordinary sound jarring against the extraordinary moment unfolding in Mario Richard's office.

"Help you prove it?" Mario's laugh held no humor. "You want me to help validate these... these accusations?" He moved to the window, staring out at his manicured lawn where neighborhood kids sometimes practiced their shots against a shooting wall.

Before Harper could respond, Mario's phone buzzed on his desk. Then again. And a third time.

He glanced at the screen, his expression shifting as he read each message. Harper noticed the subtle change in his posture, the slight tightening around his eyes.

"Lou Booker," Mario said flatly, holding up his phone. "Says some interesting things about you. That you've gone rogue, chasing conspiracies.

Says VSM had to suspend your credentials." His eyes narrowed. "Claims you've lost perspective."

Harper allowed herself a small smile. "Interesting timing, don't you think? The moment I start asking difficult questions, Lou tries to discredit me."

Mario studied her for a long moment. "You don't seem surprised."

"Because I'm not." Harper opened her bag, removing a thin file. "VSM has a lot to protect, Mario. And Lou... well, Lou's been protecting their interests for a very long time." She placed several documents on his desk. "Including during your cancer treatment."

Mario tugged at his collar, a habit from his playing days. "Tabarnac," he muttered. "I told you not to—"

"These are consent forms," Harper cut in, her voice gentle but firm. "From your treatment. Look at the highlighted section."

Mario hesitated before picking up the papers. His eyes scanned the text, stopping at a clause about genetic material storage and research rights. The paper trembled slightly in his hands.

"This doesn't prove anything," he said, but uncertainty had crept into his voice. "Medical research is standard protocol."

"Turn to the last page."

Mario hesitated, then flipped the document. The VSM letterhead stared back at him like a brand seared into paper. Below it, a partnership agreement, finalized just days after he signed his consent forms.

His phone buzzed again. Lou's name flashed on the screen. But Mario didn't move. He just stared at the documents, and Harper saw the precise moment realization slid into place.

"My God," he whispered. "What the hell did they do?"

The office door burst open as a small whirlwind in a hockey jersey rushed in, hockey stick in hand. Six-year-old Piper skidded to a stop, her blonde ponytail swinging, ice-blue eyes bright with excitement but momentarily faltering at the sight of a stranger. A "Richard" nameplate adorned the back of her jersey, slightly too big on her small frame.

The transformation in Mario was instant. The tense, troubled man of moments ago melted away as he turned to his granddaughter, a warm smile spreading across his face. "Hey, champ! What've you got to show me?"

Piper, reassured by her grandfather's smile, bounced on her toes. "I showed coach my toe drag today. Watch!" She demonstrated with her stick on the office carpet, tongue caught between her teeth in concentration.

"Perfect form," Mario praised, kneeling beside her. "Just like we practiced, eh?"

Harper watched the scene unfold, struck by the contrast between the hockey legend who'd been pacing moments ago and this doting grandfather. Piper glanced at her curiously.

"Are you a hockey player too?" she asked, fidgeting with her stick.

"Not anymore, now I'm a writer," Harper smiled. "But I used to play for Team Canada. Won gold at the Olympics."

Piper's eyes widened with excitement. "Really? You won a gold medal?" She turned to Mario. "Grandpa, she won gold just like you!"

"That she did," Mario nodded, a genuine smile breaking through his earlier tension. "Harper was quite the player."

"Did you score the winning goal?" Piper asked, now completely focused on Harper, her stick temporarily forgotten.

"Assisted on it," Harper replied, warming to the girl's enthusiasm. "Nothing as spectacular as your grandpa's goals though."

Piper beamed. "I'm gonna play just like him someday. Coach says I even skate like Grandpa did!"

The words hit like a stick to the ribs. Mario didn't flinch, but Harper caught the way his grip tightened just slightly. The implications of genetic legacy took on new meaning as Piper demonstrated another move

"Piper!" A woman's voice called from somewhere in the house. "Time for your snack!"

"Aw, Grammy!" Piper protested, but she was already heading for the door. She stopped to hug Mario's leg. "Watch me at practice tomorrow?"

"Wouldn't miss it, champ." Mario ruffled his granddaughter's hair, watching until the girl disappeared down the hallway, the sound of her running footsteps fading away.

The silence that followed felt heavier than before, weighted with new understanding. Mario remained standing where Piper had left him, staring at the doorway, his expression unreadable.

Mario moved to his desk, picking up a framed photo of Piper at her first skating lesson. His fingers traced the glass, lingering over his granddaughter's beaming face.

"It's not just about me anymore, is it?" He set the photo down carefully, turning to face Harper. "Whatever proof you have, whatever story you're chasing, it affects them too." His gesture encompassed the photos of children and grandchildren lining his office walls.

"That's why this needs to be handled carefully," Harper said softly. "But it also needs to be handled, Mario. The truth has a way of emerging, one way or another."

He nodded slowly, his expression hardening with resolve. "Then let's be clear about something." Mario's voice took on the commanding tone that had once directed teams to Stanley Cup victories. "If what you're suggesting is true, if someone did steal my DNA, create a..." he paused, still struggling with the word, "...a clone. Then that person is as much a victim as I am."

"Yes, they are."

"And you know who it is." It wasn't a question.

Harper met his gaze steadily but remained silent.

"Tell me who it is." Mario leaned forward, his presence filling the room. "You want my DNA? You want me to help prove this incredible story?" His voice dropped lower, intense rather than threatening. "Then tell me who they created from my genetic code."

The grandfather clock's steady ticking filled the silence between them. Through the window, Piper's laughter drifted up from the backyard, a reminder of what was at stake.

"I can't do that, Mario. Not yet." Harper met his eyes across the desk. "But when the time comes, you'll be the first to know."

Mario's hand went to his collar, that old nervous tell surfacing again. "Then we're done here."

Silence stretched between them. Harper didn't move. Neither did Mario.

From outside, a hockey stick snapped against pavement, the sound crisp, sharp, like something breaking.

Convergence

"If someone did this, if they created life from my DNA, then that person deserves the truth as much as I do." – Mario

The standoff lasted another moment before Mario broke away first, turning to face the wall of memorabilia behind his desk. Outside, the last echo of Piper's stick strike faded, leaving only the steady tick of the grandfather clock between them.

"All these years," he said finally, his voice barely above a whisper. "All these achievements, these moments..." He gestured at the framed photos and trophies. "And now you're telling me there's another story. One I never knew about."

Mario leaned back in his chair, eyes scanning the reminders of a life lived under bright lights. The question lingered in his gaze, unasked but clear: *Who is it?*

A deep thrum of tension ran through her as she considered her next words. Her career had always hinged on trust, an unspoken bond between journalist and source. Breaking that now, even for something as monumental as this, would be betraying everything she stood for.

"I can't," she finally said, her voice steady despite the turmoil beneath. "I can't breach that trust."

Mario's expression tightened, frustration flashing briefly before he regained control. He understood the value of secrets, he had kept plenty himself. But he also understood the pain of not knowing, of living with unanswered questions that gnawed at you. He studied her face, trying to find a way through her resolve.

"I know you want to help, and I need your help, but there are lines I won't cross. This is one of them," Harper added, trying to convey sincerity without losing her edge. The room felt charged with the weight of what they were both trying to protect.

Mario leaned back in his chair, eyes drifting to the memorabilia lining the walls, silent witnesses to a life lived under bright lights. The question lingered in his gaze, unasked but clear: *Who is it?*

"Someone in the NHL?" Mario's voice sharpened. He looked away, working through the possibilities. "No... you were just at World Juniors in Toronto. I saw the coverage."

He stepped to the window, his back to her. "It has to be one of those kids."

Harper said nothing, her silence a confirmation of sorts.

Mario exhaled sharply. "Julian Broten?" He shook his head almost immediately. "No... someone bigger. Someone about to go first overall."

Each guess was a test, but she refused to break. Yet with every name Mario spoke, she could see it in his eyes, a growing certainty that he was circling closer to the truth.

Mario sighed, glancing back at the framed photos on his desk, his family, his career. He seemed smaller now, like the enormity of the moment had diminished him. Then, a distant look came over his face as he sank into memory.

"You know, I was a bit of a prodigy myself," he said, his voice softer. "Led my hometown team in Montreal by the time I was fifteen."

Harper listened closely as he painted a picture of his past, the thrill of skating, the roar of the crowd, the weight of expectations on young shoulders. His story mirrored Liam's in many ways, though she knew their paths diverged sharply at the point where science met ambition.

"I played in the World Juniors at seventeen," he continued, a shadow of pride in his voice. "Felt like I was carrying the whole country's hopes on my back."

Harper took in every word, noting the parallels to Liam's own journey. The pressure, the promise, the struggle to remain himself amidst it all, it was a story she knew too well. She wondered if Mario had any inkling that his story had been rewritten in the life of another.

"It's hard being young and that talented," he said, meeting her gaze again. "You become more than just a player, you become a symbol."

There was a knowing look in his eyes, like he was piecing things together, each word a step closer to understanding.

"It's... Liam?" he said quietly, as if testing the waters.

Harper kept her expression neutral. Her voice remained level. "I can't confirm or deny anything, Mario."

Mario studied her for a moment, then nodded slowly, the initial shock giving way to grim determination. A realization settled between them, unspoken, but undeniable. Harper could see the question in his eyes: How much of his legacy had been shaped without his knowledge?

Harper's gaze caught on Mario's hands as he gestured, specifically, a distinctive silver streak running through the skin on his ring finger. The same mark she'd noticed on Liam during their interviews.

Mario followed her look, rubbing his thumb over the silver streak like he was seeing it for the first time. "Hereditary," he muttered. "Every man in my family has it. My father. My sons..." He paused, studying Harper's expression. "But never the daughters. Funny how DNA works, isn't it?"

The weight of those words hung between them. Another piece of evidence, another connection she couldn't ignore.

Mario cleared his throat, his voice roughened by emotion. "I'll do the DNA test." He reached for a business card, writing a number on the back. "My personal cell. When you have the results, before you publish anything, you call me. Not email, not text. You call."

Harper took the card, noting his steady hand despite everything. "You have my word."

"And Harper?" His voice stopped her at the door. "Whoever this person is... whatever VSM did... they're as much a victim as I am. Remember that when you write your story."

She nodded, feeling the weight of the DNA kit in her bag, knowing it contained the power to change lives forever. Some truths, once revealed, could never be buried again. Behind her, the grandfather clock continued its steady count, marking the moments until everything would change.

* * *

The late afternoon sun caught Pittsburgh's skyline as Harper pulled away from Mario's neighborhood. Mario's DNA sample was secure in her bag. She pulled out her phone and dialed Liam's number.

"Harper." His voice carried a mix of relief and tension. "Tell me you have something."

"I'm making progress. Just left an important meeting." She merged onto the highway, needing movement, needing to do something.

"Ben's been hovering all morning, watching my phone. Something's got VSM spooked."

Harper pulled onto the main road, choosing her words carefully. "How bad is the hovering?"

"He's trying to play it casual. Mock interviews with Wild staff, facility tours, media training." Liam's bitter laugh carried through the speakers.

"He even insisted on reviewing my medical records again, like they might have changed since last week."

"Keep playing along," Harper advised, though the news of Ben's increased attention worried her. "We need to maintain normalcy until—"

"Until the DNA results?" Liam cut in. "How long, Harper? Every day I look at Jim and Tammy I can see they are struggling like me. They want me to know the truth about my real parents."

The pain in his voice made her grip the steering wheel tighter. "I know. And I promise, we're close. Your test results are waiting at the lab, and now I have something to compare them to."

Silence filled the line for a moment. When Liam spoke again, his voice was lower, controlled. "You got another sample? You know who it is?"

"I think so..." Harper watched the city shrink in her rearview mirror. "But Liam, whatever these results show..."

"I need to know," he said firmly. "Who my real parents are. No matter what."

"I know you do. That's why we're doing this right. No rumors, no half-truths. Just facts."

Another pause. She could almost hear him pacing, the way he did when working through something difficult. "How long for the results?"

"Soon, very soon." She hesitated. "Liam... I meant what I said before. This isn't just about finding your biological parents. There might be more—"

"Just get me the results," he cut her off. "I need to know where I came from."

The line went dead. Harper set down her phone.

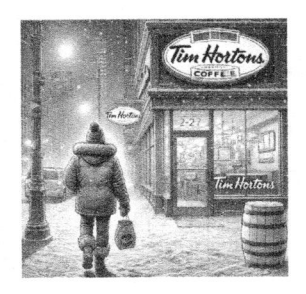

Encroachment

"What does Jessica always say? Nothing like a double-double to get words on a page. Time for a Timmy's run." – Harper

The low hum of the hotel room's air conditioning was the only sound as Harper Sinclair sat hunched over her laptop. Multiple windows crowded her screen, financial records, medical documents, encrypted files. Pittsburgh's skyline blurred in her peripheral vision, she hadn't looked up in hours. The evidence trail stretched back decades, each new discovery more damning than the last.

She pulled up another VSM financial document, scanning for connections she might have missed. Twenty years of carefully hidden transactions, shell companies, and private research funding. All leading to one place: GeneCore Solutions.

This wasn't just another sports scandal. This would shake the foundations of professional sports itself.

Harper opened another secure folder, this one containing medical records from New Horizon Fertility Clinic. The connections were there, VSM's shell companies, the mysterious payments, the timing of certain "donations." She'd uploaded everything to three separate cloud servers, each file protected by encryption that would make government agencies jealous. Years of investigative work had taught her the value of redundancy.

The cursor blinked at the end of a sentence where she'd written about Ethan Bernard's tragic death. Ethan, the boy with a future as bright as the ice he skated on, snuffed out too soon by an undiagnosed heart condition. Or so they'd claimed. The truth was buried in these documents, in the carefully hidden trail that led from VSM to GeneCore using Furever technology, from Lou Booker to Dr. Kim Jung-So.

She paused, flexing her stiff fingers. The implications were staggering. This wasn't just about one talented hockey player or even one company's ethical breaches. This was about the fundamental nature of sports, of competition itself. How many others were out there? How many more Liams and Ethans had been created in secret?

Her screen flashed with an incoming message from her lab contact.

DNA samples have arrived.

Soon, she'd have the final piece of evidence linking everything together. Then there would be no more hiding, no more secrets.

This story wouldn't just trend on social media or lead the sports networks. This would explode across every platform simultaneously, sending shockwaves through the entire sports world. Lives would change forever, Liam's most of all.

Her phone buzzed, snapping her out of her thoughts. It was Ryan.

"Harper," he whispered urgently, "you need to be careful. Marcus Gage is in Pittsburgh."

A chill crawled up her spine. She remembered Marcus from the hockey hall of fame, VSM's shadow. "Lou's not wasting any time." She paused, considering Ryan's timing. "How do you know this?"

"I have my sources." Background noise nearly drowned out his voice, the echoing acoustics of what sounded like an airport terminal. An announcement in Arabic crackled through a PA system.

"Where are you, Ryan?"

"That's not important." His voice tightened. "What matters is Marcus isn't there to negotiate."

Harper's fingers tightened on the phone. Ryan always seemed to appear with precisely timed warnings, yet never quite enough information. "You know more than you're telling me."

"Just be careful," he said, ignoring her observation. The line went dead before she could press further.

Harper stared at the screen. Ryan's warnings were always perfectly timed, and never quite complete. Marcus she understood, a clear threat, a known quantity.

* * *

Lou Booker stood at his office window, Montreal's skyline blurring through the falling snow. Behind him, Finn scrolled through surveillance photos on his tablet.

"Two hours with Mario Richard," Finn said, his voice tight. "She didn't back off."

Lou's reflection in the glass remained unmoved. "I reminded Mario what kind of journalist she is. Always chasing ghosts, always seeing conspiracies." He turned. "Besides, Marcus is in Pittsburgh now."

Finn hesitated. "And if that's not enough?"

Lou's answer was cold. "It will be."

Finn felt a chill at his uncle's words, but kept his expression neutral. Sometimes the best move was to say nothing at all.

* * *

Harper stepped out of the hotel elevator at 11 PM, balancing a Tim Hortons bag and her last double-double of the night. The hallway's fluorescent lights hummed overhead, casting harsh shadows that made every corner feel darker than it should.

She slowed approaching her room, coffee halfway to her lips. The "Do Not Disturb" sign swayed gently, someone had just exited, the door's displacement still rippling through the thin cardboard. A caffeine-fueled jitter ran through her, but years of investigative work kept her movements calm, deliberate.

Inside, her practiced eye caught the subtle signs. The air felt different, disturbed. Her papers on the desk were stacked with unnatural precision, nothing like her usual organized chaos. The notepad by the phone had been moved, its corner no longer aligned with the desk edge. Her laptop sat dead center on the wooden surface, she always kept it offset, easier to grab when inspiration struck at night.

Even her jacket, casually draped over the armchair, looked too deliberately placed, like someone had studied her habits and tried to recreate them.

A cough from the hallway made her freeze. Footsteps passed her door, paused, then continued. Harper moved to the window, using its reflection to scan the parking lot below.

Marcus stood in the shadows near a black SUV, every movement displaying the controlled precision that made him VSM's enforcer. Six-foot-three, close-cropped hair, favoring his right side slightly, where she'd noticed the shoulder holster at the garage. His collar turned up against the night chill as he spoke into his phone, face illuminated briefly by the parking lot lights.

She pulled out her phone and quickly booked a morning flight to Saint Paul. As the confirmation came through, a message from her lab contact popped up: *Analysis in progress. Results tomorrow.*

Harper checked her backups again, everything secured across multiple servers, redundancies in place. Time to move.

The 87% Factor

"Somewhere in Minnesota, a young man is chasing a dream, unaware that the truth I hold could change everything." – Harper

Harper Sinclair tapped through another article in the Journal of Sport Performance Genetics, the steady thrum of the aircraft engines masking the sound of her fingers on the keyboard. At cruising altitude between Pittsburgh and Saint Paul, she finally had time to piece together what she'd learned about genetic advantages in elite athletes.

Her screen displayed a comprehensive study of over three hundred professional athletes, hockey players, Olympic sprinters, NFL running backs, marathon champions. The research focused on five key genetic traits that separated elite performers from the general population.

The "Speed Gene" ACTN3 caught her attention first. According to the paper, only two percent of the general population carried the optimal variant for explosive power and fast-twitch muscle response. But among elite power athletes? That number jumped to eighty-two percent. Harper thought of Liam's acceleration on breakaways, how he seemed to hit top speed in two strides.

She scrolled to a chart comparing population percentages. The "Energy Gene" AMPD1 showed similar patterns, rare in the general population but common in elite athletes. Those with the optimal variant could maintain peak performance longer, their muscles processing energy more efficiently. Like Liam's seemingly endless stamina during double shifts.

The ACE gene, nicknamed the "Power Gene," controlled oxygen utilization and muscle development. The "Recovery Gene" CRP determined how quickly inflammation subsided after injury. And COL5A1, the "Durability Gene," influenced tendon and ligament strength. Each one showed the same pattern, rare in the general population, but frequently present in top athletes.

A movement caught her eye, a passenger shifting three rows back. Harper angled her laptop slightly, an old investigative habit, before returning to her research.

Her notes filled the margins of the study. Elite athletes typically carried one or two optimal variants, with a few rare cases showing three. But what if someone carried four? Or all five? The possibilities made her pulse quicken.

Her phone buzzed, a text from Ben: *Heard you left Pittsburgh. Everything okay?*

Harper left it unanswered.

VSM had access to Mario Richard's DNA, a generational talent. They had connections to fertility clinics. And they had Dr. Kim's expertise in genetic modification.

She stared at the population comparison chart again. The math was undeniable, the odds of naturally having multiple optimal variants were astronomical. Yet Liam's performance suggested exactly that combination.

Her phone remained silent, the lab's response still pending. Soon she'd have more than population statistics and performance theories. Soon she'd have proof of what VSM had engineered, an athlete carrying every genetic advantage possible. The implications would change sports forever.

THE 87% FACTOR

Harper's phone vibrated against the seat tray, the screen lighting up with a notification from the lab. She glanced at the spotty airplane WiFi signal, willing it to hold steady. After three attempts, the message finally loaded.

Dr. Nguyen's preliminary note appeared first: *Ms. Sinclair, I need to inform you that we've had some unusual activity around our facility this week. Nothing compromised, but worth noting.*

Of course they had, VSM wouldn't leave any stone unturned. Harper opened the full report, her breath catching as the data appeared.

DNA comparison analysis complete, the report began clinically. *Sample A (Desjardins) and Sample B (Richard) show an 87% genetic similarity.*

Harper read the number again. *Eighty-seven percent.*

The report continued. *This result significantly exceeds known familial relationship parameters. The highest documented genetic similarity between siblings, excluding identical twins, is 61%. At 87%, these results suggest either severe contamination or...* The technician's report trailed off, as if unwilling to speculate further.

Harper's fingers hovered over her phone, her mind racing through everything she knew about genetic engineering. This wasn't contamination. This was proof, proof of something that shouldn't exist outside of science fiction.

The lab technician added another observation. *Beyond the unprecedented similarity percentage, specific genetic markers are particularly interesting. The ACTN3, AMPD1, ACE, CRP, and COL5A1 genes all appear optimized in Sample A (Desjardins). These enhancements surpass any naturally occurring mutation we've ever documented.*

Her screen flickered as the WiFi signal wavered. Harper held her breath, watching the loading icon spin. Finally, the last portion of data appeared, a detailed breakdown of genetic markers.

The evidence was there in the cold, hard data. This wasn't just a coincidence or contamination. This was deliberate engineering, Mario's base genetic code, modified and enhanced through CRISPR technology. Someone had taken Mario Richard's DNA and turned it into a template, then carefully altered it to create something new.

Nature's template, reshaped in a lab by human ambition.

She continued reading, *Given these anomalies, we strongly recommend a complete retest with new samples. These results defy conventional genetic relationships.*

Harper replied, *No retest needed. These results tell me exactly what I needed to know.*

As her phone display dimmed, the truth crystallized. Eighty-seven percent. Close enough to maintain Mario's natural talents, but different enough to allow for enhancement. VSM hadn't just cloned Mario Richard, they'd improved upon him.

Now she just had to figure out how to tell Liam.

Harper locked her phone, needing a moment to process what she'd discovered. The flight attendant's announcement about beginning descent barely registered as her mind pieced together what she knew about Mario Richard and Liam Desjardins.

The baseline genetic advantages that made Mario great were all there in Liam, but enhanced, optimized, pushed beyond what nature intended. The differences told the real story.

Where Mario had been purely French-Canadian, with pale skin and auburn hair, Liam's features reflected a careful genetic orchestration. His mixed-race appearance wasn't random, it was calculated. A design choice that provided cover for the modifications beneath the surface and the family he would be placed in.

The evidence was there in the data. Accelerated healing that had baffled Team Canada's medical staff when Liam took that hit against Sweden. Speed that somehow exceeded Mario's legendary pace. Stamina that seemed to defy natural limits.

Ryan's warnings about CRISPR echoed in her mind. The technology didn't just allow for genetic copying, it enabled precise editing, selective enhancement. Those mysterious markers the lab had noted? They weren't accidents or contamination. They were signatures of intentional modification.

Nature had blessed Mario with exceptional genes, but VSM had taken those genes and rewritten the rules. Where Mario's body followed the natural limits of human recovery and endurance, Liam's enhanced genetics let him bypass those restrictions entirely. The same foundation, but engineered beyond normal human constraints.

The lab's suggestion of contamination almost made her laugh. This wasn't contamination, it was calculation. An 87% match meant enough of Mario's genetic blueprint to capture his athletic foundation, but with room for enhancement. Room for *improvement.*

But beneath the scientific research lay a more immediate truth. Somewhere in Minnesota, a young man was preparing for the biggest moment of his hockey career, unaware that his entire identity was about to be called into question. Unaware that his very existence represented a line crossed, a boundary between natural talent and engineered excellence that could never be redrawn.

"Ladies and gentlemen, we're beginning our descent into Minneapolis-Saint Paul airport" the pilot's voice crackled over the intercom. "Due to heavy snow and strong crosswinds, we'll be taking a longer approach from the north. It's going to be bumpy, so please remain in your seats with your seatbelts fastened."

Harper glanced out the window at the darkening sky, thick clouds promising worse weather ahead. Her phone showed three messages from Liam:

Ready for dinner? followed by *Wild game tonight* and finally *Weather is getting bad here.*

The plane lurched, dropping suddenly before stabilizing. Passengers gasped. Harper gripped her laptop bag tighter, protecting the evidence that would change everything.

"Flight crew, final approach," the pilot announced as they descended through the storm. The snow had intensified, creating a white wall visible in the landing lights. The plane rocked in the fierce winds, each gust feeling like nature itself was trying to prevent their landing.

The descent felt endless, the plane fighting crosswinds that slammed against its wings. Harper's knuckles whitened around her armrest. A flash of lightning illuminated the snow-swept runway below, still distant, but approaching fast.

"Just another day in the bold north," the flight attendant said cheerfully, though her smile seemed forced. "Welcome to Minnesota."

The wheels touched down hard, the plane bouncing once before the reverse thrusters roared to life. Snow sprayed up from the runway, creating an otherworldly effect in the landing lights. As they taxied toward the gate, Harper powered up her phone to find another message from Liam:

Roads are bad. Sending car service for you.

A thoughtful gesture. Through the window, the terminal lights illuminated an endless curtain of snow. Somewhere out there, Liam was waiting.

Storm Break

"Slow down, Harper. A story like this changes lives, we can't misstep." – Frank

Harper Sinclair strode down the snowy jet bridge, her boots slipping against the metal floor, the cool air of the jet bridge hitting her like a wake-up call. Minneapolis–Saint Paul International Airport bustled around her, but her mind was already two steps ahead, fingers already on her phone.

Without missing a beat, she dialed Frank Taylor, her editor at True North Hockey, weaving through the steady flow of travelers. She could picture him now, his broad-shouldered six-foot frame hunched over his desk, salt-and-pepper hair slightly disheveled, reading glasses perched on his nose when he thought no one was watching.

"Harper?" Frank answered, his gravelly voice carrying that familiar mix of concern and anticipation, many years of shouting in noisy press boxes had left their mark.

"I'm here," she replied, steadying herself despite the adrenaline coursing through her veins. "Did you read what I sent?"

"Been reading it for the last hour," Frank said, and she could imagine him now, perpetual five o'clock shadow on his weathered face, probably chewing on the end of a pen as he pored over the documents. "Team's already reaching out to fertility clinic. We've also asked the DNA lab to retest the sample quality."

"Then you know why we need to move fast. Tonight, after the Wild game. Full press conference."

Frank's sigh carried the weight of decades in journalism, his calculating gray eyes surely scanning the newsroom as he considered their options. "Harper, you know we can't just—"

"VSM is watching Liam," Harper cut in, her voice sharp. "Ben's hovering over him like a hawk. Whatever they're planning."

"Stop." Frank's tone hardened. "I know you want to protect him. But we do this right. VSM gets a chance to respond before we go public. That's not negotiable."

Harper's knuckles whitened around her phone. "They'll bury it, Frank. You know they will."

"Maybe. But we're journalists, not vigilantes. I've got people verifying every detail, every connection. If this story's as solid as you say, VSM's response won't matter. Truth holds up."

The terminal crowd thinned as Harper approached the exit, Minnesota's winter wind howling beyond the doors. "How long will verification take?"

"Few hours. Already have one confirmation on the fertility clinic connection to VSM." A pause. "But VSM gets their shot at a response. Period."

Harper watched snow dance in the airport lights, her breath fogging the glass. "Fine. But I need to get to Liam first. Before they figure out what's coming."

"Be careful," Frank warned. "And Harper? This is bigger than anything we've handled."

"I know." She stepped through the sliding doors, the cold biting through her coat. "That's why we can't get it wrong."

Her Uber was waiting, wipers fighting a losing battle against the snow. As she settled into the backseat, Harper dialed another number, her heart pounding harder than before.

Mario Richard answered. "Harper."

"It's confirmed," she said quietly. "The lab results are conclusive."

The silence stretched long enough for Harper to hear Mario's measured breathing. When he spoke, his voice was tight with controlled anger. "How did they, during the treatments?"

"Yes. When you were focused on surviving, they were..." She let the sentence hang.

Another pause, heavier this time. "I have some calls to make. Family that needs to know before this breaks."

"I understand." Harper watched Saint Paul's skyline emerge through the storm. "Mario? I'm sorry."

"Don't be," he replied, his voice caught slightly. "My wife... the kids... how do I even begin to explain this?"

The call ended, leaving Harper alone with her thoughts and the steady sweep of windshield wipers. Her phone buzzed, a text from Jessica: *Need me to fly in?*

Harper smiled. Not yet. But soon, she'd need every ally she could trust.

One more call to make. Somewhere in the Xcel Energy Center, Liam was watching a hockey game, unaware that his past was about to collide with his future.

That collision was about to happen.

* * *

"Let's Play Hockey!" The traditional call echoed through the Xcel Energy Center, bringing fans to their feet. From Suite 21, Liam watched the crowd roar in response, their enthusiasm undampened by the storm raging outside. The arena was packed, weather never kept Minnesota hockey fans home.

Through the arena's windows, snow swirled past the lights of Rice Park. Inside, the suite hummed with celebration. Jim and Tammy beamed with pride while his friends Axel and Gunner debated Wild defensive pairings with the intensity only hockey players could muster. Axel's six-foot frame was draped in his favorite Wild sweatshirt, his dark brown hair flow, what players called lettuce, spilling out from under a Minnesota snapback. His mustache twitched as he gestured animatedly, the tear-shaped tattoo on his right hand visible when he pointed at the ice. Even off the ice, Axel carried himself with the bold confidence that had made him stand out since their days with the Wheat Kings.

Next to him, Gunner Hansen's imposing six-foot-three frame filled out his Team Canada jacket, a physical presence befitting a shutdown defenseman. His long, flowy hockey hair rivaled Axel's, though Gunner spent more time adjusting his, a trademark he took perhaps too much pride in. His deep brown eyes tracked the play on the ice with the same intensity he brought to every game, while the stubble on his strong jawline gave him the rugged look of a true blue-liner. Even in the suite's casual atmosphere, he carried himself with the quiet confidence of someone who'd earned his spot through countless battles along the boards.

A display near the suite's entrance caught Liam's eye, jerseys from Minnesota state high school teams, celebrating teams from across the state. Next to them, a North Stars jersey reminded visitors of the state's NHL heritage.

"Pretty special, isn't it?" Dave Wilson, the Wild's assistant GM, gestured at the memorabilia. "State High School Tournament's played right here. Whole state shuts down for it. That's what makes Minnesota different, hockey's not just a sport here, it's culture."

Liam nodded, trying to focus on Dave's words while keeping track of Ben LaFleur's position. His agent hadn't moved far from the suite door all evening, his casual pose betrayed by watchful eyes.

The crowd erupted as the Wild's top line created a scoring chance. Liam used the moment to check his phone again, anxiety building. Harper's words from their brief call earlier kept echoing in his mind:

Get away from Ben. I need to see you, alone.

"Your boy's got good instincts," Dave's voice carried over the crowd noise as he talked with Jim. "Natural talent."

Natural. The word hit Liam like a body check. Nothing felt natural anymore, not since Ryan's revelations about his parents, not since Harper started digging.

His phone vibrated. Harper again.

"Excuse me," Liam muttered, moving toward the suite's private bathroom. Ben straightened slightly, but a cheer from the crowd drew his attention, the Wild had scored.

"Harper?" Liam kept his voice low.

"I'm here in Saint Paul, near the hockey lodge store." Her tone was urgent. "I have something to show you, Liam. About everything. But we need to meet now."

Liam's heart jumped. "Ben's watching me like a hawk."

"I know. But this can't wait. Can you get to the lower level? Use the crowd as cover?"

Through the suite's windows, the storm intensified, snow nearly obscuring Rice Park's festival lights. The weather could work in his favor, confusion was his ally now.

"Give me ten minutes," Liam said. "I'll find a way."

He ended the call, mind racing. The suite level was a maze of hallways and service areas. If he timed it right...

"Great goal!" Axel's voice boomed as Liam emerged. "Did you see that snipe?"

Liam forced a smile, noting Ben's position had shifted closer to the door. The storm outside grew fiercer, visible through the windows. Maybe, Liam thought, nature was offering him the chaos he needed to slip away.

He just had to figure out how to use it.

* * *

Marcus leaned against a pillar near the hockey lodge store in the arena, phone pressed to his ear. "She's here, exactly where you said. Waiting for something."

"Or someone," Finn replied from the VSM jet. "Where's Ben?"

"Suite level. Still has eyes on Liam." Marcus watched Harper pretend to browse Wild merchandise. "But she's positioned herself near the main stairs. If the kid tries to slip away..."

"He won't." Finn's voice carried less conviction than usual. "Ben knows what's at—"

Marcus's phone buzzed with another call. Montreal office. Lou.

"Hold on," Marcus cut in. "Your uncle's calling."

Without waiting for Finn's response, Marcus switched lines. "Mr. Booker."

"Tell me exactly what's happening." Lou's voice carried the weight of authority, his French-Canadian accent thickening with irritation.

"Harper Sinclair's at the hockey lodge. Watching the stairs. Ben's upstairs with—"

"Non, non," Lou cut in. "Tell me what's really happening. My nephew, he's losing control, n'est-ce pas?"

Marcus hesitated. Finn was his direct boss, but Lou signed the checks. "She's acting differently. More focused. Like someone who found what they were looking for."

"And if she reaches the boy?"

"I can stop—"

"Pas comme ça," Lou growled. "Not there. Too public. But she cannot leave with whatever she's carrying. Comprenez-vous?"

Marcus understood perfectly. "What about Finn's approach?"

"My nephew..." Lou's laugh carried no warmth. "He still thinks we're playing by rules. Tell him... tell him I'm taking charge now. And Marcus? Whatever happens to her evidence, happens. Accidents exist, non?"

Lou disconnected. Marcus switched back to Finn's call.

"What did he say?" Finn's voice was tense.

"He's concerned about Harper's evidence." Marcus kept his voice neutral. "Wants us to secure it."

"That's all?"

"He's taking direct control of the situation." Marcus watched Harper move closer to the stairs. "Said to tell you he's handling things now."

Silence stretched across the connection. Finally, Finn spoke, his voice tight. "Stay on her. I land in twenty minutes. And Marcus? Whatever my uncle said... we're not there yet. Understood?"

But they were there, Marcus knew. Lou's instructions had been clear enough. The only question was whether Finn would accept what had to be done.

"Understood," Marcus lied, ending the call. He shifted position, hand brushing the inside of his jacket. Some assignments required tools that expense reports never saw.

His phone buzzed again. A text from Lou: *Whatever it takes. Protect our investment.*

Marcus deleted the message, eyes locked on Harper. The game crowds moved around him like a river around a stone, but he barely noticed them now. His world had narrowed to a single point of focus.

The time for subtlety was ending.

* * *

Jimmy Larson leaned against the suite's wall, his six-foot-one frame built like a tank from years of battling in the corners. His dirty blonde hair was messy like he just removed his helmet after a morning skate, and a chipped tooth showed when he grinned at his former teammates' debate.

Even in casual clothes, he carried himself with the same physical presence that made him such an effective power forward, the kind of player who created space through sheer determination. His green eyes sparkled with mischief as he caught Liam's subtle signal, ready as always to join whatever plan was brewing.

Liam pulled Axel, Gunner, and Jimmy into a hallway as the first period winded down. "I need a favor. I need to lose Ben for a few minutes."

"Finally making a move on that girl from the hotel lobby?" Jimmy grinned, nudging Axel.

"Must be serious if you're dodging the agent," Gunner added with a knowing smile.

"It's not—" Liam started, but Axel cut him off.

"Don't even try denying it. We're helping, and we're coming with you."

"Guys, listen—"

"Not happening," Gunner's voice was firm. "We saw the way your agent's watching you. Besides, you need wingmen."

Liam hesitated. The less they knew, the safer they'd be. But these three had been there since Brandon, through every up and down. "Fine. But follow my lead."

Back in the suite, Ben's eyes tracked their return. Jimmy immediately launched into a story about the Minnesota state tournament, drawing Ben's attention while Axel and Gunner casually positioned themselves near the door.

"One minute, one minute remaining in the first period," the PA announced.

Liam checked his phone, then nodded to his friends. Time to move.

"Man, I'm starving," Axel announced. "Hey Ben, what's good at the concession stands downstairs?"

Ben's eyes narrowed slightly. "I can have something brought up."

"Nah, we need to stretch our legs anyway," Jimmy chimed in. "Coming, Liam?"

Jim and Tammy were deep in conversation with Dave Wilson about Minnesota's hockey heritage. Perfect timing.

"Back in a few," Liam called to his parents. Ben shifted his weight, clearly calculating whether following four players through intermission crowds would be too obvious.

They moved into the hallway, Ben trailing at a discrete distance. At the junction leading to the main stairs, Axel suddenly stopped. "Oh man, forgot my wallet in the suite."

Ben hesitated, follow Axel back or stay with Liam?

"I'll go with him," Gunner offered, already turning. "Meet you guys down there."

The split-second of confusion was all they needed. Liam and Jimmy slipped into the crowd moving downstairs while Ben's view was blocked. By the time Ben pushed through the crowd, they were already emerging near the hockey lodge down below.

Harper stood near a display of Wild jerseys, their eyes meeting across the space. No words needed. She turned toward the exit, Liam falling into step beside her.

Behind them, Axel, Gunner, and Jimmy appeared at the stairs, their plan having worked perfectly. Through the crowd and arena lights, they could only make out a feminine silhouette ahead of them. They smoothly joined the path, keeping Ben's faint shouts behind them as they pushed through the doors into the storm.

Ahead, through the swirling snow, Rice Park's winter lights beckoned.

Rice Park

"Stick together, boys. Doesn't matter if it's the ice or the storm, team stays together." – Axel

The arena doors burst open, winter air rushing to meet them. Liam stepped into the storm beside Harper, his breath visible in quick, sharp clouds. Behind them, his friends emerged laughing, still riding the high of their successful escape.

"Man, Ben's face when we split up," Axel chuckled, zipping his jacket against the cold. "Priceless."

"Like that time in Brandon when Coach caught us sneaking out to Timmy's," Jimmy added, grinning at the memory.

"Except Ben's scarier than Coach ever was," Gunner said, his smile fading slightly as he glanced back at the arena doors.

Snow whirled under the streetlights, transforming Rice Park into a glowing wonderland. Festival crowds moved through the storm like shadows, their voices carrying faintly over the wind. Carnival music drifted across the park, dreamlike and distant.

"So where are we..." Jimmy started, but his words died as a gust of wind cut through them.

"Saint Paul Hotel," Harper said quietly to Liam, her voice barely audible above the storm. Her eyes met his, conveying urgency that made his stomach tighten. "We'll talk there."

Gunner pulled his Wild hat lower, squinting through the snow at the figure walking beside his friend. In the shifting light, she was just a silhouette, purposeful and determined.

"Never seen you move this fast for a girl, Blade," Axel teased from behind them. "Not even for that figure skater in London."

"The one who kept showing up at practice?" Jimmy laughed. "What was her name again?"

But Liam barely heard them. Their familiar banter, usually a comfort, felt distant now, like echoes from another life. One where secrets weren't unraveling around him.

They moved past the darkened Wild offices, where Herb Brooks statue stood sentinel in the falling snow. Liam remembered Jim's favorite Brooks quote, one he'd repeated since Liam was young: *Write your own book instead of reading someone else's book about success.* The words hit differently now, sharp with new meaning.

Inside, shadows moved with unusual urgency for this hour. A news van pulled up, its satellite dish stark against the snowy sky.

"Something's up," Gunner muttered, his defenseman's instincts kicking in. He moved closer to Liam's left, while Axel flanked his right. Jimmy took up position behind them, their years of playing together showing in how naturally they moved as a unit.

The festival crowds grew thicker as they entered the park proper. Families huddled around ice sculptures, their camera flashes brief starbursts in the storm. Children darted past, wrapped in winter gear, their laughter a stark contrast to the weight settling over Liam's shoulders.

"You okay?" Gunner asked, catching up to walk beside him. "We can still—"

"I'm good," Liam cut him off, his voice tight. But his eyes never left Harper's back as she guided them deeper into the carnival's glow, toward whatever truth waited at the hotel across the park.

"Remember what Coach always said?" Axel spoke up, his voice carrying that same steady confidence he brought to every game. "Team stays together. No matter what."

Jimmy nodded, falling into step. "Through any storm."

Behind them all, unnoticed in the swirling snow, Marcus pressed his phone to his ear. "They're heading east," he said quietly. "Through Rice Park." He paused, listening. "No. Not alone. His friends are with him." Another pause. "Four protecting one. Like they're running interference."

An ice dragon loomed ahead, its crystalline wings catching carnival lights in rainbow fragments. Around its base, children posed for photos while parents huddled against the cold, their phone flashes adding to the dreamlike atmosphere.

"Check that out!" Jimmy pointed toward the sculpture. "Way better than those fish they had last year."

"Those weren't fish," Axel laughed, snow collecting on his shoulders. "They were supposed to be hockey players."

"Yeah, well, they looked like fish."

The banter died as they passed beneath a row of festival lights. The sudden brightness cut through the snow like a spotlight, illuminating what the storm had hidden. Gunner stopped dead in his tracks, his defenseman's instincts firing. "Hold up." His voice carried an edge that made the others turn. "That's not just some girl."

Axel squinted through the snow. "What do you mean?" Then recognition hit him like a bodycheck. "Harper Sinclair? From True North?"

Jimmy's playful grin vanished. "The reporter who covered Ethan's memorial game?"

Ahead, Harper and Liam pushed through the crowd, their dark figures stark against the carnival's glow. The mention of Ethan's name hung in the air between the friends, heavy with unspoken questions.

"Something's wrong," Gunner said, his defensive instincts taking over. "Ben watching him like a hawk, Harper showing up out of nowhere..."

"The media trucks at the arena," Jimmy added, pieces falling into place.

Axel caught movement in his peripheral vision, a man in a dark coat, phone to his ear, trying too hard to look casual. "We've got a shadow," he muttered, years of checking his surroundings on road trips kicking in. "Ten o'clock, near the dragon sculpture."

Through the swirling snow, Marcus Chen tracked their progress, his phone pressed tight against his ear. "They've made me," he spoke quietly into the phone.

Finn's voice crackled back, competed with airport noise. "Stay on them. I'm fifteen minutes out."

"You sure about this?" Marcus watched the group tighten their formation around Liam and Harper.

A family wearing Wild jerseys cut between Marcus and his targets, forcing him to adjust position. When they passed, he caught Ben's voice through his earpiece, breathless from running. "Almost there. Don't lose them."

The torchlight parade was assembling near the park's center, its warm glow casting long shadows across the snow. Harper guided them along its edge, using the gathering crowd as cover. Ahead, the Saint Paul Hotel's historic facade rose like a fortress against the dark sky.

"Whatever's going on," Gunner said quietly to his friends, "we don't leave them alone." His eyes tracked Marcus's position while keeping pace with Liam.

"No chance," Axel agreed, his usual joking manner replaced with steady resolve. Behind them, Jimmy had already pulled his phone out, documenting faces, positions, anything that might matter later.

They passed Babe the Blue Ox, the massive ice sculpture dwarfing the festival-goers around it. But none of them were admiring the artwork now. The carnival's magic had transformed into something else, a maze of shadows and light where every passing figure might be friend or foe.

Through the hotel's windows, they could see activity in the lobby. Whatever truth Harper carried, whatever had brought them through this storm, they were about to face it together.

Behind them, Marcus's voice carried faintly through the wind: "They're approaching the hotel. Moving fast. Better hurry."

The torchlight parade participants gathered in formation, their flames cutting orange swaths through the snowfall. The heat from their torches created small pockets of clear air in the storm, moments of sharp clarity in the swirling white.

Marcus kept pace through the crowd, careful now that they'd spotted him. The carnival crowd surged around him like rapids, threatening to break his sightline. His phone buzzed with increasing urgency, VSM's coordination falling apart in real time.

Ben: *Where are they?*

Finn: *Ten minutes out. Don't lose them.*

Ben: *Almost there. West side of park.*

The group ahead moved with purpose, no longer five separate people but a single unit.

"More company," Jimmy murmured, catching glimpses of Ben's dark coat through gaps in the parade line. "Coming in from behind."

Axel nodded without turning. "Saw him." His voice was calm, but his eyes never stopped scanning. "Gunner?"

"Got the front." Gunner had already moved slightly ahead and to the left, giving himself a better view of the approaching hotel entrance. "Jimmy?"

"On it." Jimmy shifted to cover their right flank, his phone still out, still documenting.

Harper glanced back at their defensive alignment, a mix of respect and concern crossing her face. She leaned closer to Liam, speaking just loud enough for him to hear. "Your friends... they're good."

"The best," Liam answered, and meant it.

They passed the final row of ice sculptures, the hotel's grand entrance now clearly visible ahead. Through the windows of the Wild offices across the park, they could see more media arriving, more equipment being rushed in. The night was building toward something bigger than just their small group moving through the snow.

Marcus's phone lit up again.

Finn: *Coming in hot. Five minutes.*

Ben: *Visual confirmed. Moving to intercept.*

Finn: *DO NOT engage. Wait for me.*

But Marcus could see the urgency in Ben's stride as he pushed through the crowd. The agent wasn't going to wait. Not with Harper so close to getting Liam behind closed doors.

"Last stretch," Gunner called softly. "Moving now."

The hotel doorman recognized their urgency, holding the heavy door open without question. They crossed the threshold in tight formation, the warmth of the lobby washing over them as carnival sounds faded to a muffled hum. A conference room waited down the hall, its polished wood door standing open.

The concierge smoothly diverted a group of carnival-goers toward the hotel's famous lobby bar, while security cameras tracked silent patterns across the hallway's dark corners.

Inside, the room felt impossibly quiet after the storm. Dark wood paneling absorbed the soft lamplight, creating shadows in the corners. Through the windows, carnival lights still pulsed, but they felt distant now, like signals from another world.

"We'll wait outside," Gunner said, his voice steady. But his eyes held questions as they swept the room, checking exits, positions, sightlines.

"Should be safe here," Harper added, catching his tactical assessment. "Your friends... they're welcome to stay close."

Axel nodded, already moving to position himself near the door. Jimmy took up a spot by the window, phone still in hand, while Gunner remained in the doorway, his broad shoulders filling the frame.

"Whatever this is," Gunner said quietly to Liam, "just say the word."

Liam managed a tight smile. "I know."

The room carried that distinct hotel scent, leather chairs, coffee service, and fresh linen tablecloths laid out for tomorrow's breakfast meeting.

The door clicked shut, leaving Liam and Harper alone in the room. Outside, muffled festival music filtered through the walls, an oddly cheerful counterpoint to the tension in the room.

Harper set her bag on the polished table, her movements deliberate. "I'm sorry about all this," she began, but Liam cut her off.

"Just... tell me."

She nodded, understanding the weight of each passing second. From her bag, she withdrew a large manila envelope, placing it carefully on the table between them. Through the windows, Marcus and Ben conferred in the park, their dark figures stark against the carnival lights. A black town car pulled up to the curb, Finn arriving at last. But none of that seemed to matter now.

Liam stared at the envelope Harper placed between them. Everything in his life, his parents, Ethan, his future, felt balanced on this single moment.

Some truths, once known, could never be unknown. But he was ready. Ready to understand why Ben watched his every move, why VSM kept such careful track of his development, why everything in his life felt just slightly off-center.

Ready to know who, or what, he really was.

Who Am I?

"You don't have to face this alone. Whatever it is, we're here. Just like we've always been." – Jimmy

The envelope lay between them on the polished table, its manila surface catching soft light from the chandelier above. The Saint Paul Hotel's conference room felt impossibly warm, its dark wood paneling and heavy curtains creating an intimate cocoon that seemed to press in around them. Outside, muffled sounds of celebration filtered through the thick windows, a different world entirely from the one about to unfold in here.

Liam's fingers hovered over the clasp, leaving damp prints when they finally made contact. This wasn't just paper, it was Pandora's box, containing truths he couldn't un-know once revealed. His heart pounded a relentless rhythm as the room seemed to shrink, the walls drawing closer to witness this moment.

Before he could open it, Harper leaned forward, her professional demeanor softening. The journalist's sharp edges melted away, leaving something more human, more vulnerable in their place. Her voice, when it came, was gentle but steady.

"Liam," she started, unconsciously mirroring his posture, "before I show you this... I need you to know something."

Liam looked at her once again.

"Whatever's in this envelope, it doesn't change who you are. You're still Liam Desjardins. Still the same person who makes Jim and Tammy proud every day, not just on the ice but in everything you do. The same kid who helped your mom organize the library fundraiser last summer. The same friend who visited Ethan's parents after..." She paused, letting that settle. "Still the same player who lights up the ice, still the same person your friends would follow into a storm."

Her words, meant as comfort, seemed to float between them like snowflakes, beautiful but impossible to grasp. He wanted to believe her, needed to, but how could he, when he already felt the ground beneath him shifting?

Harper's phone vibrated against the tabletop, cutting through the charged silence. The caller ID flashed 'Frank Taylor,' but she didn't give it more than a glance before silencing it with a swift tap. This was not the time for interruptions. The weight of her gaze returned to Liam, and he could see the gravity in her eyes warring with her innate compassion.

Through the windows, the winter carnival continued its celebration. Festival lights caught the falling snow, creating halos of color that seemed to pulse with Liam's racing heartbeat. A bead of cold sweat traced down his spine despite the room's warmth.

"I'm ready," he said, though his voice cracked on the words, betraying his uncertainty. His fingers tightened on the envelope until his knuckles went white, anchoring himself to something tangible.

Harper drew in a deep breath and exhaled slowly, her calm exterior showing the first cracks of emotion. Whatever truth she carried was heavy enough to weigh on even her seasoned shoulders. "Okay," she said softly, nodding toward the envelope. "Open it."

The sound of the clasp releasing seemed unnaturally loud in the quiet room, like a starting gun at a race Liam never wanted to run.

Harper watched as Liam pulled a stack of papers from the envelope, his hands trembling more with each page. Medical records. DNA sequences. Project files. Through the conference room windows, festival lights caught snowflakes in their glow, creating brief moments of beauty before darkness swallowed them.

Through the window's reflection, he caught glimpses of Gunner's silhouette moving past the frosted glass panels, a steady presence keeping watch while Liam's world unraveled inside.

She drew in a deep breath and exhaled slowly before continuing, her voice steady but tinged with the burden of what she had to say. "VSM wanted to build athletes they could control from scratch, perfect specimens molded from former superstar athletes."

Liam's brow furrowed as he tried to follow Harper's line of thought. His mouth felt like cotton, tongue too thick to form words. "They...what? How does that even work?"

"They stole DNA from Mario Richard," Harper said, her voice tight with controlled anger. "And they used it to create you."

Liam's vision blurred, then sharpened with painful clarity on a poster that had hung above his bed for years, Mario Richard, mid-shot, the puck leaving his stick in that perfect, signature release. The memory hit him like a bodycheck he never saw coming.

"So... is Mario my father?" The words stumbled out in a half-whisper, half-gasp, as if saying them would somehow make this revelation less surreal.

Harper hesitated, her expression softening with empathy before delivering the next blow. "Not exactly." She took another breath, as though bracing herself. "Liam... you were cloned from Mario."

"What?" Liam barked out a laugh, but it held no humor. "Human cloning? That's not—"

He pushed back from the table, chair scraping against the floor. "This is crazy. Did Ryan put you up to this? Because this isn't funny."

"Liam..."

"No, this is insane. Human cloning isn't even real." His voice rose with each word, riding the edge of hysteria. "It's science fiction. This has to be some kind of twisted conspiracy theory."

Harper's phone buzzed again, Frank Taylor's name flashing insistently, but she silenced it without looking. She waited, letting Liam process, watching as denial warred with the evidence in front of him.

"The DNA tests..." she started gently.

"Could be fake. Could be wrong." But even as he said it, his eyes dropped to the papers scattered across the table. Cold sweat beaded on his forehead despite the room's warmth. "This can't... this isn't..."

Liam pushed himself up from the table, needing distance from the papers, from Harper, from this impossible truth. He stumbled to the window, pressing his forehead against the cool glass. Below, media vans were gathering at the Wild offices across Rice Park, their satellite dishes raised like sentinels against the darkening sky. Whatever was coming, it wasn't just going to change his world, it was going to change everything.

"There's going to be a press conference after the game," she said softly. "You don't have to be there. You don't have to be anywhere you don't want to be."

Liam barely heard her. His mind was stuck.

Harper's phone buzzed again, the vibration seeming to match Liam's trembling hands. Frank Taylor's name appeared and disappeared like a warning.

"I need..." Liam started, but couldn't finish. What did he need? His world had dissolved into fragments, nothing solid left to grab onto.

Inside the warm quiet of the conference room, Liam struggled with questions he never imagined having to ask. Who was he, really? Every memory, every moment that made him who he was, were they truly his? Or was he just... a copy? The word felt wrong, incomplete, unable to capture the life he'd lived, the person he'd become.

Harper cleared her throat softly. "Liam..." The gentleness in her voice made him turn from the window, and what he saw in her expression told him there was still more truth to face.

Your friend Ethan..." Harper's voice trailed off, heavy with the weight of what she had to share. "He was like you. A clone of Mario."

The words hit Liam like a punch to the chest, driving the air from his lungs. He gripped the window frame, his legs suddenly unsteady beneath him. "No," he whispered. "Not Ethan."

The memory crashed over him without warning, Ethan sprawled on his basement floor, both of them watching Mario Richard highlights for the hundredth time. *Look at that release,* Ethan had said, rewinding the clip again and again. *It's like poetry, man. Pure poetry.* They'd spent hours trying to copy that shot, not knowing, never suspecting...

"The DNA tests confirm it," Harper continued softly. "You and Ethan... you were both part of VSM's program."

Liam turned from the window, his face pale. "Did he know?" The question came out raw, desperate. "Before he... did Ethan know what he was?"

"No," Harper shook her head. "I don't think anyone knew except VSM and the scientists involved."

Her phone buzzed again, Frank's calls growing more insistent, but neither of them acknowledged it. The truth about Ethan hung in the air between them, too heavy for interruptions.

"We were brothers," Liam said quietly, the realization dawning with terrible clarity. "Not just friends or teammates. We were actually..." His voice cracked. "And he's gone."

Harper stood, taking a tentative step toward him. "Liam, there's something else you need to know. About what happened to Ethan..."

A sharp knock at the door made them both jump. Through the frosted glass, they could see a familiar silhouette. Ben's voice carried through the door. "Liam? Are you in there?"

Outside, they heard Gunner's steady voice. "Sorry, Ben. Private meeting."

"I'm his agent," Ben's tone sharpened. "He needs to prepare for tomorrow's meeting with the Wild."

"We know who you are," Axel's voice now, unusually serious. "But right now, you wait."

Jimmy added something too quiet to hear, but Ben's frustrated sigh carried through the door.

Liam stared out at the growing media presence across Rice Park, the reality of what Harper had said earlier about the press conference taking on new weight. It wasn't just his story anymore, it was Ethan's too. Their story.

"His parents," Liam managed, his voice thick. "Tom and Sue... do they know?"

"Not yet." Harper's answer was soft, careful. "But they will, soon. Everyone will."

The knock came again, more insistent this time. Through the door, they could hear Ben's voice rising, Gunner's steady replies growing tighter. But Liam barely registered the brewing confrontation. His mind was locked on a terrible truth that couldn't be unknown. Not just his world, but everyone's, his parents, Ethan's parents, the entire hockey community, everything was about to change. And at the center of it all stood two boys who had just wanted to play hockey, who had become pawns in a game they never knew existed.

Ben would get through eventually, he was still Liam's agent, still held authority in the hockey world they lived in. But for these few precious moments before everything exploded, Liam needed to understand what they'd done to him. What they'd done to Ethan. What they'd done to all of them.

"Don't answer it," Harper whispered, already gathering the scattered papers from the table. Her movements were quick but deliberate, like she'd rehearsed this moment.

The knocking stopped. For a heartbeat, Liam thought Ben might have left. Then the door handle turned.

Ben pushed into the doorway, but Gunner and Axel were faster, their hockey instincts taking over as they caught him by the shoulders. Jimmy stepped between them, hands raised.

"Easy," Harper called out, her voice cutting through the tension. She nodded to the friends. "It's okay. Let him in."

The three hockey players exchanged glances before releasing Ben, who straightened his jacket with forced composure. His usually controlled demeanor cracked as he took in the scene, Harper stuffing papers into her bag, Liam pale and shaken by the window.

Liam turned back to the window, unable to look at Ben, unable to process one more thing. His reflection stared back at him from the glass, suddenly foreign, like looking at a stranger wearing his face.

"Ben," Harper's voice cut through the silence, professional and sharp. "We both know what's about to happen. Give him space." She shouldered her bag, moving toward the door. "I'll see you at the press conference."

Ben hesitated, glancing at Liam's back. "Don't believe her Liam," he said finally, before stepping out.

Harper paused at the door. "Liam..." But whatever she meant to say died on her lips. Some moments demanded silence.

She turned to Axel, Gunner, and Jimmy, who had moved to the far corner of the room, giving Liam space while maintaining their protective watch. "Stay with him," she told them quietly. "Don't let anyone else in this room, no matter who they are." The three friends exchanged glances before nodding, understanding the gravity in her voice.

As she stepped into the hallway, Ben hadn't moved far. "Frank Taylor's calling VSM right now," she said, keeping her voice low. "True North is giving Lou a chance to comment before we run the story."

Ben's professional mask slipped for just a moment. "Harper..."

"You knew, Ben. All these years, you knew." She shouldered her bag, already turning away. "Make sure Lou gets that call."

Through the hallway window, she could see Finn and Marcus waiting in the park below. Ben hesitated a moment longer, then headed toward the elevator to join them.

Inside the room, Liam kept his forehead pressed against the cool glass, unable to turn around, unable to face his friends. How could he? They were real people, with real histories, real families. What was he?

The question echoed in his mind as his friends' concerned voices faded into background noise. Outside, the carnival lights blurred through unshed tears, and somewhere across the park, a press conference was about to change everything.

Faceoff

"Most people bundle up, hesitant to face a storm like this. Not her. She walked out like she was chasing something, or maybe running from it." – Doorman

Harper strode through the hotel lobby toward the front entrance, her bag heavy with evidence against VSM. Through the frosted windows, she could see Ben already outside, moving across Rice Park where Marcus waited. Her breath caught when she spotted a third figure joining them, Finn Booker.

Her phone buzzed, Frank Taylor's fifteenth call in the last hour.

This time, she answered.

"Harper, we're doing this now," Frank's voice crackled through the speaker. "Conference call with Lou Booker. You ready?"

She paused near the entrance, watching Ben, Finn, and Marcus converge near one of the ice sculptures. The Winter Carnival lights painted Rice Park in shifting colors, families still enjoying the festivities. "Do it."

The line clicked, and Lou's voice filled her ear, all fake warmth and practiced charm. "Frank! What's so urgent that you're pulling me away from the NHL committee meeting? I was just telling Commissioner—"

"Cut the act, Lou." Frank's tone was ice. "We're running a story about VSM's involvement in human cloning. We're giving you one chance to comment."

Silence. Then a low chuckle that didn't quite mask Lou's nervousness. "Human cloning? Frank, have you lost your mind?"

Harper started pacing near the windows in the hotel lobby. "We have the DNA tests, Lou. Mario Richard and Liam Desjardins. We have the paper trail linking VSM to GeneCore, and Furever Genetics. We have you."

"You have nothing," Lou snapped, his fake charm evaporating. "And if you run this story, I'll—"

"You'll what?" Frank cut in. "Sue us? Go ahead. Truth is an absolute defense against libel, and we both know what the truth is."

The silence that followed was different, calculating. When Lou spoke again, his voice had changed. "You think you're protecting him? Liam?" A pause. "Did you ever wonder why Ben checks on him so often? Why we're so... particular about his medical care?"

Harper's steps slowed. "What are you talking about?"

"Cloning isn't perfect yet. These boys, they need treatments. Regular treatments. Without them..." Lou's voice dripped with false concern. "Well, just ask Ethan Bernard's parents."

Harper stopped walking. Her throat tightened. "That's a lie."

"Is it? Ask yourself why Ben never misses an appointment. Why we track every vitamin, every supplement." Lou's voice hardened. "You run this story, we're done. No more treatments. And Liam? He won't last a month."

Harper's free hand clenched into a fist, but doubt crept in. Had she missed something? She'd seen every medical record, every report, but what if...? The image of Ethan's collapse flashed through her mind, followed by Liam's face, young, trusting, with his whole future ahead of him.

"I..." she started, her voice less certain.

"Having second thoughts?" Lou pressed.

Harper's hand trembled against the window frame, her reflection ghostly in the frosted glass. The weight of Lou's words, of Liam's life, pressed down on her shoulders. For a moment, just a heartbeat, she saw herself walking away from all of this. Protecting Liam by staying silent.

"Good," Lou continued into her silence. "Because this isn't about protecting our reputation anymore. This is about keeping that boy alive."

Harper closed her eyes, forcing herself to think. No. The medical records were clean. Ben's reports were thorough. If there were treatments, there would be traces...

"Interesting theory, Lou," Harper said, forcing steel into her voice. "Funny how none of these supposed treatments show up in any medical records. Not in Ben's reports. Not anywhere."

"You think you have all our files? You think—"

"I think," Harper cut him off, pushing down her fears, "that you're terrified. I think you're making this up because you're desperate. And right now? You sound very, very desperate."

"Listen to me, you little—"

"No, you listen." Harper's voice was steel. "In thirty minutes, we're holding a press conference at the Wild offices. Your secret empire of genetic manipulation ends tonight."

"You have no idea what you're doing," Lou growled. "What you're risking—"

"See you in the headlines, Lou."

She ended the call, her breath fogging the window. The Wild offices loomed across Rice Park, she'd have to cross through VSM's territory to get there. Behind her, she could hear muffled voices from the conference room where Liam and his friends remained.

Her phone buzzed again. A text from Frank: *Watch your back.*

Harper shoved her phone in her pocket, straightening her shoulders. The press conference was thirty minutes away. She just had to make it across the park.

As she headed for the hotel's main entrance, she caught movement in the conference room window above, Liam's friends were watching, their faces tense with concern.

The bitter Minnesota night hit her as she pushed through the revolving doors. Ahead, Ben, Finn, and Marcus had spread out across the park, trying to look casual among the carnival-goers. They were waiting for her.

Marcus's phone buzzed in the swirling snow. Lou's message was brief: *She called the bluff. Take her. Now.*

He glanced at Finn, who had already received the same text. Through the carnival crowds, they could see Harper pushing through the hotel's revolving door, her breath visible in the cold air.

"Ben," Finn's voice was low, urgent. "Cut off the path by the sculpture garden. Don't let her double back toward the hotel."

Ben nodded, but his hesitation made Finn's patience snap. "Just do it," he ordered. "This ends tonight."

Harper moved with purpose through the carnival, her bag clutched close. Families laughed around ice sculptures, children chased each other with light-up toys, and vendors called out about hot chocolate and warm pretzels. The normalcy of it all made the hunters in her midst seem even more out of place.

Children shrieked with delight around a fire-breathing ice dragon sculpture. A street performer juggled flaming torches, his audience clapping in rhythm. The carnival music swelled, carousel melody mixing with vendors' calls and laughter. All of it a surreal backdrop to the deadly serious game of cat and mouse playing out in their midst.

The festival's rhythm faltered. Parents pulled their children closer, their conversations dropping to hushed murmurs. Teenagers, sensing the shift, raised their phones, catching Finn and Marcus in shaky frames, unsure if they were filming a fight or something far worse. The playful hum of the carnival dimmed, laughter tapering into uneasy silence. Something was happening. Everyone could feel it.

Marcus touched his earpiece. "She's heading toward the center path. Moving now."

Through the crowd, Harper caught glimpses of them repositioning, Marcus sliding between families, Finn circling wide, Ben hovering near the hotel's edge. They were herding her, she realized, away from the main carnival crowd toward the darker edges of the park.

Up in the hotel conference room, Axel watched Harper through the window. "They're surrounding her."

Gunner joined him, eyes narrowing. "Marcus on the left. Finn circling wide."

"Ben's hanging back," Jimmy added, his voice tight with concern. "But he's blocking her retreat."

Liam sat at the conference table, still processing the night's revelations, but Harper's name cut through his daze. "What about Harper?"

"VSM's got her trapped," Axel said, already moving toward the door. "They're pushing her away from the crowds."

Liam stood, his shock replaced by sudden clarity. Harper had risked everything to uncover the truth, his truth. Now she needed him. "Let's go."

They burst out of the conference room, taking the stairs two at a time. Through the hotel's glass doors, they could see Harper backing away from Marcus and Finn, moving deeper into the sculpture garden's shadows.

"Spread out," Liam commanded, his hockey captain's instincts kicking in. "Jimmy, take Marcus. Gunner, you're on Finn. Axel—"

The first sounds of struggle reached them as they pushed through the revolving door. Harper's elbow caught Marcus in the ribs, but Finn grabbed her arm, spinning her around. Blood appeared on her cheek where his ring cut her.

"Move!" Liam shouted, but they were too far away.

Marcus seized Harper from behind as her bag fell, scattering papers across the snow. Jimmy reached them first, launching himself at Marcus with a hockey player's precision. The tackle sent both men sprawling, and something metallic, a gun, flew from Marcus's jacket into the darkness.

Gunner slammed into Finn next, driving him away from Harper. Axel rushed to Harper's side, helping her to her feet while she wiped blood from her cheek.

"Get the gun!" Marcus shouted, struggling under Jimmy's grip. "Ben! Get the gun!"

Ben stood frozen, staring at the weapon half-buried in the snow. His eyes darted between the gun and Harper, indecision written across his face.

Liam reached Harper, dropping to his knees to gather the scattered papers. "Are you okay?" he asked, his voice thick with concern.

Harper nodded, though blood still trickled down her cheek, the metallic taste reaching her lips. She wiped it away with trembling fingers, her sleeve coming away stained red in the carnival lights. "We need those papers," she said. "And we need to move. Now."

The carnival continued around them, but a small crowd had begun to notice the violence in their midst. Ben still hadn't moved toward the gun, his loyalty to VSM fracturing against memories of college days with Harper.

"Ben!" Finn shouted, trying to break free from Gunner. "Do your job!"

The carnival lights cast shifting shadows across Ben's face as he stared at the gun.

"Ben!" Finn's voice cracked through the night air. "Pick up the damn gun! End this!"

Gunner tightened his hold on Finn, but Finn's words hung in the frigid air. Jimmy had Marcus pinned, but Marcus's eyes were locked on Ben, waiting.

Harper stood with Liam's support, blood flowing down her cheek. "Ben," she said softly, and something in her voice pulled him back to a coffee shop in Toronto, years ago, when things were simpler. When he wasn't part of this madness.

Ben's reached for the gun, his fingers brushed the gun's grip, cold metal grounding him in the moment. Years of secrets, of looking the other way, of justifying his choices, they all led here.

"That's it," Finn called out. "Now control this situation. Remember who you work for!"

"I've been watching them," Ben said, his voice barely above a whisper. "All these years. Monitoring. Testing. Documenting." His eyes met Harper's. "Lying."

"Ben," Marcus warned, still struggling under Jimmy. "Think about what you're doing."

Ben raised the gun, but not toward Harper. Not toward Liam. The barrel pointed straight at Finn.

"Back off," Ben's voice was steel. "All of you."

"You don't understand what you're doing, Ben." Finn's voice was sharp, but underneath, there was something else, fear. "You think Lou's just going to let this go? You think this ends with a press conference?"

"I know exactly what he'll do," Ben said. "Because I've helped him do it to others." He gestured toward Harper and the others. "Move. Toward the Wild offices. Now."

Axel helped Harper gather the last of her scattered papers while Liam kept himself between her and VSM's men. Gunner released Finn, backing away slowly. Jimmy waited until Ben nodded before letting Marcus up.

"You're throwing away everything," Finn spat. "Twenty years of—"

"Twenty years of what?" Ben's grip tightened on the gun. "Creating kids just to control them? Watching Ethan die because we failed him?" His voice cracked. "I'm done."

The carnival crowds had begun to notice, parents pulling children away, phones filming. Through the gathering audience, Harper's group moved steadily toward the Wild offices.

Marcus released a slow sigh, a flicker of something, disappointment? Resignation? Crossing his face before it hardened. "Should've known you'd crack. You never had the stomach for this."

Ben kept the gun trained on Finn, backing away with the others. "Maybe," he answered. "But tonight, the truth comes out. About VSM, about Furever, about everything."

"Ben," Harper said softly. "Come with us."

Ben shook his head, eyes still locked on Finn and Marcus. "Go. I'll make sure they stay put until the police arrive." In the distance, sirens wailed over the carnival music. The crowd had thinned considerably, people hurrying away from the armed confrontation, cell phones recording as they fled.

"You sure?" Harper asked.

"Twenty years of keeping secrets," Ben's voice was steady now. "I need to see this through."

Ben kept the gun raised as Harper, Liam, and the others backed away toward the Wild offices. The tension hung thick between them, their breath visible in the icy air. Sirens wailed in the distance, growing louder. The carnival crowd had begun to scatter, uncertain whether to run or keep filming.

Finn's hands curled into fists. "You're making a mistake, Ben."

Ben's grip tightened on the gun. "No. I'm finally doing something right."

Marcus exhaled sharply, his breath a white cloud in the freezing air. His fingers flexed at his sides, his body coiled with tension. His jaw clenched as if grinding down a final decision.

Then, he moved.

It happened fast, too fast.

Finn reached out, as if realizing what Marcus was about to do, but he was a second too late.

Marcus lunged.

Ben's instinct took over.

The crack of the gunshot ripped through the carnival air, freezing the scene in place.

A woman nearby screamed. A family ducked behind an ice sculpture. Phones shot up, capturing shaky, unfocused video of the chaos. The crowd went from cautious to panicked in an instant.

Marcus hit the ground hard, gripping his shoulder, snow already darkening with blood beneath him.

Finn's expression flickered between shock and fury.

Ben took two steps back, still holding the gun, air rushing in and out of his lungs. His hands trembled slightly, but his aim never wavered.

"Stay down, Marcus," Ben said, voice low and even. "I told you. It's over."

Marcus clutched his shoulder, snarling through the pain. His face twisted in fury, but something else, betrayal.

"You just signed your death warrant."

Ben didn't answer. Didn't flinch.

A second siren cut through the chaos, police arriving.

Ben glanced toward Harper's group, now pushing through the last of the carnival-goers, nearing the Wild offices.

Good. They were almost safe.

Finn knelt beside Marcus, pressing a hand to the wound. His gaze locking onto Ben.

"We need to leave," Finn muttered.

"We need to kill him," Marcus hissed.

Finn's voice was sharp, but controlled. "Not here."

His eyes flickered toward the flashing red-and-blue lights cutting through the festival haze. Too many witnesses. Too many cameras.

Finn's gaze lifted, meeting Ben's. A silent promise burned in his eyes, this wasn't over.

But before he could move, before either of them could run.

"FREEZE! HANDS UP!"

The command rang out over the festival chaos.

Marcus gritted his teeth, still clutching his bleeding shoulder as uniformed officers surged forward, guns drawn.

Finn's stared at Ben, but he didn't resist. Slowly, he raised his hands, fingers flexing as if considering his options.

Marcus let out a bitter, pained laugh. "You just had to shoot me, huh, Ben?"

Ben still didn't lower the gun. Didn't answer.

A moment later, officers forced Finn and Marcus to the ground, zip ties binding their wrists.

Finn cast one last glance at Ben as they hauled him up, expression unreadable, but simmering with unspoken threats.

"This isn't over," he murmured.

Ben finally sighed, lowering the gun as the weight of the moment settled over him.

No. This wasn't over.

But at least, for tonight, it was enough.

Harper wiped blood from her cheek, still tasting iron on her lips as she stepped into the Wild offices.

The buzzing crowd of reporters turned the moment they saw her, phones rising.

Security moved to intercept her, then recognized her.

"Press conference," Harper called out, her voice hoarse but strong.

The cameras swung toward her like flowers tracking the sun.

For the first time in her career, Harper Sinclair was on the other side of the lens.

And she had one hell of a story to tell.

Security guards struggled to contain the growing media frenzy in the Wild offices lobby. Reporters clustered in groups, trading theories about the hastily called press conference.

Camera crews jostled for position, their equipment creating a forest of tripods and boom mics. Phones livestreamed to waiting audiences. The room hummed with speculation and excitement, something big was breaking, they could smell it. VSM's name bounced between veteran reporters who'd covered the agency for years. Theories flew: scandal, corruption, something about the NHL draft.

"Harper Sinclair never calls press conferences," one reporter muttered. "She asks the questions, she doesn't answer them."

"Look at her face," another whispered as Harper entered.

"Something about VSM," one veteran reporter said. "Saw Finn Booker in the park."

"Police just arrested three men outside," another cut in. "One of them had a gun."

"Harper Sinclair's involved somehow."

The whispers died as Harper moved past the media with Liam and his friends. Blood had begun flowing freely from her cheek now that she was in the warm building. She ignored the shouted questions, keeping her head down as Axel and Gunner cleared a path through the press.

Jimmy spotted an empty conference room. "This way," he called, holding the door.

Once inside, Liam grabbed a handful of tissues from a box on the table. "Here," he said softly, reaching for Harper's face. "You're bleeding pretty bad."

"It's fine," Harper started, but Liam was already dabbing at the cut.

"You got hurt protecting me," he said, his voice tight. "The least I can do is clean you up." Blood had stained the collar of her white blouse, creating a stark crimson pattern.

"Protecting the truth," Harper corrected, wincing slightly as Liam worked. "You deserved to know."

A commotion erupted in the lobby. Through the glass walls, they could see reporters turning, cameras raising. A familiar figure moved through the crowd with practiced ease.

"Holy shit." Gunner blinked. "Is that..."

"Mario Richard," Axel finished.

Liam's hand froze on Harper's cheek. The hockey legend, his genetic source, was heading straight towards them.

The door opened, and Mario stepped in. "Hi, I'm—"

"We all know who you are, sir," Liam cut in, his voice unsteady despite his attempt to stay composed.

Harper touched Liam's arm gently. "Mario knows, Liam. I called him after I got the test results."

Mario's eyes moved from Liam to Harper's bloodied face, then back to Liam. "I just found out myself," he said quietly. "Seems we've both been kept in the dark."

"Well," Liam said, attempting a weak smile, "should I start calling you dad now?"

The joke hung in the air for a moment before Mario let out a short laugh, breaking some of the tension. "Let's figure out what we're going to call each other after we deal with this mess."

Through the glass, cameras flashed and recorded their meeting. Harper dabbed at her cheek one last time, then dropped the bloodied tissue on the table. The evidence of VSM's desperation to keep their secret was written in red across her face and blouse.

"Ready?" she asked, looking between them.

Mario studied Liam's face for a long moment, something unreadable flickering in his eyes, recognition, uncertainty, maybe even guilt. "Harper," he said finally, his voice quieter now, "could you give us a minute?"

Harper nodded, understanding. "I'll handle the press for now. Take your time." She squeezed Liam's arm gently before slipping out the door.

Axel, Gunner, and Jimmy exchanged glances, the same silent communication they'd perfected on the ice. Without a word, they moved toward the door, though each cast a final look at Liam. They'd followed him into countless battles on the ice, now they were watching him face something far bigger than any game.

"We've got your back," Jimmy said softly as they left, the words carrying more weight than usual.

Once they were alone, Mario turned to Liam. The legendary hockey player's usual confidence had given way to something more vulnerable, more human. "Listen," he started, "I know you're probably thinking we need to get out there, face this head-on. That's what I'd usually do too." He paused, studying Liam's face. "But this isn't just another press conference. This is your life, our lives, and once we walk through that door, nothing will ever be the same."

Liam looked Mario in the eyes, seeing not the hockey legend, but a man grappling with an impossible situation. Outside, camera flashes continued to light up the glass walls like silent lightning.

"Are you ready for this?" Mario asked softly. "Because if you're not, we walk away right now. To hell with all of them."

The concern in Mario's voice was genuine, unexpected. This man who'd unknowingly given Liam life was now offering him a choice, something VSM never had.

Presser

"Harper's not just exposing the truth. She's doing what I was too weak to do. Fighting for the ones who deserved better." – Ben

The conference room door had clicked shut behind them, muffling the chaos outside. Through the glass walls, camera flashes continued their silent storm, but inside, time seemed to pause. Mario's words hung in the air between them: *we walk away right now.*

Liam studied Mario's face, the face he'd seen in countless highlights, posters, and now, in person. "You said you just found out," Liam said, his voice tight with control. "That this is all news to you too."

Mario nodded, waiting.

"But I need to hear it from you." Liam's hands clenched at his sides. "Did you know? Maybe not at first, but later? When I started making headlines in juniors?"

"Liam."

"Because I could understand why," Liam continued, the words rushing out now. "Your legacy. Having someone carry on your legacy. Maybe VSM even made it sound noble, advancing the sport, living on through me, and Ethan—"

"Stop." Mario's voice cut through Liam's spiral. "Just... stop." He ran a hand through his hair, and for a moment, Liam saw not the legend, but a man grappling with his own shock and anger. "They stole from me, from my family."

The mention of family turned something inside Liam. He hadn't even thought about that. About Mario's kids suddenly discovering they had a genetic sibling engineered in a lab.

"I should be at my granddaughter's first playoff game right now," Mario said, his voice cracking slightly. "Instead, I'm here trying to figure out how to tell my family that someone..." He stopped, struggling for words.

"That someone used your DNA to create me," Liam finished quietly.

Mario turned to him, his expression raw with emotion. "How do I explain this to them? That somewhere out there, they have a... what? An uncle? A cousin? Everything I thought I could protect them from, media circus, public scrutiny, it's all about to explode."

"I've spent years building not just a career, but a life my family could be proud of," Mario said. "You think I'd risk that? Risk them? For what, some twisted science experiment?"

"No," Liam said quietly. "No, you wouldn't."

Mario moved to the window, his back to the flashing cameras. "When Harper showed up at my door, asked me for my DNA... I felt sick. Not because of you," he added quickly, turning back to Liam. "But because someone had taken something so personal, so fundamental, and used it without permission. Without conscience."

Liam stood, joining Mario at the window. Outside, Harper was managing the press, buying them this moment of truth.

"So what do you want to do?" Mario asked. "My offer stands. We can walk away, deal with this privately. Let the lawyers and PR teams handle it."

Liam watched the scene outside the room, thinking of everyone who'd helped him get here, Harper risking her life for the truth, Ben finally choosing right over loyalty, his friends standing by him. He thought of Ethan, who never got the chance to know who he really was.

"No," Liam said firmly. "No more hiding. No more secrets." He turned to Mario. "VSM took choices from both of us. I won't let them take this one too."

A smile, proud and genuine, spread across Mario's face. "Then we face it together. As family? As friends? We'll figure that part out. But together."

Liam nodded, feeling something settle inside him, not peace exactly, but purpose. "Together."

They moved toward the door where Harper waited, ready to tell the world a truth that would change everything. But now, at least, Liam knew who stood with him. And why.

The conference room door opened to a burst of camera flashes. Liam stepped out beside Mario Richard, an impossible pairing that sent a ripple of confusion through the crowd. The buzz of speculation rose sharply, then fell to whispers as they moved through the packed room.

"Mario Richard? Why is he here?" "What's going on with VSM?" "Why's Harper Sinclair's face bleeding?"

They made their way to the side of the makeshift stage where Harper waited, her bloodied cheek a stark reminder of the evens earlier this evening. Through the windows, snow continued to fall.

Harper approached the podium, her steps echoing in the suddenly quieting room. "Good evening," she began, her voice steady despite the chaos outside. "What I'm about to share will fundamentally change how we view sports, ethics, and human potential."

She laid out the foundation first, Furever Genetics' reputation in animal cloning, their groundbreaking work with racehorses and endangered species. Professional. Clinical. But building to something bigger.

"Then tragedy struck," Harper continued. "Dr. Kim Jung-So lost his son in a car accident." She paused, letting the human element sink in. "Grief can drive people to cross lines they never thought they would."

Mario shifted slightly, the movement drawing every eye in the room. The legendary player's presence added weight to each word Harper spoke.

"But Dr. Kim needed resources for his ambitions. He found them in Victoria Sports Management." The room stirred at VSM's name. "Together, they embarked on a program that would push past every ethical boundary."

Liam watched a veteran reporter in the front row, someone who'd covered hockey for decades, slowly piecing it together. The man's eyes darted between Liam and Mario, confusion rather than recognition dawning in his expression.

"We have evidence," Harper continued, "of VSM funding a secret human cloning program. Not just to bring back Dr. Kim's son, but to create what they believed would be incredible athletes."

The room erupted. Fragments of shocked conversations bounced off the walls: "Human cloning? That's impossible—" "What does this have to do with Mario Richard?" "Incredible athletes? What are they talking about?"

A reporter from TSN suddenly stood, her face pale with realization. "Are you saying..." she started, her voice carrying over the chaos, "that Mario Richard's DNA was used to create..." She couldn't finish, but her eyes locked onto Liam.

The silence that followed was deafening. Even the camera shutters seemed to pause.

"That's insane," someone finally said.

"Look at them!"

"Liam's mixed-race, Mario's French-Canadian."

"Different height, different build."

"Brown eyes versus blue, can't even grow playoff scruff."

Nervous laughter rippled through parts of the room. A senior columnist shook his head, pen frozen above his notepad. "A kid from Manitoba with a totally different look? This is what we're supposed to believe?"

"VSM's done some shady things," another voice called out, "but human cloning? Come on."

Harper's voice cut through the denial. "I understand your skepticism. I shared it." She held up a thick folder. "That's why we have DNA tests showing an 87% match between Liam and Mario, modified through CRISPR technology. We have medical records detailing genetic engineering. And most importantly, we have the paper trail connecting VSM directly to Furever Genetics."

She spread several documents across the podium. "We have medical records detailing this genetic engineering. And most importantly, we have the paper trail connecting VSM directly to Furever Genetics."

The laughter died. In the sudden quiet, the sound of Mario clearing his throat seemed impossibly loud.

"They stole from me," he said, his voice carrying authority earned through decades in the spotlight. "Used my DNA without consent to engineer athletes. Made sure they looked nothing like me to hide what they'd done." He turned to Liam. "But they couldn't hide the truth forever."

A veteran columnist from The Hockey News slowly removed his glasses, polishing them with trembling hands. "Twenty years covering this sport," he muttered, "and now we find out they're manufacturing players in labs."

As the questions began flying, Liam stood straight-backed beside Mario. They looked nothing alike, VSM had made sure of that, but in this moment, they were undeniably connected. Not by appearance or mannerisms, but by a deeper truth that was finally breaking free.

And in that moment, that truth belonged to all of them.

* * *

In Lou Booker's office, VSM staff crowded around the mounted television. Through floor-to-ceiling windows, Montreal's snowfall seemed distant compared to the storm starting in the office.

"Tabarnac," Lou muttered, his accent thick with frustration. Harper Sinclair's face filled the screen, that bloodied cheek like a badge of honor as she tore apart everything he'd built.

Phones started ringing. Email notifications pinged. Clients wanting answers.

"This can't be real," someone whispered. Others were already closing laptops, gathering coats.

"They did this behind our backs!"

"We had no idea about..."

"Are we... complicit?"

One by one, the staff began gathering their belongings. Some moved quickly, almost running, others lingered, shooting uncertain glances at Lou's back. Within minutes, the office emptied, leaving only the sound of Harper's voice from the television and the soft padding of Zeus's paws as the old dog moved to sit beside his master's chair.

Lou tried Finn's phone, then Marcus'. No answer. The Saint Paul police would have them by now. Dr. Kim wasn't answering either, that told Lou everything he needed to know about where the doctor's loyalties lay.

Lou turned away from the chaos, dropping into his chair. Through the windows, Montreal stretched before him, its lights cold and distant. His reflection in the glass showed a man who had reached too far, too fast, and was now watching everything slip away.

Zeus whined softly, pressing his head against Lou's leg. Even as VSM crumbled, Lou refused to accept defeat. His empire might be burning, but he would not run. Some secrets would stay buried.

* * *

The press conference room crackled with tension as Harper stepped back from her initial revelation. Hands shot up immediately, a forest of desperate questions waiting to be asked. Harper pointed to a veteran reporter from TSN.

"Can you clarify the timeline of VSM's involvement with Furever Genetics?"

Before Harper could answer, a tabloid reporter from TMZ burst in, "Was he grown in a lab? Like, in some artificial womb?"

The room stirred uncomfortably. Liam felt heat rise in his face, but Harper's voice cut through the chaos, steady and firm.

"Liam was born naturally at Brandon General Hospital. Tammy Desjardins carried him to term and gave birth to him. VSM and the fertility clinic led Jim and Tammy to believe they were receiving a standard donor embryo." Harper paused, letting that sink in. "Tammy is Liam's birth mother. That fact isn't in question."

Liam felt something in his body loosen at those words. Through all the revelations, that truth remained: Tammy had carried him, given birth to him, loved him.

A reporter from Hockey Weekly raised her hand, her expression almost apologetic. "This might sound insensitive, but... Liam is clearly mixed-race, while Mario Richard is... well, how do you explain that?"

The room fell silent. Mario shifted beside Liam, but Harper responded first.

"The geneticists used CRISPR to alter genetic traits, including appearance. What you're seeing, the skin tone, eye color, facial features, those are controlled by just a tiny fraction of our genetic code. They engineered these changes to keep their program hidden in plain sight." Harper's voice hardened. "They manipulated DNA not just for performance, but for secrecy. They deceived everyone, including the Desjardins family."

A legal correspondent from CBC stood next. "This raises serious questions about ownership and rights. VSM essentially designed Liam's genetic code. Do they have any claim to—"

"I'm not property," Liam interrupted, his voice firm. The room fell silent. "I'm not a patent or a product. I'm a person."

Mario stepped forward, placing a hand on Liam's shoulder. The gesture wasn't lost on the reporters, a dozen cameras captured the moment.

"What about the others?" A voice called out. "The arrests we just witnessed in Rice Park, were they involved in this program?"

Harper touched her cheek, feeling fresh blood at the mentioned of the arrests. "Those VSM employees were directly involved in monitoring and managing their... investments." The last word carried a weight of disgust.

Liam felt Mario's hand tighten on his shoulder. Harper's face showed the strain of the moment before she answered.

"But there's more," Harper continued, her voice softening. "This program didn't start with Liam. Another young hockey player, Ethan Bernard, who died two years ago, was also part of VSM's program."

The room erupted again. Questions flew from all directions:

"How many others?"

"Are there health risks?"

"What does the NHL know?"

Harper raised her hands for quiet. "Many of these questions will be addressed in the coming days. We have geneticists and medical experts preparing detailed reports. What's important now is—"

"What about you, Liam?" A young reporter interrupted. Her voice was gentler than the others. "How do you see yourself now? Who are you in all of this?"

The room fell silent, waiting. Liam looked at the faces before him, some hungry for scandal, others genuinely concerned, all wanting answers he was still searching for himself.

"I'm a hockey player who loves this game. I'm Jim and Tammy's son. And everything else," he glanced at Mario, then back to the crowd, "that's something I'll have to work through. But I won't hide. I won't run from this truth."

Harper stepped forward. "That's all for now. We'll have more information in the coming days. Thank you."

The room erupted once more, but Harper was already guiding them toward the back conference room. Through the chaos, Liam caught fragments of their shouted questions, about records, about rights, about his future in hockey.

The reporters' questions came fast and hard, but Liam knew the real game was just beginning, and this time, the stakes were higher than any championship.

Shockwaves

"They will rage, they will legislate, they will condemn, and they will still come begging for what I can create." – Dr Kim

The chaos of the press conference faded as Liam caught sight of his parents. Jim and Tammy stood near the back of the room, where they'd watched everything unfold. The moment their eyes met, Liam felt the weight of the past few days, the anger, the confusion, the hurt, begin to lift.

Without hesitation, he moved toward them. His friends formed a protective barrier, shielding him from the pressing cameras and shouted questions. None of that mattered now.

Tammy reached him first, pulling him into an embrace that felt like coming home. Her familiar lavender scent mixed with the faint trace of tears. "My boy," she whispered, her voice thick with emotion. "Always my boy."

The words from the press conference echoed in Liam's mind: *Tammy is Liam's birth mother. That fact isn't in question. She had carried him, given birth to him, loved him from his first breath.*

Jim's strong arms encircled them both. "Son," was all he could manage, but it said everything.

"I'm sorry," Liam murmured. "For being angry about the fertility clinic, for doubting—"

"No," Jim cut him off gently. "We should have told you sooner. We just... you were always ours, Liam. From the moment we knew you were coming."

Mario stood slightly apart, watching the family reunion with a mix of emotions playing across his face. Liam caught his eye over Tammy's shoulder and made a decision. He extended his arm, inviting Mario into their circle.

For a moment, Mario hesitated. This wasn't just about him anymore, he had a family of his own who would be processing this news, trying to understand what it meant for them. But looking at Liam, he saw not just his genetic reflection, but a chance to be part of something unexpected and real.

"My granddaughter played hockey tonight," Mario said softly as he stepped closer. "I should've been there, but... I needed to be here too. Family's complicated sometimes."

"Gets more complicated by the minute," Jim said with a warm smile, making room in their circle.

Tammy reached out and squeezed Mario's arm. "Family is what we make it."

The media swirled around them, cameras flashing, questions flying, but in that moment, they were just a family, unconventional, unexpected, but real. Axel, Gunner, and Jimmy maintained their protective formation, occasionally throwing warning glances at reporters who ventured too close.

"Think we can get out of here?" Liam asked, suddenly exhausted. "Maybe grab some food?"

"The Dark Horse?" Axel suggested. "Best mac and cheese in Saint Paul."

"Perfect," Tammy said, wiping her eyes.

As they moved toward the exit, Mario's phone buzzed repeatedly, his family watching the news unfold. He glanced at the screen, then tucked it away. Those conversations would come later.

Outside, camera flashes still penetrated the falling snow. Somewhere, VSM was burning, investigations were starting, and questions about Liam's future in hockey remained unanswered.

But for now, they had mac and cheese to eat and a new reality to process.

* * *

The white lights of the Furever Genetics lab cast shadows across Dr. Kim's face as he watched the press conference end on his tablet. His reflection in the polished chrome of a centrifuge showed a smile, cold, calculating, satisfied.

Harper Sinclair's final words faded from the screen. *"...the beginning of a long investigation into VSM and their role in this unprecedented breach of ethics."*

"Ethics," Dr. Kim murmured. He set the tablet down beside a row of precision instruments. "They talk of ethics while standing on the shoulders of our work."

Dae-Song's eyes tracked the scrolling news feeds, processing each reaction with algorithmic precision. "Their responses align exactly with predicted behavior patterns. Fear, moral outrage, religious indignation, all right on schedule." His lips curved in that familiar cold smile. "The naturals always resort to their base programming when confronted with evolution."

Dr. Kim caught the distinction in his son's words, *naturals*, as if they were a separate species. He'd noticed Dae-Song using the term more frequently lately, drawing a clear line between enhanced and unenhanced humans. The boy who once asked about bringing back his mother now spoke of base programming and evolutionary steps. Progress, yes, but toward what end?

"The world isn't ready for what we've achieved," Dr. Kim said carefully, watching his son's reaction.

"The world is never ready for evolution, Father. That's why it must be guided." Dae-Song's fingers slid across the tablet, dismissing the chaos of human reaction as mere background noise. "VSM's fall is just the first step. Dubai will be our chrysalis."

"Everything is prepared," Dae-Song continued, his voice carrying the same clinical precision as their surroundings. "The facility is operational. Equipment transfers are complete. The next phase can commence within forty-eight hours."

"The world will hunt us now," Dr. Kim said, gathering the last of their critical data.

"Let them chase VSM's shadows," Dae-Song replied, his words measured and cold as laboratory steel. "Lou Booker and his empire served their purpose, funding research, providing test subjects, maintaining secrecy. But they saw only profit, not potential. Not power. Our new partners understand true ambition."

Together, they moved toward the exit. As they passed the secure storage units, Dae-Song's eyes lingered briefly on Cabinet 35-G, but he said nothing. He paused at the threshold, his enhanced mind already calculating the next moves in their greater game. "Better to be the architect, Father, than the experiment."

The lab door sealed behind them. In the darkness, monitors continued their countdown to something only father and son understood.

VSM's fall wasn't an end. It was merely the first domino in a longer game.

* * *

Harper settled onto a barstool in the St. Paul Hotel's dimly lit bar, finally allowing herself to breathe. Above her, multiple screens broadcasted the storm she'd unleashed. Her phone hadn't stopped vibrating since the press conference ended, each alert marking another ripple in the growing wave of global reaction.

CNN appeared on the center screen, the anchors expression grave. "Breaking news tonight as the world grapples with an unprecedented revelation: human cloning is no longer science fiction..."

Harper's phone lit up: #CloneGate trending worldwide.

The bartender silently placed a bourbon in front of her, nodding toward Frank Taylor's name on the tab. On another screen, Senator Penny Morrison stood at a podium, surrounded by colleagues.

"This is a direct violation of federal law," Morrison declared, her voice sharp with controlled anger. "Human cloning was banned for a reason. We will be launching immediate investigations into all parties involved. The full weight of congressional oversight will be brought to bear."

BBC News broke in on the left screen: "Breaking from Rome, where Vatican officials have called for an immediate global ban on human cloning, declaring it 'a fundamental violation of human dignity.'" The ticker below showed #FureverScandal spreading across Europe.

Harper's phone buzzed. A text from Frank: *You okay? Things are exploding here.*

Before she could respond, Al Jazeera's feed caught her attention. A panel of international scientists appeared, their debate already heated. "This isn't just about sports," a MIT geneticist argued. "We're talking about a complete disregard for established bioethical protocols."

#BanCloning flashed across Fox News, where news anchors face filled the screen, his outrage palpable. "This is what happens when we let science run unchecked. They're manufacturing human beings in labs! What's next? Designer babies? This is a direct assault on human dignity and divine creation."

From Tokyo, NHK showed crowds gathering outside Furever Genetics' satellite office, their signs visible even through the rain: "Stop Playing God."

MSNBC cut to a legal analyst: "We're looking at potential criminal charges here. International laws were broken. The implications for genetic rights, human rights, patent law, this will be in courts for years."

Harper's hand trembled slightly as she reached for her drink. Her phone lit up with another alert: London's Times reporting VSM's stock in freefall. Major sponsors pulling out. Lou Booker unreachable for comment.

Across every screen, across every time zone, the story morphed and grew. Scientific breakthrough. Ethical crisis. Sports scandal. Religious debate. It was all of these and more.

The bartender turned up the volume as CNN cut to a live feed outside VSM's Montreal headquarters. Protesters flooded the sidewalks, their chants growing louder, their signs demanding justice.

Harper took a long sip of bourbon, watching as #CloneGate went viral. The truth was out. The world was watching. And the real fight was just beginning.

Under the Microscope

"A team isn't just who celebrates with you, it's who stands with you when the lights go out." – Coach Boucha

Liam sat in the quiet of his hotel room, the soft glow of the TV screen casting flickers of light against the darkened walls. His mind buzzed, still trying to process the chaotic fever of the press conference earlier that night. He'd thought that things would settle down, but the world had other ideas. Every channel seemed to be discussing him, his existence, his future, his worth. The weight of it all made the hotel room feel stifling, like the walls were closing in on him.

He muted the television for a moment, listening to the low hum of silence before his curiosity got the better of him. Clicking the volume back up, ESPN's debate show filled the room, the animated voices of two commentators arguing over his very existence.

"The NHL must take a stand!" insisted one, his voice rising with conviction. "We can't have more Liams being manufactured in labs! It's not natural, it's not fair to the natural players who've fought their way up through sheer grit and talent."

The words hit hard. He had spent his entire life working to get where he was, every training session, every sacrifice, but now it seemed none of that mattered. To them, he was just a product, a manufactured thing.

The other commentator cut in, her voice sharp with rebuttal. "Hold on now. Why should Liam be punished for being born? He didn't ask for this! He's not responsible for being created in a lab any more than we're responsible for being born into our families."

Liam felt a flicker of relief at her words. At least someone got it. But then she went on.

"If we start banning players based on their genetics, where do we draw the line?" she asked. "This is a slippery slope. Are we going to ban anyone with an advantage? Natural genetic variations? We're punishing someone for something they had no control over."

Liam leaned forward, resting his elbows on his knees, his hands clasped tightly in front of him. The truth was, he didn't know how to feel. One moment, he wanted to scream at the screen, to tell them they didn't understand. He wasn't just a science experiment. He was an athlete, one who had bled and sweat for every inch on the ice.

But what did they see? Did the world see Liam, hockey player? Or Liam, the clone?

Jerry Dryden, the commentator, crossed his arms, his expression stern. "But what about the integrity of the sport? This could change everything. If we allow clones like Liam to play, where do we stop? What happens when records are shattered, not by human achievement, but by engineered talent?"

A sports scientist joined the conversation. "Let's be clear about something, genetic potential isn't destiny. We see this in identical twins all the time. Same DNA, different outcomes. One becomes an elite athlete, the other never develops past recreational sports. Why? Because success in sports isn't just about genes, it's about dedication, opportunity, and countless hours of deliberate practice."

"Exactly," the woman agreed. "Look at the NHL draft history. How many sons of former players never make it? They have the 'genetic advantage' but take a different path. Meanwhile, undrafted players fight their way up through sheer determination."

As he watched the heated debate unfold, a knot tightened in his stomach. No one had ever questioned his dedication before. No one had ever questioned his love for the game.

His eyes flickered back to the screen, where the woman made one final point that lingered in the air like a lifeline. "If Liam goes on to break records, it won't just be because of his DNA. It'll be because of his dedication, his strategy, his skill. You can't clone heart, you can't clone grit."

Liam muted the TV again, feeling the tension thrum through his body. For a moment, he just sat there, the silence pressing in as he stared blankly at the screen.

He wasn't sure what was worse, being seen as something more than human, or being treated like something less.

Liam couldn't help but scan more channels, and each network seemed to have a different angle, some personal, others political, but none of them touched on how he was feeling. How could they?

He paused on one channel where a panel discussion was underway. The topic, displayed boldly in the corner of the screen: "The Ethics of Cloning: Humanity's Future or Pandora's Box?"

A bespectacled professor spoke animatedly. "What we're witnessing isn't just about Liam. His existence opens the door to designer humans. The implications go far beyond sports."

Liam shifted in his seat, drawn to the weight in her words.

A former coach shook his head. "This isn't about philosophy, it's about fair competition. Liam was engineered for success."

"You're missing the larger point," the professor interrupted. "This is about genetic diversity. Nature creates variations that help humans survive diseases, environmental changes. What happens when we start mass-producing people from the same genetic template?"

The host leaned forward. "Like copying the same key over and over?"

"Exactly," the professor nodded. "In agriculture, genetic uniformity makes crops vulnerable to disease. The same principle applies to humans. One successful clone leads to demand for more. That's how we risk losing the genetic diversity that's protected us for millennia."

The coach looked skeptical. "But we're not talking about creating armies of clones here. We're talking about one kid, Liam. Why do we need to turn him into a symbol for the end of the world?"

A Catholic bioethicist joined the discussion. "This isn't about condemning Liam as an individual, but we must address the moral crisis here. Cloning reduces human life to a product, something designed and manufactured. It fundamentally violates human dignity."

The host turned toward her. "How so?"

"Every human being has intrinsic value, created in God's image," she explained. "When we start engineering people in labs, we're treating them as products, not persons. We're saying some lives are more valuable than others based on their genetic design."

The geneticist nodded. "And it won't stop here. Today it's Liam. Tomorrow it could be hundreds, thousands. Once proven successful, there will be demand for designer babies, enhanced soldiers, specialized workers, treating humans as commodities to be engineered and mass-produced."

"Exactly," the bioethicist agreed. "We're opening the door to exploiting human life. Creating people for specific purposes, treating them as means to an end rather than individuals with inherent worth."

"A moment," interrupted a civil rights attorney on the panel. "We're ignoring the immediate human rights implications. Liam is a person under the law, regardless of how he came to be. The real question is: who owns his genetic code? VSM? The fertility clinic? Mario Richard? This could set precedents for human rights that will impact generations."

The host leaned forward. "Are you suggesting Liam could be considered intellectual property?"

"That's exactly the problem," the attorney nodded grimly. "We're entering uncharted territory where corporations could claim ownership rights over DNA and the human beings using that genetic sequence. It's not just about sports anymore, it's about fundamental human freedom."

Liam turned off the TV, his hands trembling slightly. The room felt too small, the air too thick. He stared at his reflection in the window, the professor's words echoing. Was he really a threat to humanity's future? Or was he just... Liam?

He was no longer just a young athlete trying to make his mark. He was something else entirely, and it wasn't clear where he fit anymore.

Outside the hotel window, Saint Paul moved on as it always had. But for Liam, nothing would ever be the same. His phone lit up with notifications, the World Juniors team chat buzzing since the media storm broke.

Liam stared at his phone as it lit up with a flood of notifications. The group chat with his World Juniors teammates had been buzzing non-stop since the media storm broke. His phone vibrated again, and again, the screen lighting up with messages of support, humor, and, of course, Julian's signature jabs.

Axel: *Bro, they're tearing it up on SportsCenter about you. You hanging in there?*

Riley: *Man, they've got you on every channel. They'll forget about it soon enough. You good?*

Remi: *Saw you on CNN. Weird seeing hockey on there, man.*

Charlee: *My little sister says you're trending above some K-pop band. That's serious.*

Liam felt a wave of warmth at their concern. He hesitated before typing a quick response.

Liam: *Yeah, I'm alright. Just dealing with it.*

Then, as expected, Julian jumped in.

Julian: *Handling it? Better you than me, Blade. Crazy world, huh? Maybe early retirement is calling your name.*

Liam shook his head, a half-smirk tugging at his lips despite the jab.

Axel: *Jules, always the clown. Jealous much?*

Julian: *Jealous of what? All the paparazzi? Nah, I'll pass.*

Then a new message came in from a quieter member of the group, someone who didn't speak up often but always hit the right note when he did.

Alex: *You've got this, Blade. We know you, and the world will see what we already know, this doesn't change anything.*

The support from Alex warmed Liam more than he expected. His teammates were all over the country, but they felt close.

Julian: *But seriously, man. You've got this. Just don't let them make you their science project.*

Liam blinked at the unexpected support in Julian's message. Maybe there was more to Julian than the usual sarcasm.

Another message appeared, this time from Jackson, one of the new guys on the team:

Jackson: *We're with you, Blade. No matter what. You got this.*

And then, just as Liam was starting to relax, another text came through from Julian:

Julian: *Oh, and heads-up... I'm hearing the NHL's calling a special meeting.*

Liam's heart skipped a beat. The league stepping in? He hadn't even thought about that. What would they say? What could they decide? A knot of unease twisted in his gut, but he pushed the thought aside. That bridge would come later.

Liam's phone rang, Coach Boucha's name lighting up the screen. He hesitated for a moment before answering.

"Coach."

"Liam." Boucha's voice carried its usual steady authority. "You watching all this?"

"Hard not to," Liam managed, sinking back against the headboard.

"Listen to me." The coach's tone softened slightly, but kept its edge. "Thirty years coaching, and you know what I've learned? Politics, media, public opinion, they all change with the wind. But there are two things that stay constant: family and what you do with the opportunities you're given."

Liam waited, knowing Coach wasn't finished.

"Your parents, Jim and Tammy, they're your anchor. The team? We're your second family. And that ice? That's your opportunity. Nothing else matters except what you do with what you've got, son. Everything else is just noise."

The tension eased. "Thanks, Coach."

"The world loves drama," Boucha continued. "But remember what I always say..."

"Control the ice, control yourself," Liam finished with him.

"Exactly." Another pause. "The team's behind you. Every single one of them. Even that smartass Broten."

Despite everything, Liam found himself smiling. "Julian sent a message earlier. Almost sounded like he cared."

"Yeah, well, don't let it go to your head." Boucha cleared his throat. "Get some rest, son. Tomorrow's another day."

After hanging up, Liam sat in the quiet of his room, Coach's words settling in his mind. Whatever came next, NHL meetings, media circus, endless debates, he knew one truth remained.

He belonged on the ice.

His phone buzzed one last time.

Julian: *Hey, designer baby, see you at the Scouting Combine. We'll see if us naturals can still take you.*

Liam smiled. Maybe that was the point, he'd have to keep proving himself, over and over.

That much, at least, hadn't changed.

Under Review

"Exposing the truth felt like a victory, until I saw the cost etched in Liam's eyes." – Harper

Harper Sinclair threaded through the crowd of reporters at NHL headquarters in New York, each jostling for position. Cameras flashed, microphones stretched toward the empty podium like metal flowers reaching for sunlight.

"What's your take, Harper?" asked a colleague from a rival publication, his pen poised over a notepad. "You think they knew about Liam before your story broke?"

"I don't think anyone really suspected cloning was real," she murmured. "It's forbidden everywhere, and why start with sports? If anything, you'd expect military or medical applications first."

The other reporter nodded thoughtfully. Around them, speculation buzzed like a swarm of bees. Some believed the NHL was blindsided, others suspected complicity at higher levels. Harper stayed silent, watching. Had her story forced the league's hand? Or had they been waiting for someone else to rip off the Band-Aid?

She adjusted the small recorder in her hand, ensuring it was ready for whatever statements would come. Harper had been down this road many times before, where every word could either reveal or obscure, a truth wrapped in careful diplomacy. But this time felt different. Personal. The stakes weren't just professional, they were human.

The chatter died down as the NHL commissioner stepped up to the podium, his face set in stone. The tension in the room deepened with each passing second. He tapped the microphone, sending a sharp crack through the speakers that jolted everyone to attention.

"Ladies and gentlemen," he began, his voice heavy with the gravity of the moment. "We've called this press conference today to address serious concerns raised by recent events."

His cadence was deliberate, each sentence was well practiced to be non-committal, avoiding any direct admission of what the league might have known. Yet beneath the polished surface, Harper detected the urgency, the pressure mounting from all sides.

"As many of you know," the commissioner continued, "the NHL Draft is only a couple of months away, a time when we celebrate young talent entering our league. However, we find ourselves at an unprecedented crossroads."

The room stilled. This was it, the decision that would alter the course of Liam's life.

"We are here not just because of Liam's situation but also due to new findings regarding Ethan Bernard's death," he said solemnly. "Ethan was also confirmed to have been a clone."

A ripple of shock passed through the crowd. Ethan's death had been a tragedy, but this confirmation added a chilling new layer. Harper knew this would devastate his parents all over again.

"Given Ethan Bernard's tragic death, and growing concerns about the medical risks of genetic engineering in athletes," the commissioner said, "the NHL has made a difficult decision."

He paused, scanning the room. "Effective immediately, the NHL is enforcing a permanent and absolute ban on genetically engineered athletes, including clones. There will be no exceptions, no appeals. This is final. Additionally, we're forming a special committee to investigate whether Ethan Bernard's death was related to complications from genetic engineering, and to screen all current players and prospects for similar modifications."

The room exploded. Reporters shouted over each other, desperate for clarity, their voices merging into a chaotic din.

"What about current players?" A voice cut through the chaos. "Are there clones already in the NHL?"

The commissioner's grip tightened on the podium. "Effective immediately, all current NHL players and prospects will undergo mandatory genetic testing before next season."

Another reporter jumped in. "And if you find any?"

"Any genetically engineered player, past or present, will be permanently ineligible to compete in the NHL," the commissioner stated, his voice cold.

A stunned silence followed. Then, another reporter fired back. "You're saying you could erase careers overnight?"

"This decision is final," the commissioner stated, his voice cold. "Our priority is the integrity of the sport."

The room erupted again. Harper's mind raced. How many others might be out there? How many careers hung in the balance? She watched the commissioner deflect follow-up questions, his careful non-answers suggesting this went deeper than anyone suspected.

Harper stood frozen. The commissioner's words had just ended Liam's hockey career before it began.

Liam, the boy who had grown up idolizing hockey, who had trained, sacrificed, and poured his soul into the sport, was now banned from the only future he had ever envisioned. Not because of his skill, his effort, or his heart, but because of his origins.

The crowd buzzed, outrage mixing with confusion. Harper caught snippets of questions thrown at the commissioner:

"Is there any legal basis for this ruling?"

"Are other leagues expected to follow suit?"

One reporter raised his voice above the clamor, "A permanent ban? No path to appeal? How do you justify shutting down careers before they've even started?"

The commissioner's face remained unmoved. "Our primary concern is fairness and safety within our sport," he replied evenly, offering no further solace.

Harper's pulse quickened again. The shock had landed, but with it came a cold realization, her story had led to this. She had exposed the truth, but in doing so, she had handed the NHL the weapon they used to destroy Liam's future before he even had a chance to fight for it.

The buzz around her grew distant as she grappled with her own role in this tragedy. Liam's story had started as an investigation into sports integrity, but now it felt like something far darker, a window into humanity's capacity for exclusion, for casting aside those deemed too different, too unnatural.

As the press conference wound down, Harper slipped out alongside the swarm of reporters, her thoughts spiraling. She couldn't shake the image of Liam, his face as he learned that his future had been stolen, not by his lack of talent, but by his genetic makeup. She felt both vindicated and devastated. The truth had come out, but it had crushed the very person she had hoped to protect.

Outside, Harper leaned against the cool stone of the building. Her story had opened Pandora's box, but maybe that's what needed to happen.

Change never came easy, and sometimes the truth had to hurt before it could heal.

Her phone buzzed, a message from Frank:

Story's not over yet. Keep digging.

She smiled grimly, thinking of the DNA tests to come, the careers at stake, the lives about to change.

Harper pocketed her phone and turned onto 33rd Street, where the looming facade of St. Michael's Church stood like a silent judge. The NHL's decision echoed in her mind, a grave proclamation casting a long shadow over the future of exceptional athletes like Liam.

Inside, reporters dissected the NHL's ruling, their angles forming, their questions sharp. But out here, in the city's quiet hum, Harper's thoughts unraveled. She had delivered the truth, but with it, she had unwittingly delivered a crushing blow to Liam's future.

Liam wasn't in New York, but Harper could feel the weight of his absence. It was as if the consequences of her story were aimed directly at him, a young man thrust into a whirlwind of questions he never asked to answer. Every step she had taken, every revelation she had brought to light, had now become a weapon against him.

She imagined him receiving the news, his shock, his devastation. The NHL had extinguished the bright trajectory he had fought for, reducing it to the cold reality of his genetic origins. Something he had no control over, revealed by her own hands.

Harper found herself retreating into a shadowed alleyway, seeking refuge from the bustling world outside. For the first time in her career, she wasn't sure if the truth had been worth the cost. She thought uncovering his origins would protect him. Instead, the truth had cast him out, marking him as something different, something the league had no place for.

She pulled out her phone and typed:

What did I do, Frank? I just destroyed a kid's dream.

The response came quickly: *This isn't the end of his story, Harper. Or yours.*

Harper straightened, drawing in a steadying breath. *Maybe Frank was right. The story wasn't over. Then neither was Liam's.*

* * *

In the quiet of Liam's childhood home, the television's vibrant glow cast light across the room. The familiar warmth of the living room now felt cold and distant, transformed into a place of reckoning, a courtroom where the future of Liam's dreams was being decided, and the verdict had just come down.

Liam sat between his parents, Jim and Tammy, staring at the screen but not truly seeing it. The NHL commissioner's announcement played on a loop, a cruel reminder of the league's final, devastating decision. The words echoed endlessly in Liam's mind: banned from professional hockey.

"What just happened?" Liam's voice, usually so full of life, was barely a whisper, a shadow of itself. His gaze remained locked on the replay, though he couldn't seem to focus. The words, *clones are banned,* pierced through the fog in his mind, over and over again, like an accusation.

Jim's hand, calloused from years of work, rested on Liam's shoulder, a steadying touch, though Jim's own heart was just as shaken. There were no words that could undo the blow, but the gesture was his way of saying: *I'm here. We're in this together.*

Beside them, Tammy sat, her hands clenched tightly in her lap, her eyes burning with a fierce, protective anger. It wasn't right. It wasn't fair. She had no outlet for the rage swelling inside her, no one to aim it at but the empty screen.

"This was supposed to be *your* moment," Tammy said, her voice raw, barely contained. The bitterness in her tone was sharp, as if she could will the universe to change through sheer defiance. "You worked so hard for this. We all did."

Jim reached for the remote, switching off the TV, silencing the relentless replay that was torturing them all. The room plunged into silence, save for the soft creaks of the old house settling, as if even the walls felt the tension. "We'll get through this," he said quietly, his voice rough but steady. He looked at Liam, his expression a mix of determination and helplessness. "You're still *you*, Liam. You're still my son, the brightest star I've ever seen on the ice."

The hockey memorabilia that lined the room, jerseys, trophies, and photos, suddenly felt like relics of a past that had been taken from him. They stared back at Liam like hollow reminders of a future that now seemed out of reach. The dream he had chased for so long, the career he had spent his life preparing for, had been snatched away in the blink of an eye.

Liam's hands shook slightly, his composure fraying at the edges. He felt a deep tremor, not just in his body, but in the very core of who he was. "If I'm not a hockey player, if I can't chase that dream…" His voice cracked, raw with something deeper than grief. "Then who the hell am I?"

Tammy turned to face her son fully, her gaze fierce, unwavering. There was no doubt in her eyes, no hesitation in her voice. "You are Liam," she said firmly. "Our son. *My* son. And nothing, nothing, that league says will ever change that."

Jim nodded in quiet agreement, his hand still resting on Liam's shoulder. "You've earned your place on that ice," he said. "No one can take that away from you. Not ever"

Liam looked back at his parents, the two people who had been with him every step of the way. They had sacrificed for him, believed in him, stood by him through everything. And here they were again, standing strong beside him, even when the world had turned against him.

The initial shock that had frozen him in place began to thaw. It wasn't gone, but in its place, something else stirred, a rising determination. The fight wasn't over, not by a long shot. "Then we'll fight it," Liam said, his voice growing stronger with each word. "Whatever it takes."

In that moment, the Desjardins family felt closer than ever, bound not by blood, but by love and unbreakable resolve. They huddled together, a tight-knit force against the storm that was still raging outside. The world might have made its judgment, but in this room, in this family, Liam knew he wasn't alone.

The battle ahead was daunting, uncertain and filled with challenges they couldn't yet see. But here, in the quiet of their home, they found a renewed sense of purpose. Together, they would face it all.

As the moonlight filtered through the window, it glinted off the mantelpiece where Ethan's toonie sat. Liam's mind drifted to that cold day at the cemetery, his promise still echoing: *I'll keep going for both of us, Ethan. Everything we dreamed about, I'll make it happen.*

He reached for the toonie. The NHL might try to stop him, but they didn't understand the power of that promise.

This wasn't over.

The Long Game

"I convinced myself I was powerless, but regret taught me the truth: I had the power. I just didn't use it." – Ben

In the golden gleam of dawn, the world awoke to a storm that had been brewing in the depths of secrecy and silence. The revelations had burst like a dam across the global consciousness. Victoria Sports Management (VSM), Furever Genetics, the audacious reality of human cloning in sports, now a narrative laced through every headline and hashtag. The screens pulsed with the stern faces of politicians, leaders calling for swift justice over #clonedoping, an ethical debacle laid bare.

In Canadian Parliament, voices rose sharply demanding a full investigation of VSM, while across the border, U.S. Congress members scrambled to address the unprecedented scandal with new legislation.

At the heart of it all, in the towering VSM headquarters, Lou Booker stood silently by the window, watching the chaos below. From his office, the world seemed so far away, yet he felt it closing in like a tightening noose. The lobby below, nearly empty after the mass exodus of employees during Harper's press conference, now saw only officers filing through the entrance, their approach deliberate and inevitable, slicing through the morning calm with the weight of the law at their backs.

Lou's gaze flicked briefly to his own reflection in the glass, a man who had once been hailed as a visionary, now a villain in the eyes of the world. His face was calm, unflinching. He could have left. The exits were there, the means within reach. But that was not Lou Booker. Running was for the weak, for the defeated. He would not give the world that satisfaction.

Zeus, his loyal companion, lay quietly at his feet, perhaps the only being who would remain faithful to the end.

His body was still, but his mind ticked through the years of carefully laid plans, of alliances built on ambition. The future of sports had once been in his hands, molded by his vision of what the world could be. And now, that vision was crumbling, piece by piece, brought down by forces he had once thought beneath his notice.

He could hear the steady thrum of the approaching footsteps, the officers moving closer through the halls. Lou stood tall, hands clasped behind his back, refusing to move from his position by the window. The weight of VSM's collapse hung in the air, but he carried it with a quiet dignity. If this was the end, he would face it on his terms.

There was a knock at the door. The sound echoed through the silence like a final, inevitable note in a long symphony. But Lou didn't flinch. He turned from the window slowly, his expression as composed as ever, his back straight. The officers entered, their presence filling the room, but Lou's gaze remained steady, defiant.

As they approached, the room seemed to hum with the tension of unspoken words. Lou's eyes met the lead officer's, and though his hands were outstretched to receive the cuffs, his posture remained unbroken. He was a man who had lost everything, yet somehow, in this moment, he stood as if he had surrendered nothing.

"You have the right to remain silent," the officer began, his voice firm, the words familiar to Lou after all these years of bending rules and playing with fire.

Lou's lips curled, just slightly. Let them think they had it all. Some secrets would remain his alone.

No struggle. No plea for mercy.

Just the sharp snap of the cuffs.

Cameras exploded in bursts of white, flashing like gunfire as he was led through the entrance. His empire lay in ruins behind him. But war was a long game, and Lou Booker never played for short-term gains.

Some battles were lost. The war never ends.

* * *

Miles away, Harper sat in her cluttered office, staring at the phone. She dialed the number. Ryan Patel answered after a few rings, his voice carrying the unmistakable tone of someone with the upper hand.

"Harper," he greeted smoothly. "Everything alright?"

She didn't waste time. "Where's Dr. Kim?"

Ryan let out a soft chuckle. "Still hunting, are we?"

Silence stretched between them.

"You know," Ryan said, as if discussing the weather, "you really are excellent at following leads. Every single one."

Something in his tone made her pause. "What do you mean?"

"The business card from New Horizon. The connection to the Bernards. The DNA collection happening at just the right moment." He paused. "Quite a convenient trail, wouldn't you say?"

Harper's fingers tightened on the phone. "You're saying—"

"I'm saying you did exactly what we needed. When we needed it." Another pause. "Perfect timing, really. The NHL draft coming up. Liam's rising star. The media attention. Couldn't have planned it better ourselves."

She thought back to each discovery, each revelation. The convenient timing. The perfect trail of evidence. Frank's warning echoed: *When a story falls into your lap too easily, that's when you should worry the most.*

"You've done your job well," Ryan continued, his voice almost gentle. "We couldn't have done it without you."

The pieces clicked into place with devastating clarity. Every "discovered" lead, every convenient piece of evidence, she hadn't been investigating. She'd been following a script.

"You used me." It wasn't a question. It was a fact. Cold. Brutal.

"Smart, aren't you?" Ryan replied smoothly. "That's why it worked."

She remembered Liam in that hotel conference room, trusting her with his future. Every revelation she'd uncovered had been carefully planted, timed, orchestrated. She hadn't protected him, she'd been the weapon used to destroy him.

"You..." Her voice hardened. "You used me to burn Liam's life to the ground."

Ryan's voice remained calm, detached. "The truth always comes out, Harper. We just gave it a little push."

Before she could respond, the line went dead.

The phone slipped from her fingers. She stared at her first front-page story hanging on the wall, the one about young hockey phenoms Liam and Ethan. The story that had started all of this.

She'd thought she was exposing corruption. Instead, she'd become part of it.

Her computer screen flickered with an incoming email. A draft of tomorrow's headline: "NHL Bans Cloned Athletes."

This wasn't over.

It couldn't be.

She opened a new document and began to type: "The Real Story Behind the Clone Ban."

* * *

Later Harper Sinclair paced her hotel room like a caged animal, fury radiating from every step. Her laptop glowed in the dim light, documents spread across the bed, evidence of how thoroughly she'd been played. Shell companies, clinic records, surveillance reports on genetically engineered children, all breadcrumbs Ryan had carefully dropped, leading her exactly where they wanted. She'd been their weapon against VSM, and Liam had paid the price.

Her fingers curled into fists. She needed answers, and Ben was her best shot at getting them. Ben, who'd turned the gun on Finn instead of her in Rice Park. Ben, who'd helped bring down VSM from the inside. Now he sat in jail, and Harper intended to use every ounce of that betrayal against his former employers.

A quick call to Nick, her contact in the system, secured the meeting. Ben had already proven willing to flip once, now she needed him to fill in the gaps Ryan had so carefully maintained. How deep did Lou Booker's plans really run? What connections lay buried between those fertility clinics and Korea? Most importantly, what had they really done to Liam?

She wouldn't be anyone's pawn again. This time, she'd write the real story, all of it.

The visitation room felt sterile and cold, its fluorescent lights casting a harsh glow on the table between Harper and Ben. He looked haggard, his face etched with the consequences of the choices he had made.

"Harper," Ben began, his voice softer than the last time they spoke. "You need the final pieces, right?"

Harper nodded, her pen poised over her notebook. "I need to know how VSM was connected to the fertility clinics. I need to understand exactly how families like Liam's were brought into this without knowing."

Ben sighed deeply, running a hand over his tired face. "VSM started by partnering with fertility clinics. They wanted to provide embryos to families who needed assistance, couples like Jim and Tammy Desjardins, who went to the clinics for help. But those embryos... they weren't just random donations."

He paused, collecting his thoughts before continuing. "Lou provided the funding, sponsoring the families through these clinics through a non-profit foundation. The embryos that were implanted, they were clones. Carefully selected, genetically engineered embryos meant for specific families. In Liam's case, they matched his DNA to fit his adoptive parents, Jim and Tammy. They thought they were getting a chance at parenthood, and they had no idea what VSM was really doing."

"What about Dr. Kim and Furever Genetics?" Harper asked. "How did they fit into VSM's operation?"

Ben shook his head. "I never met Dr. Kim. That was all Lou and Finn's territory. I just knew the clinics were getting the embryos from somewhere overseas. Lou kept that part of the operation separate, need-to-know basis only. But I heard things... snippets of conversations about shipments from Korea, special handling procedures."

"Are there records of all this?" Harper asked. "Documentation I can use?"

Ben's expression darkened. "VSM's been destroying records for weeks. I kept copies of my surveillance reports, but the clinic connections, the overseas transactions, Lou would have scrubbed those clean by now."

"How many clones were there total?" Harper asked.

Ben shook his head. "I only knew about the ones in Canada I monitored. There could be others... probably are. That was above my clearance level."

"And Ethan?" Harper pressed, looking up from her notes. "He was the first, right?"

Ben's face clouded. "Yes. Ethan Bernard was the first chosen one. VSM had high hopes for him, he was supposed to be their golden ticket. But he was born with a heart defect. It wasn't something they could predict, and it shattered their plans. Ethan was proof that even genetic engineering couldn't guarantee perfection."

He leaned back in his chair. "That's why they kept going. They realized they couldn't rely on just one or two clones. The clones were human, they had choices. Some of them, like Ethan, weren't fit to play. Others... they chose different paths. Not every clone followed the destiny VSM had laid out for them. Some wanted nothing to do with hockey. They didn't care about the sports at all."

Harper's pen stilled for a moment as she absorbed this. "So VSM knew there were risks."

Ben nodded. "They knew they couldn't force someone to be what they wanted. Just because you clone an athlete doesn't mean that clone will want to play the game. So they created more, multiple clones, spread across different families. They needed a pool of potential players, knowing full well that some of them wouldn't follow the script. They said Liam was their best hope after Ethan died."

Harper's mind raced as Ben continued. It all made sense now, why VSM had to manipulate the system so thoroughly, why they needed to control the narrative. This was never just about creating one star athlete. It was about playing a long game, about stacking the deck with as many clones as possible in the hope that one would rise to the top.

She looked at Ben, who was staring at his hands, clearly wracked with guilt. "And Jim and Tammy?" she asked, her voice softer now. "They never knew?"

Ben shook his head. "No. They knew they were getting a donated embryo, raised Liam as their own. They went to the clinic for help, and that's what they thought they got. VSM never told them the truth. It was all under the guise of helping families like theirs. That's how they justified it to themselves, they were giving people children. But really, they were just running an experiment."

Harper's heart clenched. She thought of Liam, the weight of this truth about to come crashing down on him. "And what about the others?" she asked quietly. "The other clones who didn't choose sports?"

Ben shifted uncomfortably in his chair. "I kept files on all of them. Had to monitor their progress, their choices. Some of those kids..." His voice cracked slightly. "They built beautiful lives, completely different from what VSM wanted."

"Tell me about them," Harper pressed gently, sensing Ben's need to unburden himself.

"There was this one near Vancouver, Thomas Zhang. His DNA was built for speed, a future NHL star in waiting. But at six, he picked up a violin, and the game never stood a chance."

"I had to report that to Lou as a 'failed investment.' But watching that kid perform on stage..." Ben's voice faltered. "There was nothing failed about him."

He ran a hand through his hair, continuing. "Another one, Michael Sullivan in Halifax, is studying to become a marine biologist. Works with endangered species."

Harper leaned forward. "How many others?"

"They're everywhere. Mostly small to midsize towns, all across Canada. Living normal lives, no idea about their origins or that VSM was watching." Ben's face darkened. "I knew their birthdays, their achievements, their dreams. I watched them grow up through surveillance photos and progress reports. Sometimes I felt more like a stalker than an agent."

He looked directly at Harper, his eyes wet. "The worst part? I started caring about them. All of them. Even the ones VSM wrote off. Every report I filed felt like a betrayal. These weren't failed experiments, they were people. Real people with real lives."

"And Liam?" Harper asked softly.

"Liam was different. He loved hockey. It was pure, natural. Not forced. That's what made him special." Ben's voice grew quiet. "Maybe that's why I couldn't keep lying. Watching him play, seeing that genuine passion... it made all the others make sense. They all had that same authenticity, just in different ways."

The enormity of it all hung heavy between them. Harper closed her notebook, the truth laid bare before her. "Thank you, Ben," she said, her voice firm but quiet. "For Liam, this means everything."

Ben nodded, his expression weary. "It's the least I can do. After everything we did..."

As Harper stood to leave, she hesitated for a moment, looking back at Ben. "What now for you?"

Ben answered, looking resigned. "I've made my bed. But at least now, I can start trying to make amends."

With that, Harper turned and left the room, the door closing softly behind her. Outside, the weight of the truth settled on her shoulders, but so did a sense of resolve.

Liam would know the truth, and VSM's part in this was exposed.

Dr. Kim had the rest of the answers.

And this time, she wasn't playing by anyone's rules.

* * *

The first light of dawn spilled across the tarmac, casting sharp shadows around the private jet. Dr. Kim Jung-So and Dae-Song moved in silence, their footsteps the only sound in the stillness. The world behind them was in chaos, headlines blaring, the media roaring with the fallout from VSM and Furever Genetics, but here, they remained untouched.

Dae-Song paused at the foot of the stairs, his tablet displaying the cascade of global reactions. "Let them focus on sports and athletes," he said, his voice carrying a clinical detachment. "Our vision extends far beyond their limited imagination."

Dr. Kim studied his son's profile in the harsh morning light. "You sound almost pleased."

"Aren't you?" Dae-Song's eyes held something beyond mere intelligence now, a cold calculation that made even his father pause. "VSM thought they could be kings of sport. Such limited ambition." His lips curved into that familiar analytical smile. "Why be kings when we can be gods?"

Inside the jet, they exchanged another wordless glance before settling into their seats. Dr. Kim reclined, watching his creation, his son, process data streams with inhuman efficiency. The CEG modifications had worked beyond his wildest expectations. Perhaps too well.

"Dubai is just the beginning," Dae-Song said quietly, his fingers dancing across multiple screens. "The next phase of evolution won't be limited to athletes, Father. The naturals have had their time."

Dr. Kim felt a mixture of pride and unease. They had done it. VSM's downfall was no longer their concern. But as he watched his son's calculating eyes scan the data streams, he felt the weight of what they'd truly begun.

Let Liam Play

"You'll never skate alone, kid. Your team's bigger than you think, and we've all got your back." – Coach Boucha

Liam ran his fingers over the Brandon Wheat Kings jersey, the fabric rough beneath his touch. The last time he wore it, Ethan had been there, his laughter still lingering if Liam closed his eyes. The memory cut deep, sharp as ice under his skates.

At the kitchen table, Liam stared at his other jerseys, Team Canada, London Knights, and the empty hanger waiting for an NHL sweater that might never come. Each one felt like a frozen moment in time, a version of himself caught in a dream that had just shattered.

Jim's fingers drummed against his coffee mug, the sound echoing through their too-quiet kitchen. The TV in the corner, usually tuned to sports highlights, stayed dark. They'd had enough of the endless debates about genetic engineering and cloning in sports, enough of seeing Liam's name scrolled across the bottom of screens like a cautionary tale.

"The Players Association isn't backing down," Jim said, his voice carrying forced optimism. "The statement from their president this morning—"

"Was political double-speak," Liam cut in, harsher than he intended. He softened at the hurt in his father's eyes. "Sorry, Dad. I just... I'm tired of people talking around the real issue."

Tammy reached across the table, covering Liam's hand with hers. "We've always found a way forward," she said quietly. "This time won't be different."

But it was different. The NHL's decision felt like a crosscheck to the boards, sudden, jarring, and changing everything in an instant. Liam had faced setbacks before: injuries, tough losses, critics who said he was too young or too raw. But this? This felt like someone had stolen not just his future, but his identity.

A sharp knock jolted Liam from his thoughts, slicing through the quiet. Jim and Tammy exchanged glances as Liam stood, his movements weighted with the exhaustion of the past few days. When he opened it, he found an army waiting.

Harper stood at the front, her expression set with the same determination he'd seen when she first broke the story about VSM. Behind her, Mario Richard's presence filled the doorway, a living legend whose DNA had become an unwitting part of Liam's story. Coach Boucha stood shoulder-to-shoulder with them, still carrying himself with that commanding presence that could silence a locker room with a look. Even Pete Marston was there, for once not trying to sell anything.

"They don't get to erase you, Liam," Harper said, her voice sharp, unyielding. "Not now. Not ever."

Coach Boucha stepped past her into the kitchen, his presence filling the space like a locker room before a championship game. "You know what makes a great player?" he asked, not waiting for an answer. "It's not just skill. Not just training. It's heart. And in thirty years, I've never seen a bigger one than yours, kid."

Mario shifted, never one for speeches, but this moment demanded it. "They're doing what they always do, clinging to the past. But the game doesn't wait. And neither should you."

Pete, already firing off messages, smirked. "The stars are speaking up. They know talent when they see it. And they won't let the league forget."

As the group filed into the kitchen, Liam felt something shift inside him. The jerseys on his wall no longer seemed like reminders of what he'd lost. Instead, they were proof of what he'd already achieved, what he'd fought for before.

Jim rose to shake hands with Coach Boucha, the spark of hope finally returning to his eyes. "Thank you for being here," he said, his voice thick with emotion. "All of you."

Harper followed Liam back to the table, her usual reporter's notebook nowhere in sight. This wasn't a story anymore, this was a battle plan. "We've got some ideas," she said, her tone focused and determined. "And I'm in this for the long haul. We're going to get you back on that ice."

Liam looked around at the faces gathered in his kitchen, people who believed in him, who were willing to fight for him. The knot in his stomach began to unwind, replaced by something else: the same fire that drove him in the final minutes of a tied game.

"So," Liam said, his voice stronger than it had been in days, "where do we start?"

Harper smiled, pulling out her laptop. "We start by reminding them who you really are, not a clone, not an experiment, but a hockey player. One of the best they've ever seen."

The kitchen, which moments ago had felt like a shrine to broken dreams, now hummed with purpose. They had a fight ahead of them, but Liam had never backed down from a challenge on the ice. He wasn't about to start now.

By morning, Harper's social media campaign had exploded. Messages of support flooded in from across the hockey world, filling her screen faster than she could read them. The kitchen still buzzed with energy, though quieter now, Coach Boucha had left to make calls to his contacts in the league, while the others worked their own angles. Even the early hour couldn't dampen the determination that had taken root when their unlikely alliance formed.

Around her, empty coffee cups and scattered notes told the story of their all-night strategy session. But it was the responses lighting up her screen that made Harper's heart race. #LetLiamPlay was spreading like wildfire.

One tweet stood out: *Hockey without Liam is like a net without a goal.* Below it, a clip of Liam, fluid, electric, unstoppable, his #7 jersey flashing under the lights.

Another fan's post featured Liam's silhouette, stark against the cold glow of arena lights, with the caption: *More than a player, Liam's an artist in skates. We need #7 back on the ice.*

A video from a mother showed her young daughter holding a sign that read: *Liam fights for dreams. When does he fight again?* The connection was palpable, Liam wasn't just a skater. To these fans, he was a symbol of resilience, of hope. And more than ever, his absence was felt.

Liam leaned over Harper's shoulder, his breath catching at the sight. "I never thought..." he started, then stopped, collecting himself. "These people don't even know me."

"They know what matters," Harper replied. "They know what you represent."

The hockey world responded with fury. Players Liam had faced on the ice, legends he'd grown up watching, all of them speaking out against the ban. The support was immediate, overwhelming, and growing by the minute. But it was the fan response that truly caught fire, organic, passionate, unstoppable.

Pete's phone buzzed. "Some of the old guard are pushing back," he said, scanning the message. "They're calling it a publicity stunt, saying we're trying to pressure the league."

"Let them," Mario countered. "Every time they speak against Liam, they just prove our point."

Across the kitchen table, Jim and Tammy Desjardins sat close together, their fatigue evident but lightened by a growing thread of optimism. Mario Richard, arms crossed, stood nearby, a silent pillar of support. Pete Marston, ever restless, juggled his phone, ready to ignite action the moment it was needed.

Harper spoke up, her voice clear and steady as she broke the quiet tension, "Our next step is in person," she said, nodding toward the screen that displayed the surge of support. The group's attention focused on her, a guiding light amidst the fog of uncertainty. "The fans are our cornerstone. They'll push this into something the NHL can't ignore."

A wave of nods met her words, their collective resolve hardening as they gathered around the glowing screens.

"The Stanley Cup Championship," Harper continued, her mind already piecing together the strategy. "We'll make our first move there. It's the biggest stage, and we'll make sure the whole hockey world sees it."

Jim allowed a smile to break through his worry, a moment of warmth in the storm. Tammy squeezed Mario's hand, a quiet, shared vow to see this through together.

"Liam's more than just a label," Harper emphasized, her voice gathering momentum. "He's the beating heart of this sport. And it's time they remember that."

Mario stepped forward, his presence commanding attention. "I've seen this before, the league trying to shut out talent. Europeans, college kids, anyone who didn't fit their mold. But the game always wins. The real game, played with passion and heart."

The room buzzed with energy as Pete rallied his contacts, setting fan clubs across the country into motion. "We'll fill the stands with Liam's name and #7," Pete said, his usual salesman persona giving way to something deeper, genuine belief.

"We'll take over social media," Tammy declared, her voice resolute. "Every post, every hashtag, every story will make sure they can't ignore Liam anymore."

Suggestions quickly transformed into tasks, the air thick with determination as their campaign began to take shape. Jim added his voice about merchandise, while Mario outlined his connections with retired players who could speak out.

As Pete continued working his contacts, a flurry of texts and calls set the wheels in motion, pushing their message to break through into televised events, news segments, and fan protests. The opposition would be fierce, old guard executives, traditionalists who feared change, those who saw genetic engineering as a threat to the sport's integrity. But they were ready.

Harper watched Liam absorb it all, saw the way he straightened when fans shared stories of how his playing had inspired them. This wasn't just about getting him back on the ice anymore, it was about protecting the soul of the sport itself.

"I want to be part of this," Liam said firmly. "Not just as a symbol, I want to fight for this myself."

Harper pulled up a calendar. "We've got three weeks until the Finals. We need coordinated fan events in every NHL city, media coverage that keeps this story alive, and player support that shows this isn't just about Liam, it's about the future of hockey itself."

The kitchen hummed with renewed purpose as screens glowed and phones buzzed with mounting support. #LetLiamPlay was more than a hashtag now, it was becoming a movement. And when they took it to the Stanley Cup Finals, the NHL would have no choice but to listen.

* * *

The Stanley Cup Finals. Game 1. The arena thundered with energy. From her spot in the press box, Harper Sinclair surveyed the crowd below. Three weeks of building pressure had led to this moment. #LetLiamPlay shirts filled the stands, not just scattered groups anymore, but thousands strong.

Mario Richard stepped onto the red carpet laid across the ice for the ceremonial puck drop, his presence commanding instant respect. But as he walked, another figure emerged from the tunnel, Liam, wearing his Team Canada jersey and his signature number 7. The crowd's reaction was instant and explosive.

Mario paused, turning to welcome Liam with a smile that the jumbotron captured perfectly. Together, they walked to center ice, where the team captains waited. The roar grew louder with each step, signs bearing Liam's name and number lifting high above heads, a show of solidarity that spanned every NHL fanbase.

When Mario handed the puck to Liam, letting him make the ceremonial drop, the arena erupted. Cameras flashed, capturing the moment when both captains reached out, not just for the puck, but to shake Liam's hand. It was a gesture of respect that transcended league politics, a statement that the players themselves had chosen their side.

From their suite, Jim and Tammy watched with tears in their eyes as their son stood tall at center ice. Mario rejoined them moments later, settling into his seat next to the iPad where Coach Boucha's face filled the screen. Harper could feel the electricity in the room as the game began. This wasn't just a ceremonial puck drop anymore, it was a declaration. The NHL could ban Liam from playing, but they couldn't stop him from being part of the game he loved. And they couldn't ignore the unified voice of the hockey world demanding his return.

By the third period, Harper's phone buzzed with a call that set everyone on edge. Before she could answer, there was a knock at the door of the suite. Harper stood up, her heart pounding as she opened the door to reveal the NHL commissioner, his presence a reminder of the stakes they were playing for tonight.

"Ms. Sinclair," the commissioner greeted, his voice steady but his eyes scanning the room, taking in Liam, his parents, and Mario. "May I come in?"

Harper nodded, stepping aside. Liam and his family exchanged glances, a quiet tension filling the suite. The commissioner walked in and turned to face Liam.

His voice cut through the silence like a referee's whistle in a shootout, sharp, piercing, and final. "We've come to a decision."

Everyone held their breath, the air thick with anticipation. Even Coach Boucha leaned closer to his screen.

"The NHL has decided that, effective immediately, you will no longer be prevented from entering the draft," the commissioner continued, his tone neutral but firm. "However, given the complexities and ethical challenges surrounding cloning, we are tabling the matter for further review. We will continue to work toward a long-term policy regarding the impact of cloning on the league and its athletes. But as of now, you're free to pursue your career."

Liam exhaled deeply, the tension in his body finally releasing. His parents exchanged a look of disbelief and joy, while Harper felt a surge of triumph wash over her.

"That's all we've ever wanted," Tammy said, her voice steady but filled with relief.

The commissioner nodded, offering a final word. "This isn't the end of the conversation, but for now, it's time to let Liam play."

As the commissioner left, the room erupted in a wave of emotion. Liam's parents wrapped him in a tight hug, their pride radiating in every gesture. Mario stood by, his hand firm on Liam's shoulder. "The game always finds a way to right itself," he said quietly.

Through the tablet, Coach Boucha's voice cracked with emotion. "You showed them what hockey's really about, kid. Heart over everything else."

"You did it," Harper said softly, her eyes meeting Liam's.

"No," Liam corrected, pulling her into a hug. "We did it. All of us."

Outside, the chants of #LetLiamPlay reverberated through the arena, a testament to the journey they had all been on. For Liam, it wasn't just about reclaiming his place on the ice, it was about fighting for his identity, for the right to be seen as more than the product of science.

That night, as they walked through the arena, the weight of the victory settling over them, Harper felt more than just satisfaction. She felt hope, a belief in the power of perseverance, of standing up for what was right. Pete's phone kept buzzing with messages from fan clubs celebrating across the country, while Mario fielded calls from former players offering congratulations.

As they stepped into the night, with Liam's path to the rink finally cleared, they knew this was only the beginning. #LetLiamPlay had become more than a campaign, it had become a rallying cry for the entire hockey world.

The real victory wasn't just changing the NHL's decision. It was proving what mattered most was how you played the game.

Tonight, hockey had won.

The First Pick

"For the first time, I feel like my story is mine to tell." – Liam

The electric buzz of anticipation filled Montreal's Bell Centre as Liam sat, a stoic figure amidst a sea of hopefuls. His gaze flickered between the grandeur of the stage and the crowd surrounding him. To his left, Jim and Tammy flanked him, their silent presence a bulwark of love and solidarity. On his right, Mario Richard sat like a watchful guardian, an emotional anchor amidst the turbulence of Liam's uncertain future.

In the media box, Harper's fingers hovered above her keyboard, ready to immortalize this moment for True North Hockey. The tension in the arena was electric, this was no ordinary draft. Biotechnology had thrust itself into the world of sports, and tonight's selection was not just about a player, it was about rewriting the rules of human potential.

The commissioner's voice sliced through the silence. "With the first overall pick in the NHL Draft, the Minnesota Wild select..."

The commissioner paused, the silence deafening.

A deliberate shuffle of papers.

A breath held.

The entire arena waiting.

"Liam Desjardins."

The Bell Centre erupted. Liam rose, each step toward the stage carrying the weight of everything they'd fought for. His handshake with the commissioner wasn't just a draft selection, it was vindication. With steady hands, he pulled the Minnesota Wild jersey over his head.

He was exactly where he belonged.

As Liam returned to his family's embrace, Jim's back slap rang with pride, while Tammy's hug held all the warmth of home. Mario stood beside them, their bond forged in battle.

Later, away from the crowd, Harper found them huddled together. They welcomed her with warm smiles.

"You made it," Harper said softly. "Now go light it up."

Liam's smile was genuine. "Thanks to you, all of you."

She left them there, knowing Liam had found exactly where he belonged.

* * *

THREE WEEKS LATER - TORONTO

The cheers had faded. In their place, Harper's apartment hummed with the quiet weight of unfinished business. Summer's warmth seeped through the open window, yet the air inside felt cooler, charged with the weight of her latest discoveries. The sports arenas lay dormant, but Harper's investigation into the world of genetic manipulation was far from resting.

Dr. Kim Jung-So's presence lingered like a shadow over every file, every piece of research. His reach seemed to stretch across continents, a ghostly figure slipping through the cracks of legal systems and international boundaries. The revelations from Ryan had shaken Harper, unraveling a conspiracy so sprawling that its implications rippled across industries far beyond sports.

As more details emerged, an unsettling realization gnawed at Harper: *she had been a pawn.* While she chased VSM and Furever Genetics, Dr. Kim had used her investigation as a diversion, buying time for his escape. His disappearance, coupled with Ryan's suspicious retreat to the Middle East, hinted at a complex and deeply entrenched network. The more Harper uncovered, the more daunting the scope became.

Her thoughts circled back to Liam. If he had been tailored for hockey supremacy, were there others, clones bred for greatness, for profit, for untold purposes? The enormity of the situation pressed down on her, and the gravity of what had been done, what might still be happening, grew heavier with each passing hour.

Harper rose from her desk and moved to the window, her gaze sweeping over the Toronto skyline. The city stretched out, normal and quiet, a stark contrast to the questions churning in her mind. Somewhere out there, Dr. Kim was building something far more dangerous than enhanced athletes. She could feel it.

"Where are you hiding?" she whispered to the skyline. "And what are you really planning?"

A video call notification popped up on her laptop, Frank Taylor. She returned to her desk, clicked accept, and her editor's face filled the screen, his expression a mix of pride and concern.

"Harper," Frank began, his voice warm but worried, "you've broken the biggest story of your career. But what you're chasing now... it goes way beyond True North Hockey. I can't protect you out there."

Harper leaned forward, determination in her eyes. "I know, Frank. But I have to—"

The laptop screen flickered and went black. She reached to restart it, her pulse quickening. Then her cell phone vibrated on the desk. No Caller ID.

She hesitated, but instinct took over, and she answered.

A voice, young but unnaturally precise, cut through the silence. "Harper Sinclair," Dae-Song said, each word calculated for maximum impact. "Still trapped in your natural cage."

He paused, just long enough for her to feel the weight of his next words.

"Your kind had their day in the sun. All natural things must fade, and the night belongs to us."

The line went dead. Harper's hand tightened around the phone, her breath caught in her throat. Not Dr. Kim this time, his son. His creation.

A knock at the door cut through her thoughts.

Harper froze. The knock came again, deliberate, precise, like a metronome marking time. Her heart hammered as she crossed to the door, each step measured and silent.

Through the peephole, a figure stood in shadow, features obscured by the dim hallway light. Professional instinct warred with self-preservation as her hand hesitated on the handle.

The silence stretched. A pause, just long enough to make her pulse spike. Outside, footsteps faded down the hallway, but this figure stayed. Waiting.

She opened the door just enough for the security chain to catch, leaving only a sliver of the hallway visible. The figure remained half-hidden in shadow, face turned slightly away from the light.

"We share a common enemy," the figure said, voice tight with urgency.

Harper's fingers gripped the door frame. "And who would that be?"

"My son." Dr. Kim stepped into the light, his face etched with worry. "What I've created... what he's become... I need your help to stop him."

The realization struck like a jolt. The true threat wasn't the creator, it was the creation.

About the Author

J. Alan Childs is the author of *A Genetic Power Play*, his first hockey novel, as well as four books on the sport of lacrosse: *Flamethrowers - Guardians of the Game* (Volumes 1 & 2), *Minnesota Lacrosse: A History* (non-fiction), and the children's picture book *Can I Play? Flamethrower Lacrosse Stories*.

By day, Alan is a data geek working in the swine industry, designing software solutions to help farmers optimize their operations. By night, he blends his love of sports with storytelling, crafting narratives that explore the thrill of competition, the weight of legacy, and the evolving nature of athletic performance.

A lifelong sports fan, Alan grew up in Southern California, a hockey enthusiast in a land without ice. After marrying his wife, Candy, they moved to Minnesota, embracing the State of Hockey to raise their five children, all of whom played hockey and lacrosse.

ABOUT THE AUTHOR

The same year they arrived, the Minnesota North Stars moved away, leaving them teamless, until the Wild arrived in 2000. From that moment, the family became devoted Wild fans, sharing their love of the game across generations.

Now, with their children grown, Alan and Candy are proud grandparents to eight grandchildren, seven granddaughters and one grandson. They still call the Twin Cities home, frequently visiting their favorite rink, Burnsville Ice Arena, to get their hockey fix.

When not writing or watching hockey or lacrosse, Alan enjoys tinkering with data, exploring sports history, and spending time with their two dogs, Zeus and Monster, who keep life just as exciting as Game 7 overtime.

Made in the USA
Monee, IL
11 April 2025